ARTEMIS FOWL
THE ETERNITY CODE

THE GRAPHIC NOVEL

Adapted by
EOIN COLFER
&
ANDREW DONKIN

Art by GIOVANNI RIGANO

Color by PAOLO LAMANNA
Color Separation by STUDIO BLINQ

Lettering by CHRIS DICKEY

$\mathcal{D}$ısnєy · HYPERION BOOKS
New York

Adapted from the novel *Artemis Fowl: The Eternity Code*

Text copyright © 2013 by Eoin Colfer
Illustrations copyright © 2013 by Giovanni Rigano

Printed in the United States of America
First Edition
10 9 8 7 6 5 4 3 2 1
V381-8386-5-13105
Library of Congress Cataloging-in-Publication Data

Colfer, Eoin.

Artemis Fowl. The eternity code / adapted by Eoin Colfer and Andrew Donkin ; illustrations by
Giovanni Rigano.—First edition.

pages cm

Summary: After Artemis uses stolen fairy technology to create a powerful microcomputer and it is
snatched by a dangerous American businessman, Artemis, Juliet, Mulch, and the fairies join forces to try
to retrieve it.

ISBN 978-1-4231-4527-1 (hardcover)—ISBN 978-1-4231-4577-6 (pbk.)

1. Graphic novels. [1. Graphic novels. 2. Adventure and adventurers—Fiction. 3. Fairies—Fiction. 4.
Magic—Fiction. 5. Computers—Fiction. 6. England—Fiction.] I. Donkin, Andrew. II. Rigano, Giovanni,
illustrator. III. Title. IV. Title: Eternity code.

PZ7.7.C645Arw 2013

741.5'9415—dc23   2013001136

Visit www.disneyhyperionbooks.com and www.artemisfowl.com

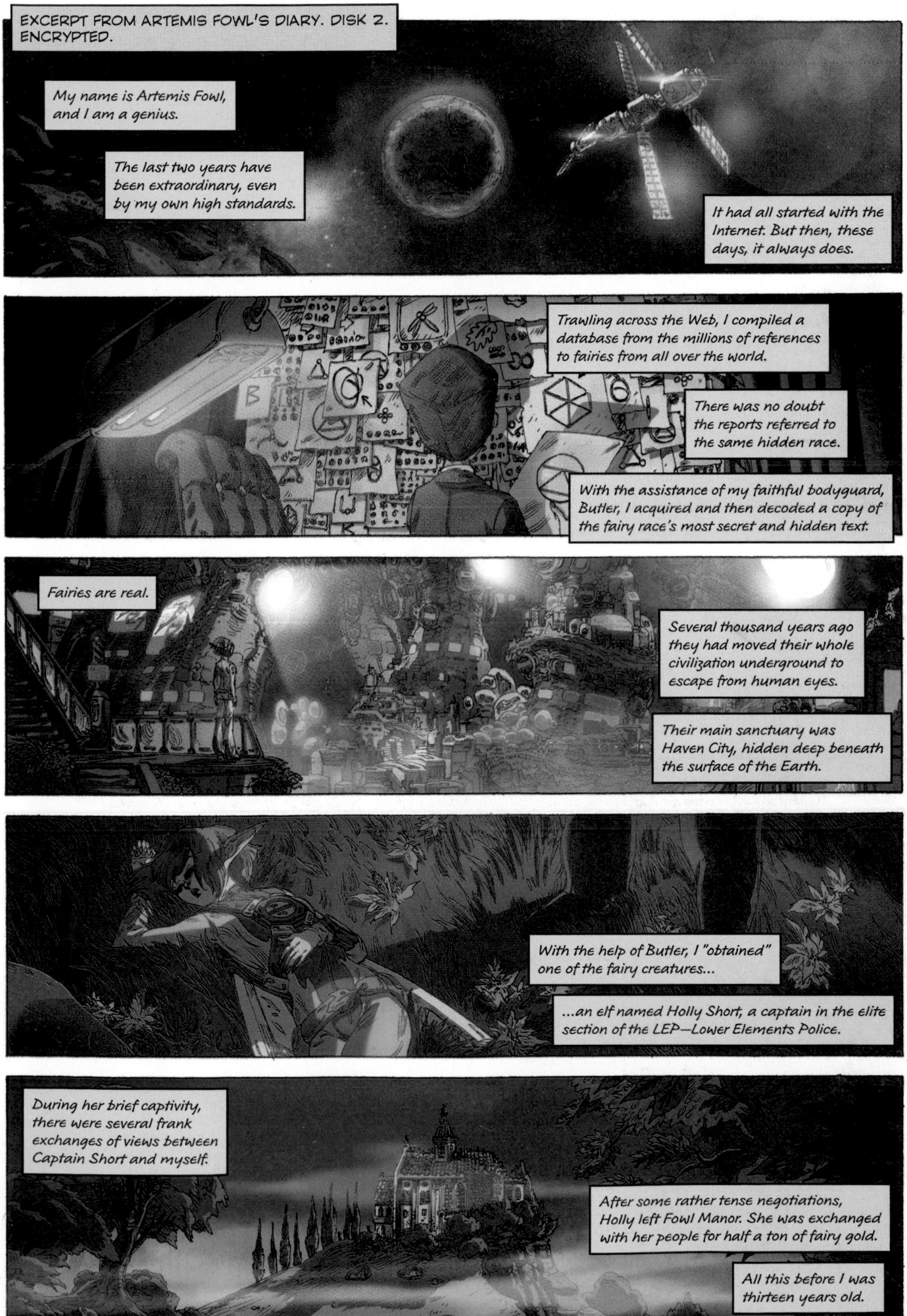
EXCERPT FROM ARTEMIS FOWL'S DIARY. DISK 2. ENCRYPTED.
My name is Artemis Fowl, and I am a genius.
The last two years have been extraordinary, even by my own high standards.
It had all started with the Internet. But then, these days, it always does.
Trawling across the Web, I compiled a database from the millions of references to fairies from all over the world.
There was no doubt the reports referred to the same hidden race.
With the assistance of my faithful bodyguard, Butler, I acquired and then decoded a copy of the fairy race's most secret and hidden text.
Fairies are real.
Several thousand years ago they had moved their whole civilization underground to escape from human eyes.
Their main sanctuary was Haven City, hidden deep beneath the surface of the Earth.
With the help of Butler, I "obtained" one of the fairy creatures...
...an elf named Holly Short, a captain in the elite section of the LEP—Lower Elements Police.
During her brief captivity, there were several frank exchanges of views between Captain Short and myself.
After some rather tense negotiations, Holly left Fowl Manor. She was exchanged with her people for half a ton of fairy gold.
All this before I was thirteen years old.

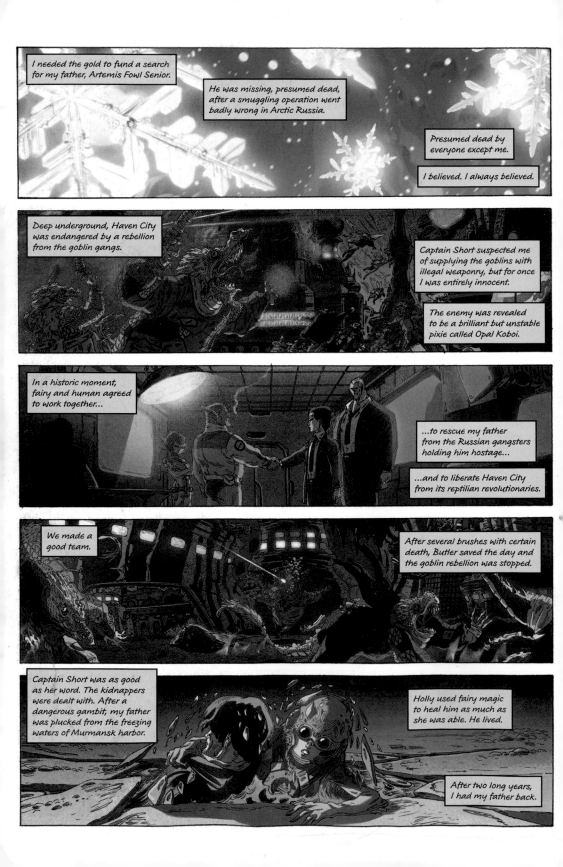

I needed the gold to fund a search for my father, Artemis Fowl Senior.

He was missing, presumed dead, after a smuggling operation went badly wrong in Arctic Russia.

Presumed dead by everyone except me.

I believed. I always believed.

Deep underground, Haven City was endangered by a rebellion from the goblin gangs.

Captain Short suspected me of supplying the goblins with illegal weaponry, but for once I was entirely innocent.

The enemy was revealed to be a brilliant but unstable pixie called Opal Koboi.

In a historic moment, fairy and human agreed to work together...

...to rescue my father from the Russian gangsters holding him hostage...

...and to liberate Haven City from its reptilian revolutionaries.

We made a good team.

After several brushes with certain death, Butler saved the day and the goblin rebellion was stopped.

Captain Short was as good as her word. The kidnappers were dealt with. After a dangerous gambit, my father was plucked from the freezing waters of Murmansk harbor.

Holly used fairy magic to heal him as much as she was able. He lived.

After two long years, I had my father back.

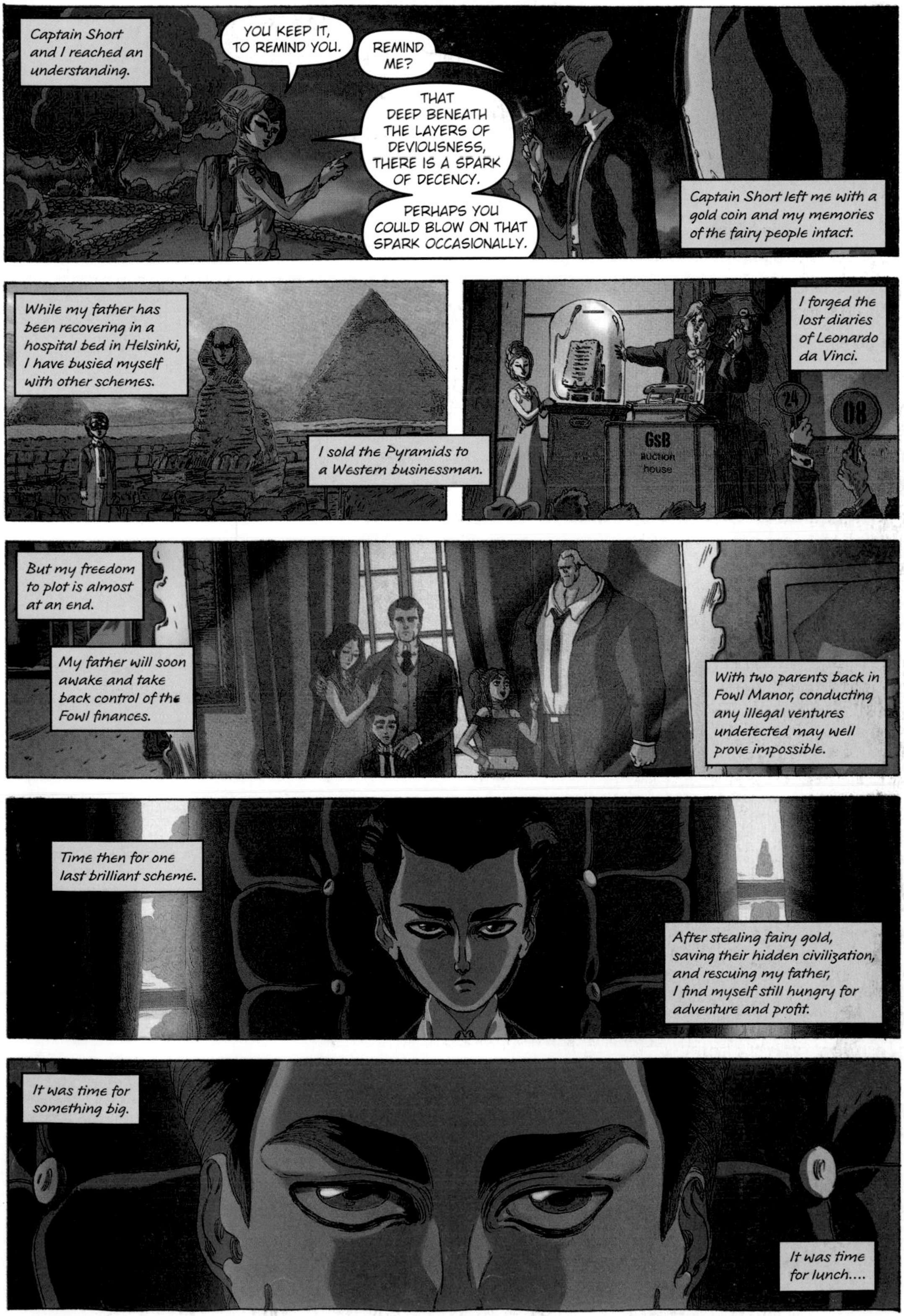
Captain Short and I reached an understanding.
YOU KEEP IT, TO REMIND YOU.
REMIND ME?
THAT DEEP BENEATH THE LAYERS OF DEVIOUSNESS, THERE IS A SPARK OF DECENCY.
PERHAPS YOU COULD BLOW ON THAT SPARK OCCASIONALLY.
Captain Short left me with a gold coin and my memories of the fairy people intact.
While my father has been recovering in a hospital bed in Helsinki, I have busied myself with other schemes.
I sold the Pyramids to a Western businessman.
I forged the lost diaries of Leonardo da Vinci.
24
08
GsB
auction house
But my freedom to plot is almost at an end.
My father will soon awake and take back control of the Fowl finances.
With two parents back in Fowl Manor, conducting any illegal ventures undetected may well prove impossible.
Time then for one last brilliant scheme.
After stealing fairy gold, saving their hidden civilization, and rescuing my father, I find myself still hungry for adventure and profit.
It was time for something big.
It was time for lunch....

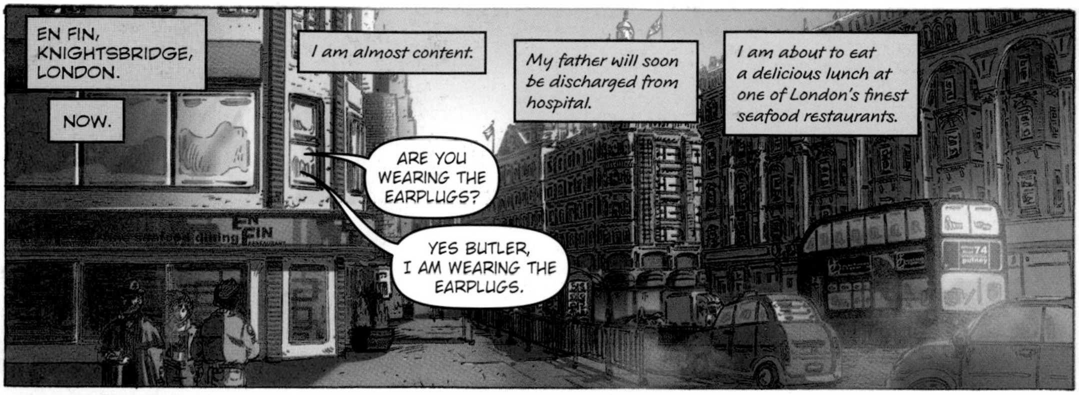
EN FIN, KNIGHTSBRIDGE, LONDON.
NOW.
I am almost content.
My father will soon be discharged from hospital.
I am about to eat a delicious lunch at one of London's finest seafood restaurants.
ARE YOU WEARING THE EARPLUGS?
YES BUTLER, I AM WEARING THE EARPLUGS.

CHAPTER 1:
THE CUBE

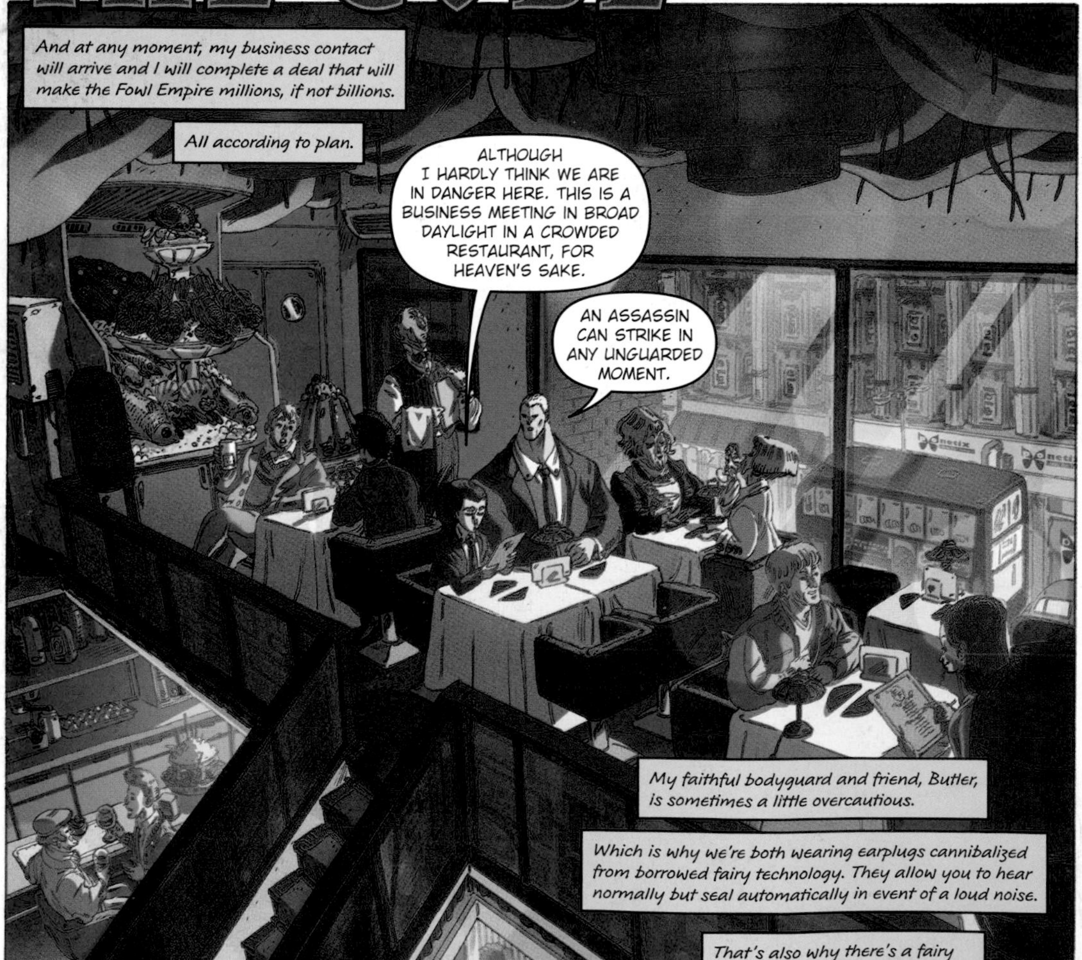
And at any moment, my business contact will arrive and I will complete a deal that will make the Fowl Empire millions, if not billions.
All according to plan.
ALTHOUGH I HARDLY THINK WE ARE IN DANGER HERE. THIS IS A BUSINESS MEETING IN BROAD DAYLIGHT IN A CROWDED RESTAURANT, FOR HEAVEN'S SAKE.
AN ASSASSIN CAN STRIKE IN ANY UNGUARDED MOMENT.
My faithful bodyguard and friend, Butler, is sometimes a little overcautious.
Which is why we're both wearing earplugs cannibalized from borrowed fairy technology. They allow you to hear normally but seal automatically in event of a loud noise.
That's also why there's a fairy sonix grenade magnetized to the underside of our restaurant table.

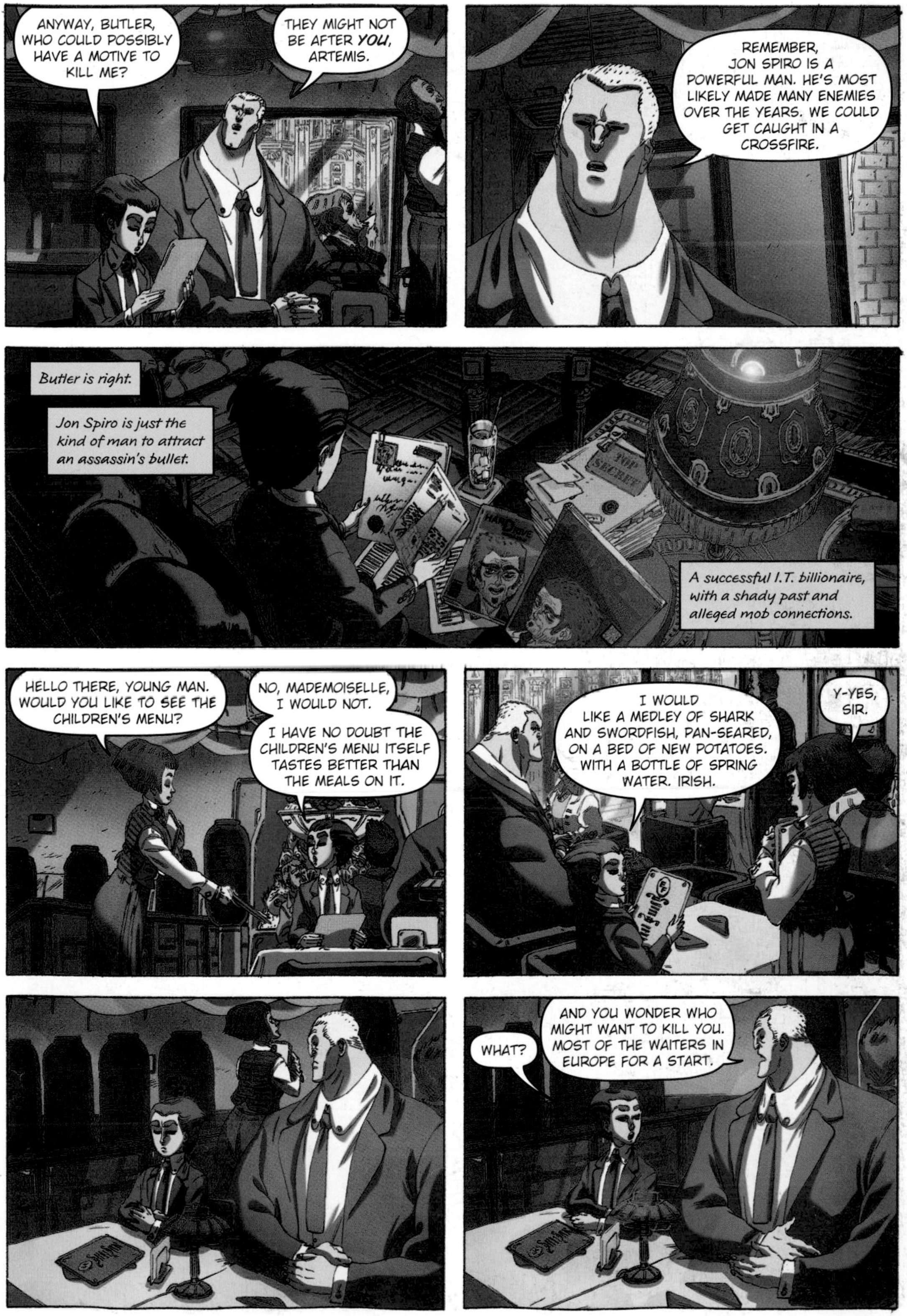
ANYWAY, BUTLER, WHO COULD POSSIBLY HAVE A MOTIVE TO KILL ME?
THEY MIGHT NOT BE AFTER *YOU*, ARTEMIS.
REMEMBER, JON SPIRO IS A POWERFUL MAN. HE'S MOST LIKELY MADE MANY ENEMIES OVER THE YEARS. WE COULD GET CAUGHT IN A CROSSFIRE.
Butler is right.
Jon Spiro is just the kind of man to attract an assassin's bullet.
TOP SECRET
A successful I.T. billionaire, with a shady past and alleged mob connections.
HELLO THERE, YOUNG MAN. WOULD YOU LIKE TO SEE THE CHILDREN'S MENU?
NO, MADEMOISELLE, I WOULD NOT.
I HAVE NO DOUBT THE CHILDREN'S MENU ITSELF TASTES BETTER THAN THE MEALS ON IT.
I WOULD LIKE A MEDLEY OF SHARK AND SWORDFISH, PAN-SEARED, ON A BED OF NEW POTATOES. WITH A BOTTLE OF SPRING WATER. IRISH.
Y-YES, SIR.
WHAT?
AND YOU WONDER WHO MIGHT WANT TO KILL YOU. MOST OF THE WAITERS IN EUROPE FOR A START.

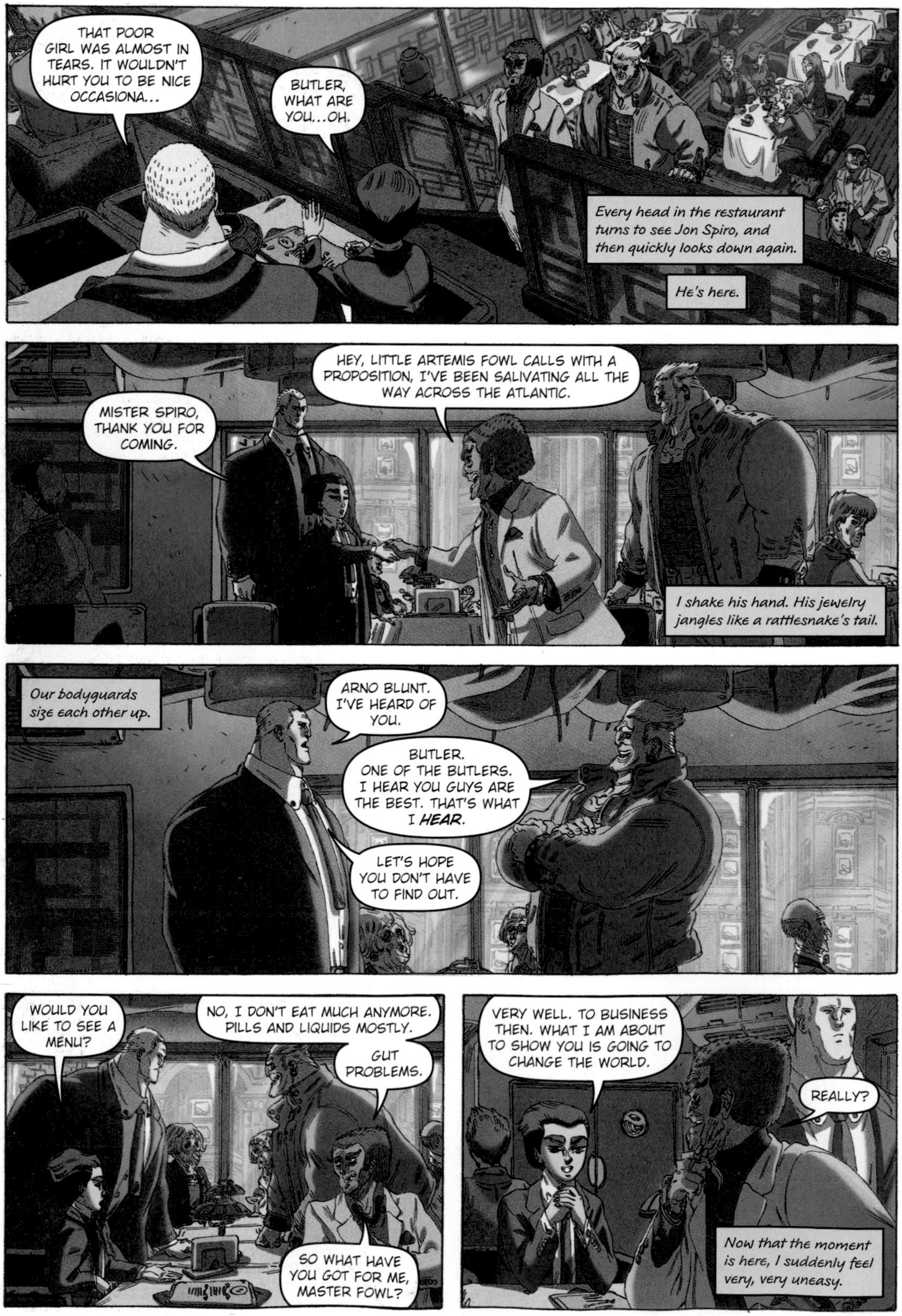
THAT POOR GIRL WAS ALMOST IN TEARS. IT WOULDN'T HURT YOU TO BE NICE OCCASIONA...
BUTLER, WHAT ARE YOU...OH.
Every head in the restaurant turns to see Jon Spiro, and then quickly looks down again.
He's here.
MISTER SPIRO, THANK YOU FOR COMING.
HEY, LITTLE ARTEMIS FOWL CALLS WITH A PROPOSITION, I'VE BEEN SALIVATING ALL THE WAY ACROSS THE ATLANTIC.
I shake his hand. His jewelry jangles like a rattlesnake's tail.
Our bodyguards size each other up.
ARNO BLUNT. I'VE HEARD OF YOU.
BUTLER. ONE OF THE BUTLERS. I HEAR YOU GUYS ARE THE BEST. THAT'S WHAT I HEAR.
LET'S HOPE YOU DON'T HAVE TO FIND OUT.
WOULD YOU LIKE TO SEE A MENU?
NO, I DON'T EAT MUCH ANYMORE. PILLS AND LIQUIDS MOSTLY.
GUT PROBLEMS.
SO WHAT HAVE YOU GOT FOR ME, MASTER FOWL?
VERY WELL. TO BUSINESS THEN. WHAT I AM ABOUT TO SHOW YOU IS GOING TO CHANGE THE WORLD.
REALLY?
Now that the moment is here, I suddenly feel very, very uneasy.

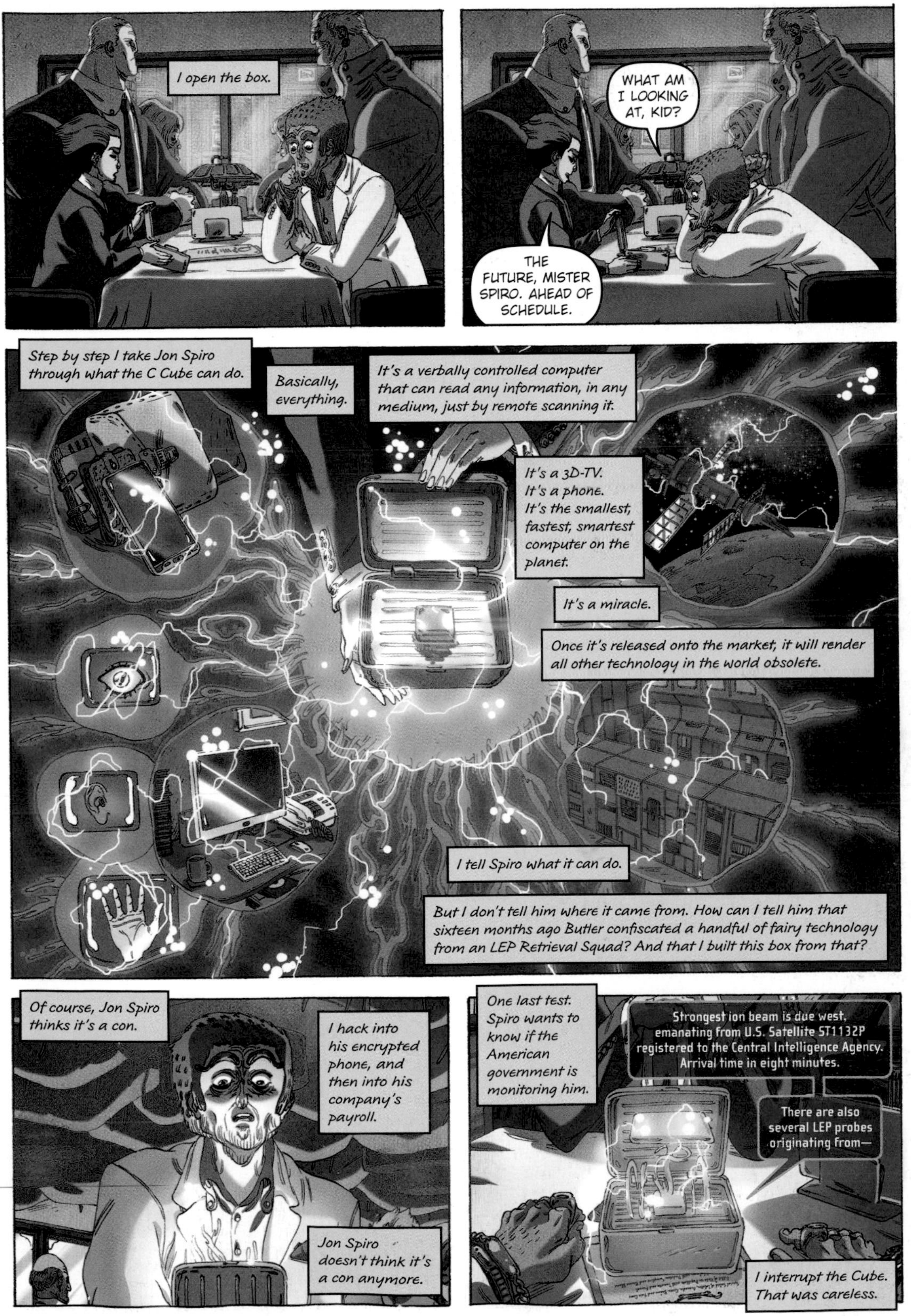
I open the box.
WHAT AM I LOOKING AT, KID?
THE FUTURE, MISTER SPIRO. AHEAD OF SCHEDULE.
Step by step I take Jon Spiro through what the C Cube can do.
Basically, everything.
It's a verbally controlled computer that can read any information, in any medium, just by remote scanning it.
It's a 3D-TV.
It's a phone.
It's the smallest, fastest, smartest computer on the planet.
It's a miracle.
Once it's released onto the market, it will render all other technology in the world obsolete.
I tell Spiro what it can do.
But I don't tell him where it came from. How can I tell him that sixteen months ago Butler confiscated a handful of fairy technology from an LEP Retrieval Squad? And that I built this box from that?
Of course, Jon Spiro thinks it's a con.
I hack into his encrypted phone, and then into his company's payroll.
Jon Spiro doesn't think it's a con anymore.
One last test. Spiro wants to know if the American government is monitoring him.
Strongest ion beam is due west, emanating from U.S. Satellite ST1132P registered to the Central Intelligence Agency. Arrival time in eight minutes.
There are also several LEP probes originating from—
I interrupt the Cube. That was careless.

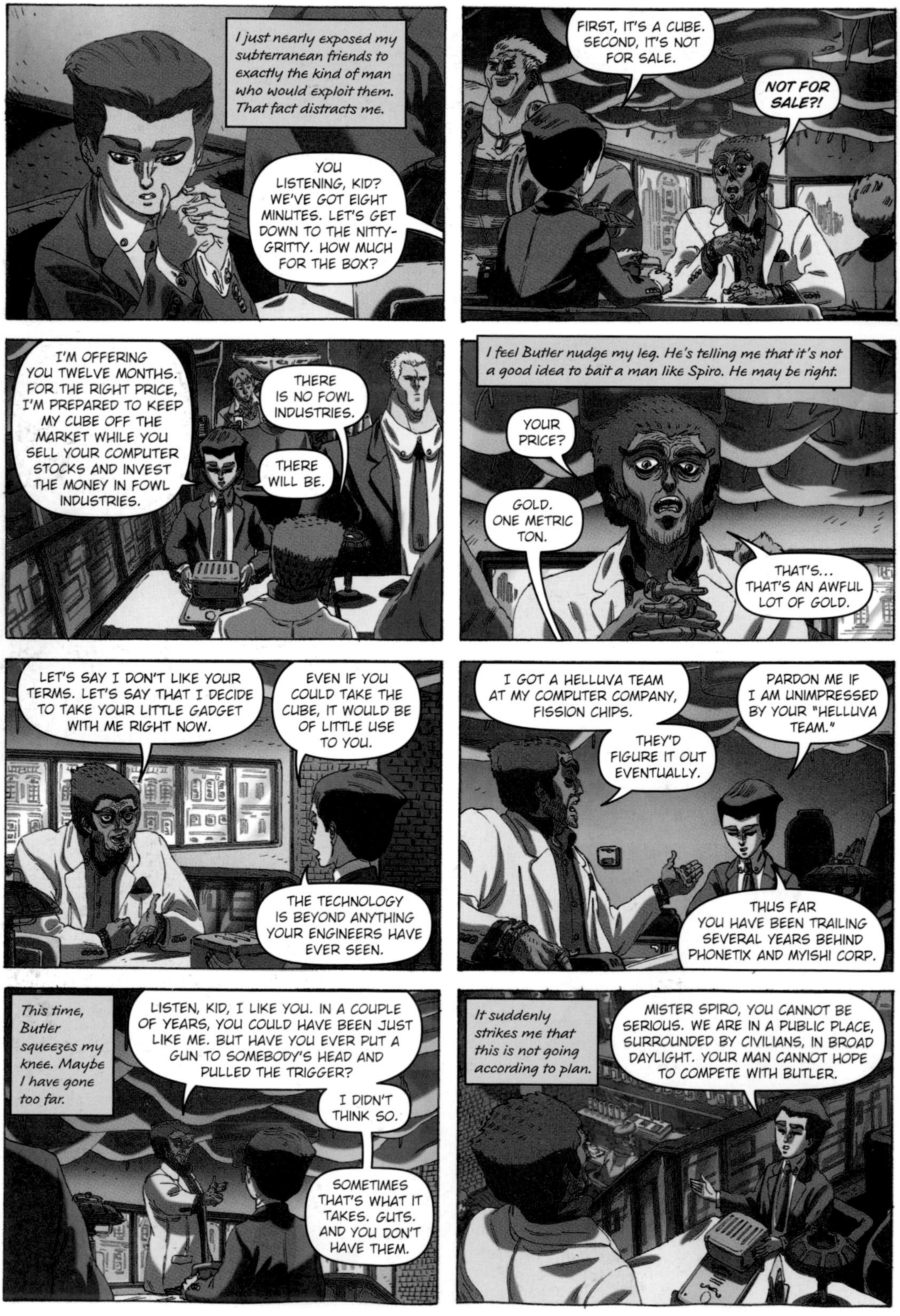
I just nearly exposed my subterranean friends to exactly the kind of man who would exploit them. That fact distracts me.
YOU LISTENING, KID? WE'VE GOT EIGHT MINUTES. LET'S GET DOWN TO THE NITTY-GRITTY. HOW MUCH FOR THE BOX?
FIRST, IT'S A CUBE. SECOND, IT'S NOT FOR SALE.
NOT FOR SALE?!
I'M OFFERING YOU TWELVE MONTHS. FOR THE RIGHT PRICE, I'M PREPARED TO KEEP MY CUBE OFF THE MARKET WHILE YOU SELL YOUR COMPUTER STOCKS AND INVEST THE MONEY IN FOWL INDUSTRIES.
THERE IS NO FOWL INDUSTRIES.
THERE WILL BE.
I feel Butler nudge my leg. He's telling me that it's not a good idea to bait a man like Spiro. He may be right.
YOUR PRICE?
GOLD. ONE METRIC TON.
THAT'S... THAT'S AN AWFUL LOT OF GOLD.
LET'S SAY I DON'T LIKE YOUR TERMS. LET'S SAY THAT I DECIDE TO TAKE YOUR LITTLE GADGET WITH ME RIGHT NOW.
EVEN IF YOU COULD TAKE THE CUBE, IT WOULD BE OF LITTLE USE TO YOU.
THE TECHNOLOGY IS BEYOND ANYTHING YOUR ENGINEERS HAVE EVER SEEN.
I GOT A HELLUVA TEAM AT MY COMPUTER COMPANY, FISSION CHIPS.
THEY'D FIGURE IT OUT EVENTUALLY.
PARDON ME IF I AM UNIMPRESSED BY YOUR "HELLUVA TEAM."
THUS FAR YOU HAVE BEEN TRAILING SEVERAL YEARS BEHIND PHONETIX AND MYISHI CORP.
This time, Butler squeezes my knee. Maybe I have gone too far.
LISTEN, KID, I LIKE YOU. IN A COUPLE OF YEARS, YOU COULD HAVE BEEN JUST LIKE ME. BUT HAVE YOU EVER PUT A GUN TO SOMEBODY'S HEAD AND PULLED THE TRIGGER?
I DIDN'T THINK SO.
SOMETIMES THAT'S WHAT IT TAKES. GUTS. AND YOU DON'T HAVE THEM.
It suddenly strikes me that this is not going according to plan.
MISTER SPIRO, YOU CANNOT BE SERIOUS. WE ARE IN A PUBLIC PLACE, SURROUNDED BY CIVILIANS, IN BROAD DAYLIGHT. YOUR MAN CANNOT HOPE TO COMPETE WITH BUTLER.

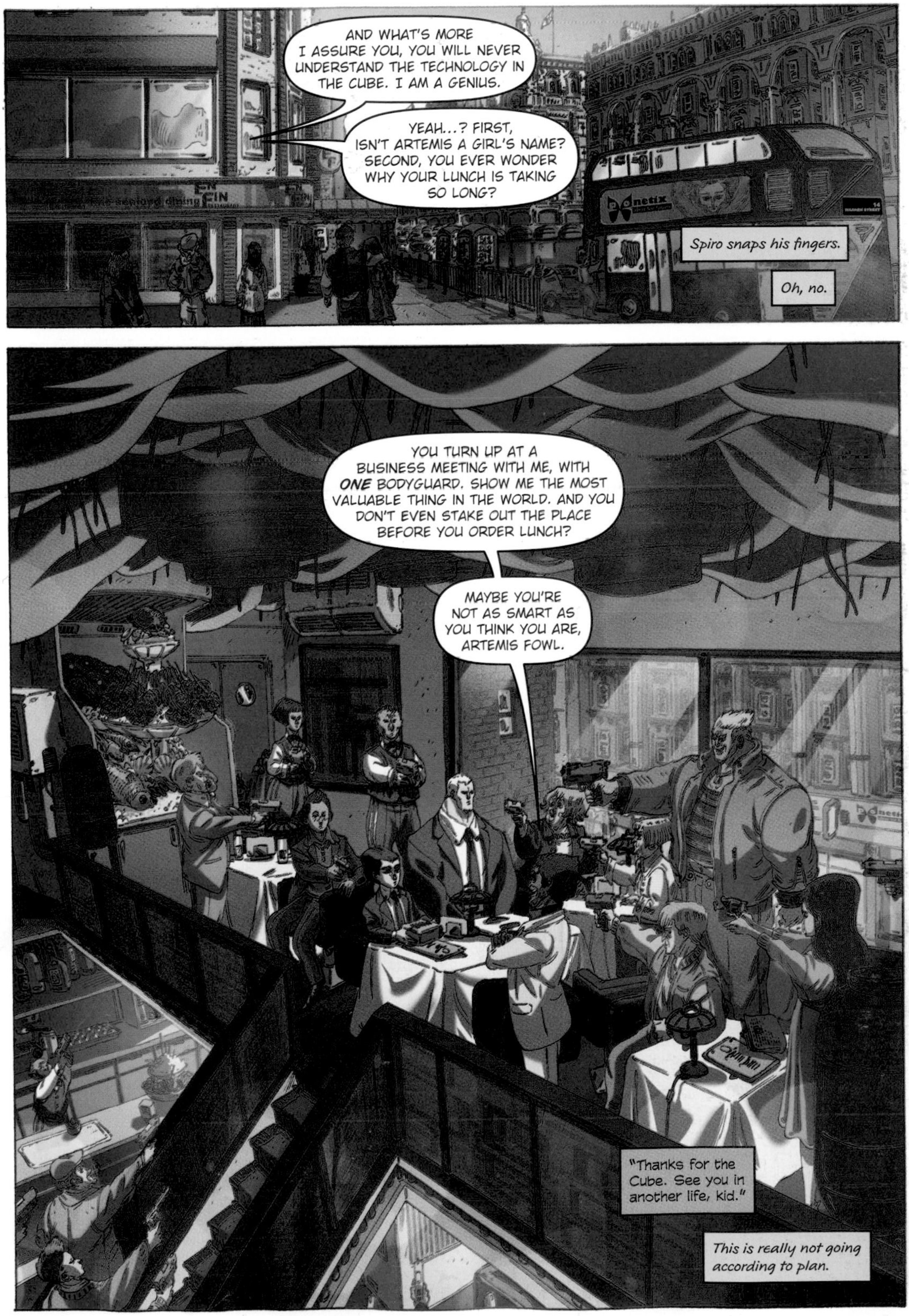
AND WHAT'S MORE I ASSURE YOU, YOU WILL NEVER UNDERSTAND THE TECHNOLOGY IN THE CUBE. I AM A GENIUS.
YEAH...? FIRST, ISN'T ARTEMIS A GIRL'S NAME? SECOND, YOU EVER WONDER WHY YOUR LUNCH IS TAKING SO LONG?
Spiro snaps his fingers.
Oh, no.
YOU TURN UP AT A BUSINESS MEETING WITH ME, WITH ONE BODYGUARD. SHOW ME THE MOST VALUABLE THING IN THE WORLD. AND YOU DON'T EVEN STAKE OUT THE PLACE BEFORE YOU ORDER LUNCH?
MAYBE YOU'RE NOT AS SMART AS YOU THINK YOU ARE, ARTEMIS FOWL.
"Thanks for the Cube. See you in another life, kid."
This is really not going according to plan.

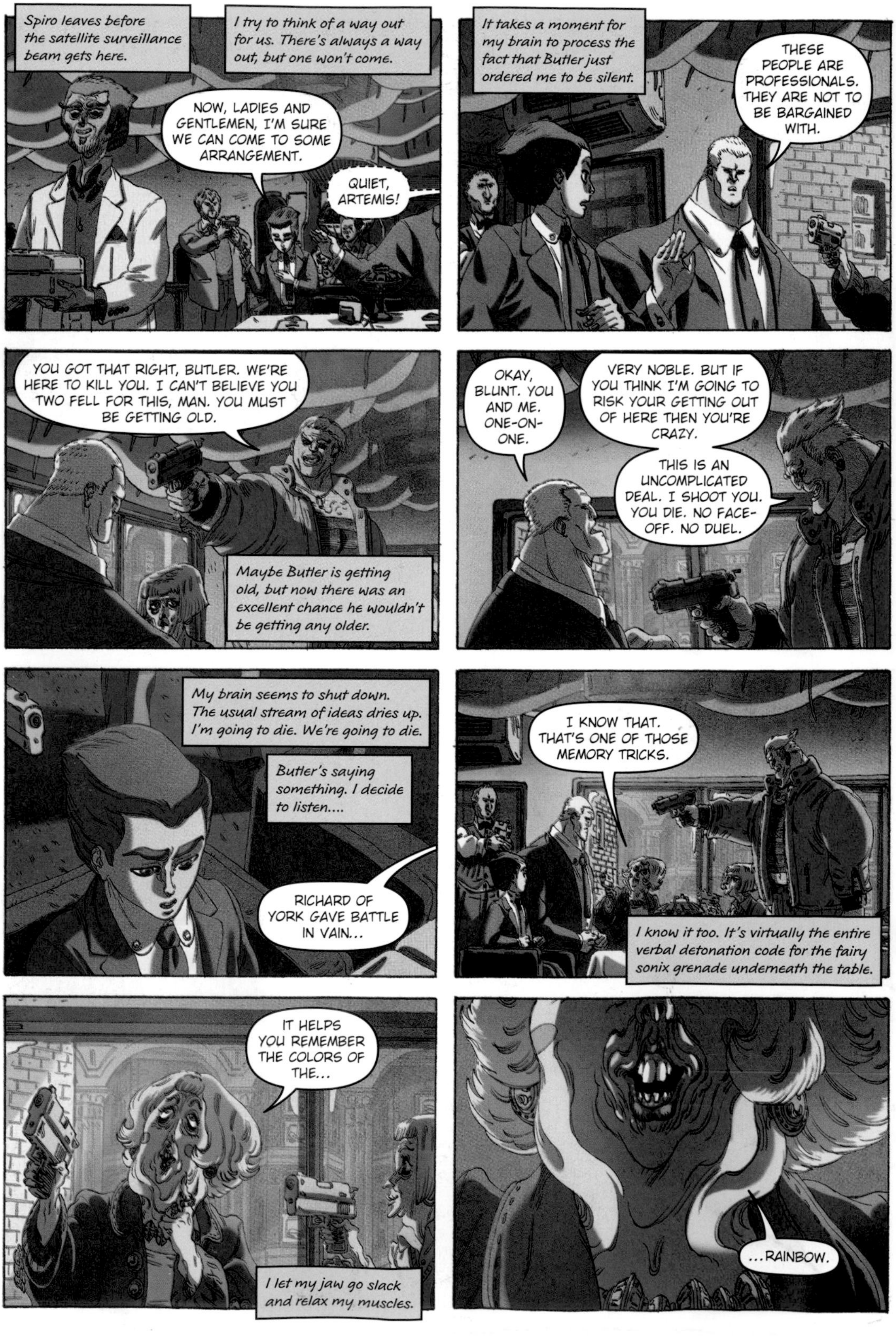

Spiro leaves before the satellite surveillance beam gets here.
I try to think of a way out for us. There's always a way out, but one won't come.
NOW, LADIES AND GENTLEMEN, I'M SURE WE CAN COME TO SOME ARRANGEMENT.
QUIET, ARTEMIS!
It takes a moment for my brain to process the fact that Butler just ordered me to be silent.
THESE PEOPLE ARE PROFESSIONALS. THEY ARE NOT TO BE BARGAINED WITH.
YOU GOT THAT RIGHT, BUTLER. WE'RE HERE TO KILL YOU. I CAN'T BELIEVE YOU TWO FELL FOR THIS, MAN. YOU MUST BE GETTING OLD.
Maybe Butler is getting old, but now there was an excellent chance he wouldn't be getting any older.
OKAY, BLUNT. YOU AND ME. ONE-ON-ONE.
VERY NOBLE. BUT IF YOU THINK I'M GOING TO RISK YOUR GETTING OUT OF HERE THEN YOU'RE CRAZY.
THIS IS AN UNCOMPLICATED DEAL. I SHOOT YOU. YOU DIE. NO FACE-OFF. NO DUEL.
My brain seems to shut down. The usual stream of ideas dries up. I'm going to die. We're going to die.
Butler's saying something. I decide to listen....
RICHARD OF YORK GAVE BATTLE IN VAIN...
I KNOW THAT. THAT'S ONE OF THOSE MEMORY TRICKS.
I know it too. It's virtually the entire verbal detonation code for the fairy sonix grenade underneath the table.
IT HELPS YOU REMEMBER THE COLORS OF THE...
I let my jaw go slack and relax my muscles.
...RAINBOW.

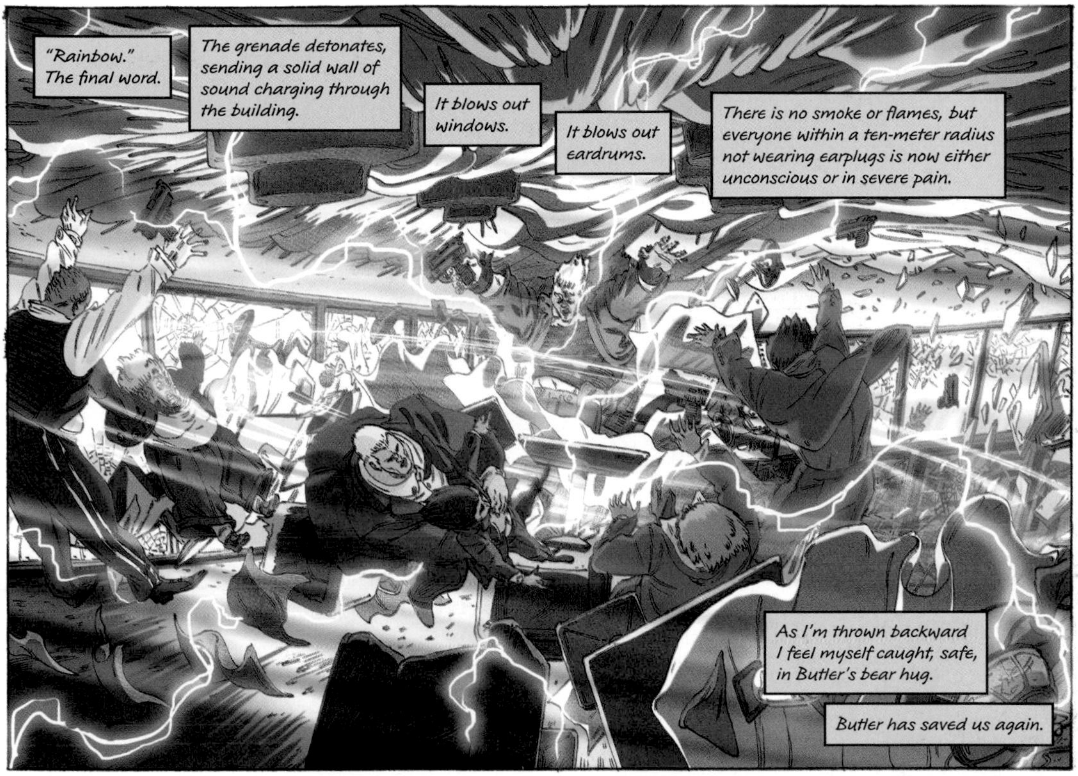
"Rainbow."
The final word.
The grenade detonates, sending a solid wall of sound charging through the building.
It blows out windows.
It blows out eardrums.
There is no smoke or flames, but everyone within a ten-meter radius not wearing earplugs is now either unconscious or in severe pain.
As I'm thrown backward I feel myself caught, safe, in Butler's bear hug.
Butler has saved us again.

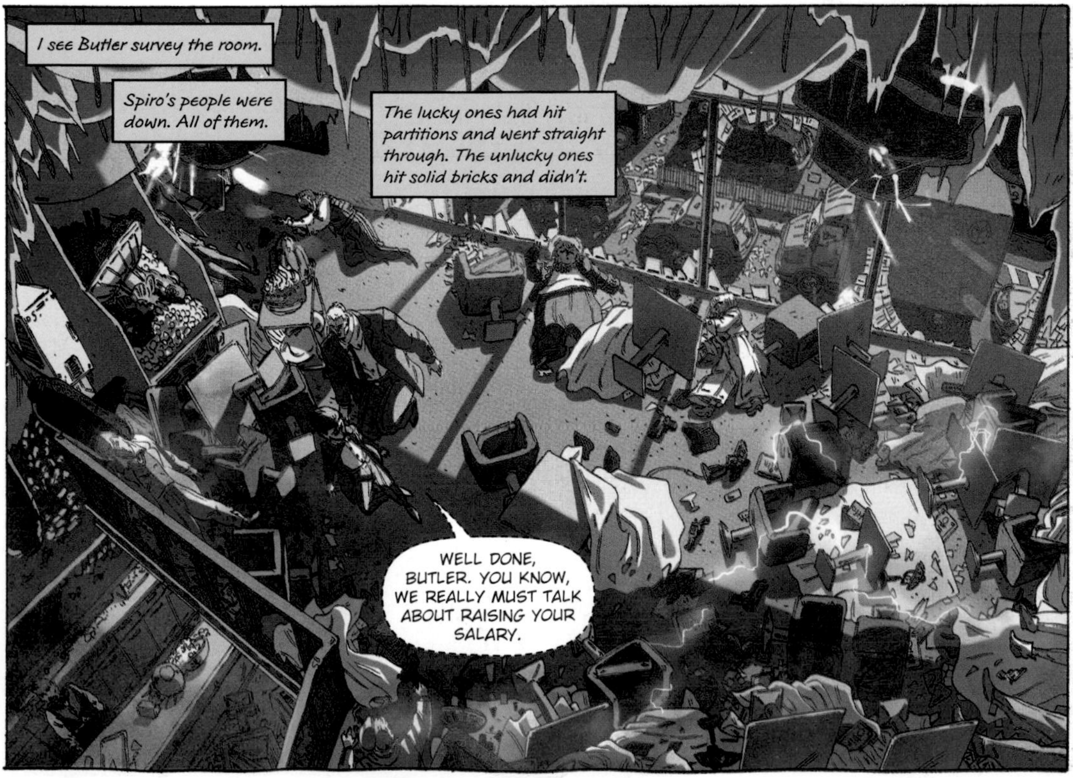
I see Butler survey the room.
Spiro's people were down. All of them.
The lucky ones had hit partitions and went straight through. The unlucky ones hit solid bricks and didn't.
WELL DONE, BUTLER. YOU KNOW, WE REALLY MUST TALK ABOUT RAISING YOUR SALARY.

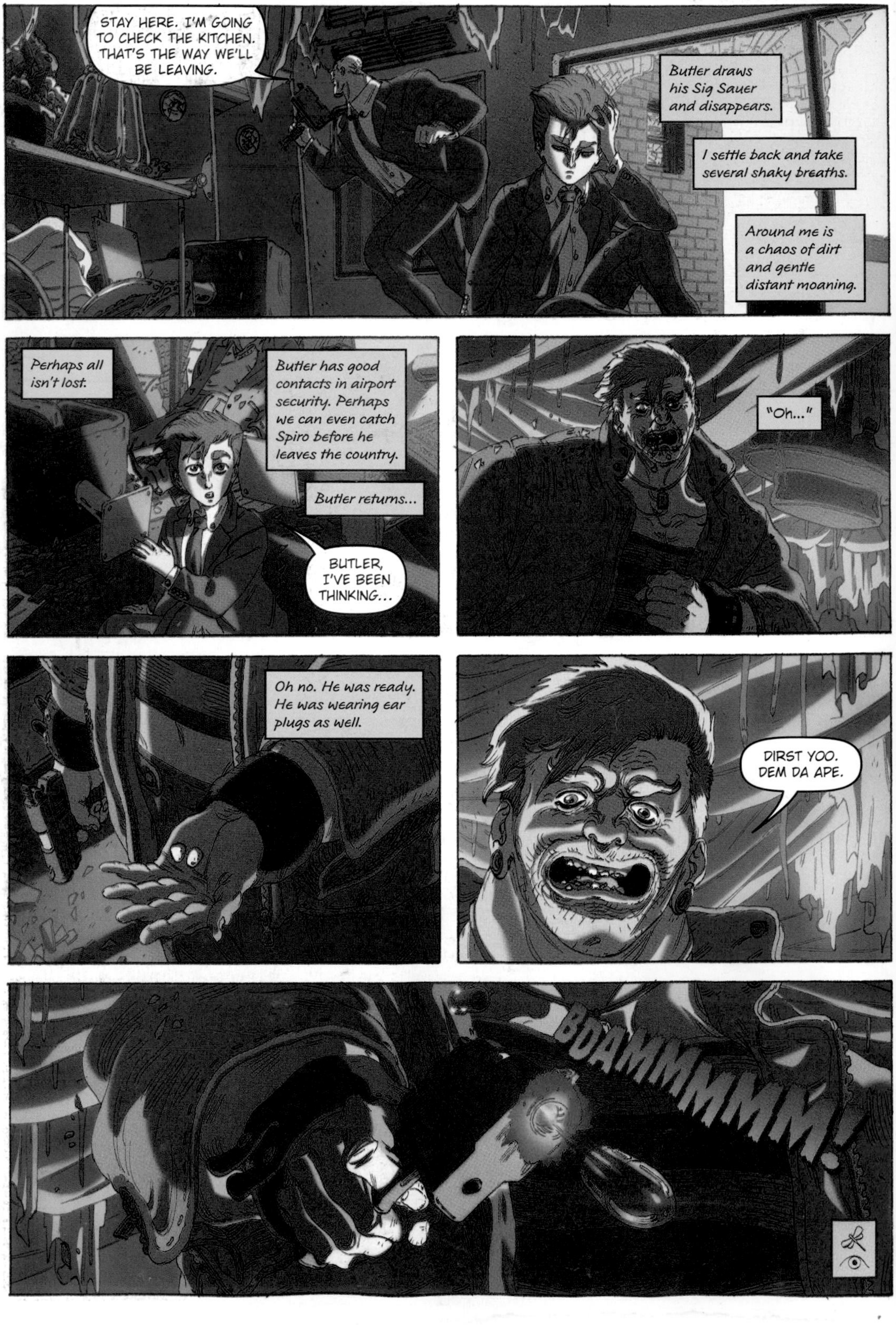
STAY HERE. I'M GOING TO CHECK THE KITCHEN. THAT'S THE WAY WE'LL BE LEAVING.
Butler draws his Sig Sauer and disappears.
I settle back and take several shaky breaths.
Around me is a chaos of dirt and gentle distant moaning.
Perhaps all isn't lost.
Butler has good contacts in airport security. Perhaps we can even catch Spiro before he leaves the country.
Butler returns...
BUTLER, I'VE BEEN THINKING...
"Oh..."
Oh no. He was ready. He was wearing ear plugs as well.
DIRST YOO. DEM DA APE.
BDAMMMMMM!

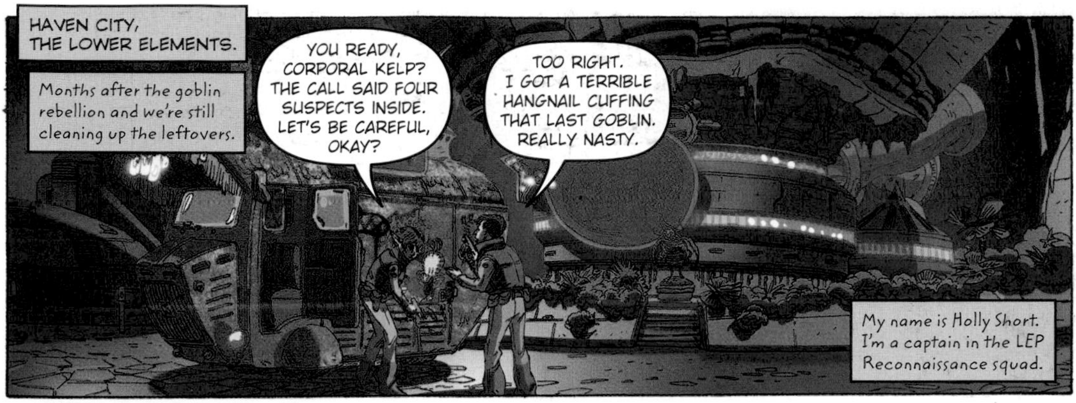
HAVEN CITY, THE LOWER ELEMENTS.
Months after the goblin rebellion and we're still cleaning up the leftovers.
YOU READY, CORPORAL KELP? THE CALL SAID FOUR SUSPECTS INSIDE. LET'S BE CAREFUL, OKAY?
TOO RIGHT. I GOT A TERRIBLE HANGNAIL CUFFING THAT LAST GOBLIN. REALLY NASTY.
My name is Holly Short. I'm a captain in the LEP Reconnaissance squad.

CHAPTER 2: LOCKDOWN

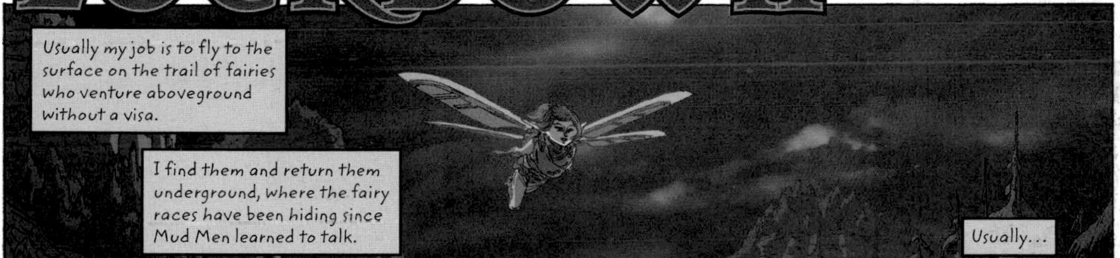
Usually my job is to fly to the surface on the trail of fairies who venture aboveground without a visa.
I find them and return them underground, where the fairy races have been hiding since Mud Men learned to talk.
Usually...

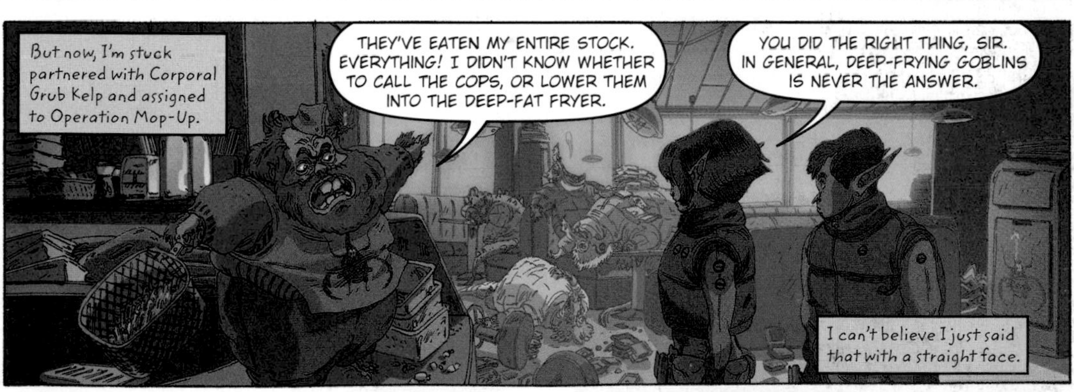
But now, I'm stuck partnered with Corporal Grub Kelp and assigned to Operation Mop-Up.
THEY'VE EATEN MY ENTIRE STOCK. EVERYTHING! I DIDN'T KNOW WHETHER TO CALL THE COPS, OR LOWER THEM INTO THE DEEP-FAT FRYER.
YOU DID THE RIGHT THING, SIR. IN GENERAL, DEEP-FRYING GOBLINS IS NEVER THE ANSWER.
I can't believe I just said that with a straight face.

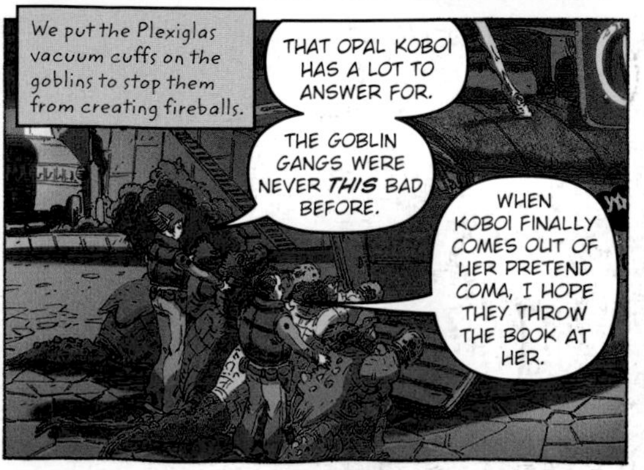
We put the Plexiglas vacuum cuffs on the goblins to stop them from creating fireballs.
THAT OPAL KOBOI HAS A LOT TO ANSWER FOR.
THE GOBLIN GANGS WERE NEVER THIS BAD BEFORE.
WHEN KOBOI FINALLY COMES OUT OF HER PRETEND COMA, I HOPE THEY THROW THE BOOK AT HER.

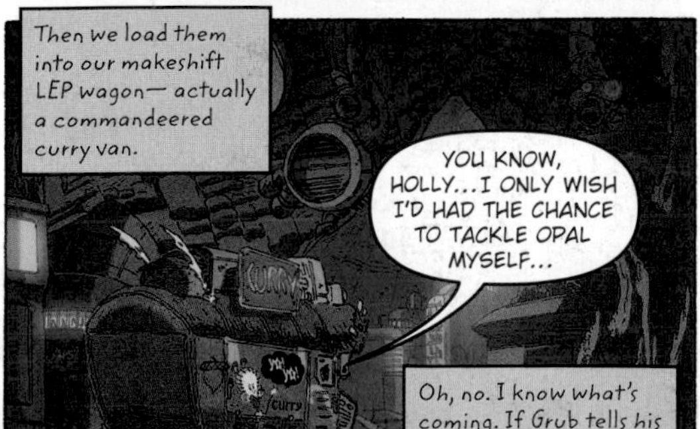
Then we load them into our makeshift LEP wagon— actually a commandeered curry van.
YOU KNOW, HOLLY... I ONLY WISH I'D HAD THE CHANCE TO TACKLE OPAL MYSELF...
Oh, no. I know what's coming. If Grub tells his Butler story again then I may have to punch his lights out.

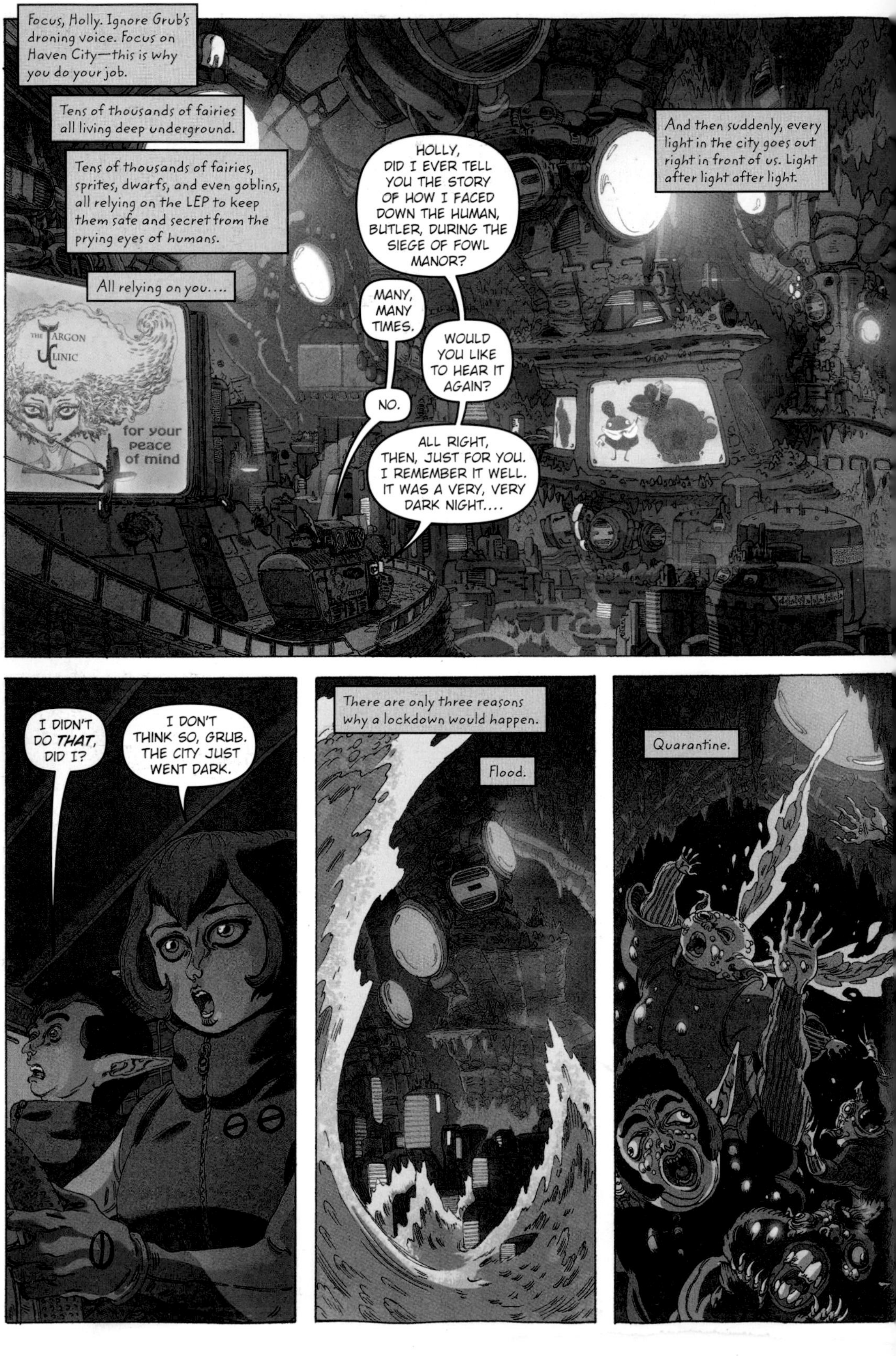

Focus, Holly. Ignore Grub's droning voice. Focus on Haven City—this is why you do your job.
Tens of thousands of fairies all living deep underground.
Tens of thousands of fairies, sprites, dwarfs, and even goblins, all relying on the LEP to keep them safe and secret from the prying eyes of humans.
All relying on you....
THE JARGON CLINIC
for your peace of mind
HOLLY, DID I EVER TELL YOU THE STORY OF HOW I FACED DOWN THE HUMAN, BUTLER, DURING THE SIEGE OF FOWL MANOR?
MANY, MANY TIMES.
WOULD YOU LIKE TO HEAR IT AGAIN?
NO.
ALL RIGHT, THEN, JUST FOR YOU. I REMEMBER IT WELL. IT WAS A VERY, VERY DARK NIGHT....
And then suddenly, every light in the city goes out right in front of us. Light after light after light.
I DIDN'T DO ***THAT***, DID I?
I DON'T THINK SO, GRUB. THE CITY JUST WENT DARK.
There are only three reasons why a lockdown would happen.
Flood.
Quarantine.

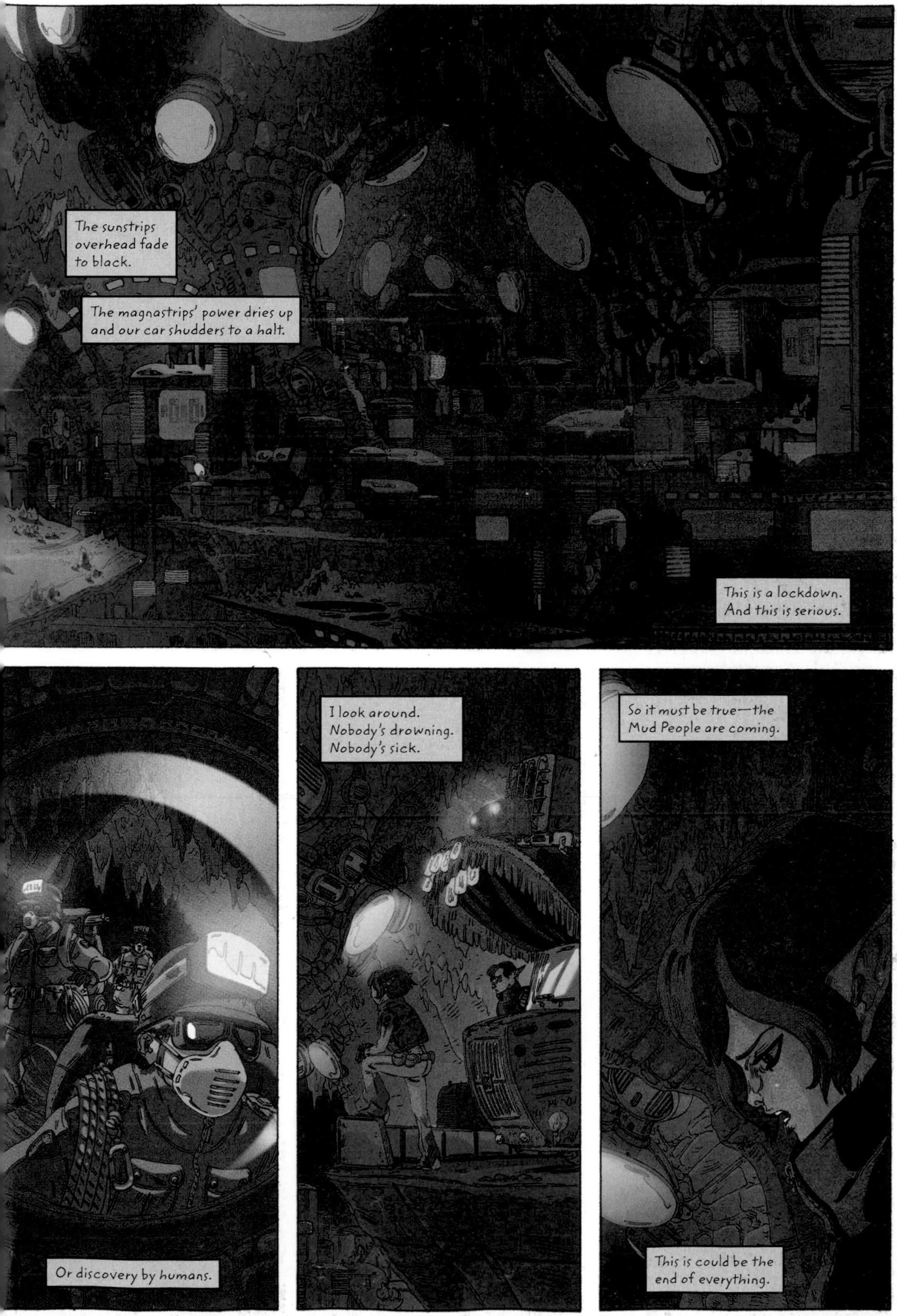
The sunstrips overhead fade to black.
The magnastrips' power dries up and our car shudders to a halt.
This is a lockdown. And this is serious.
Or discovery by humans.
I look around. Nobody's drowning. Nobody's sick.
So it must be true—the Mud People are coming.
This is could be the end of everything.

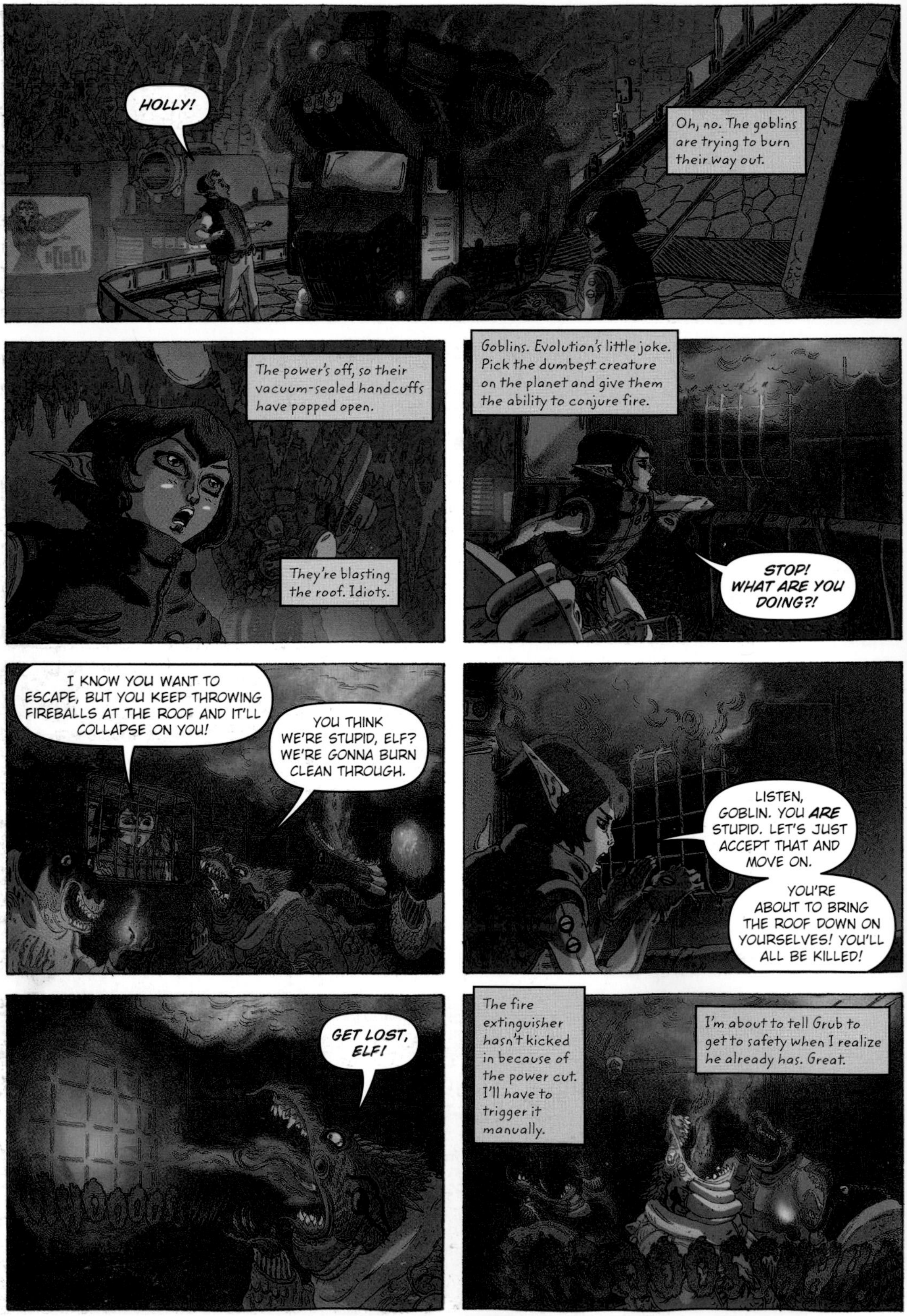
HOLLY!
Oh, no. The goblins are trying to burn their way out.
The power's off, so their vacuum-sealed handcuffs have popped open.
They're blasting the roof. Idiots.
Goblins. Evolution's little joke. Pick the dumbest creature on the planet and give them the ability to conjure fire.
STOP! WHAT ARE YOU DOING?!
I KNOW YOU WANT TO ESCAPE, BUT YOU KEEP THROWING FIREBALLS AT THE ROOF AND IT'LL COLLAPSE ON YOU!
YOU THINK WE'RE STUPID, ELF? WE'RE GONNA BURN CLEAN THROUGH.
LISTEN, GOBLIN. YOU ARE STUPID. LET'S JUST ACCEPT THAT AND MOVE ON.
YOU'RE ABOUT TO BRING THE ROOF DOWN ON YOURSELVES! YOU'LL ALL BE KILLED!
GET LOST, ELF!
The fire extinguisher hasn't kicked in because of the power cut. I'll have to trigger it manually.
I'm about to tell Grub to get to safety when I realize he already has. Great.

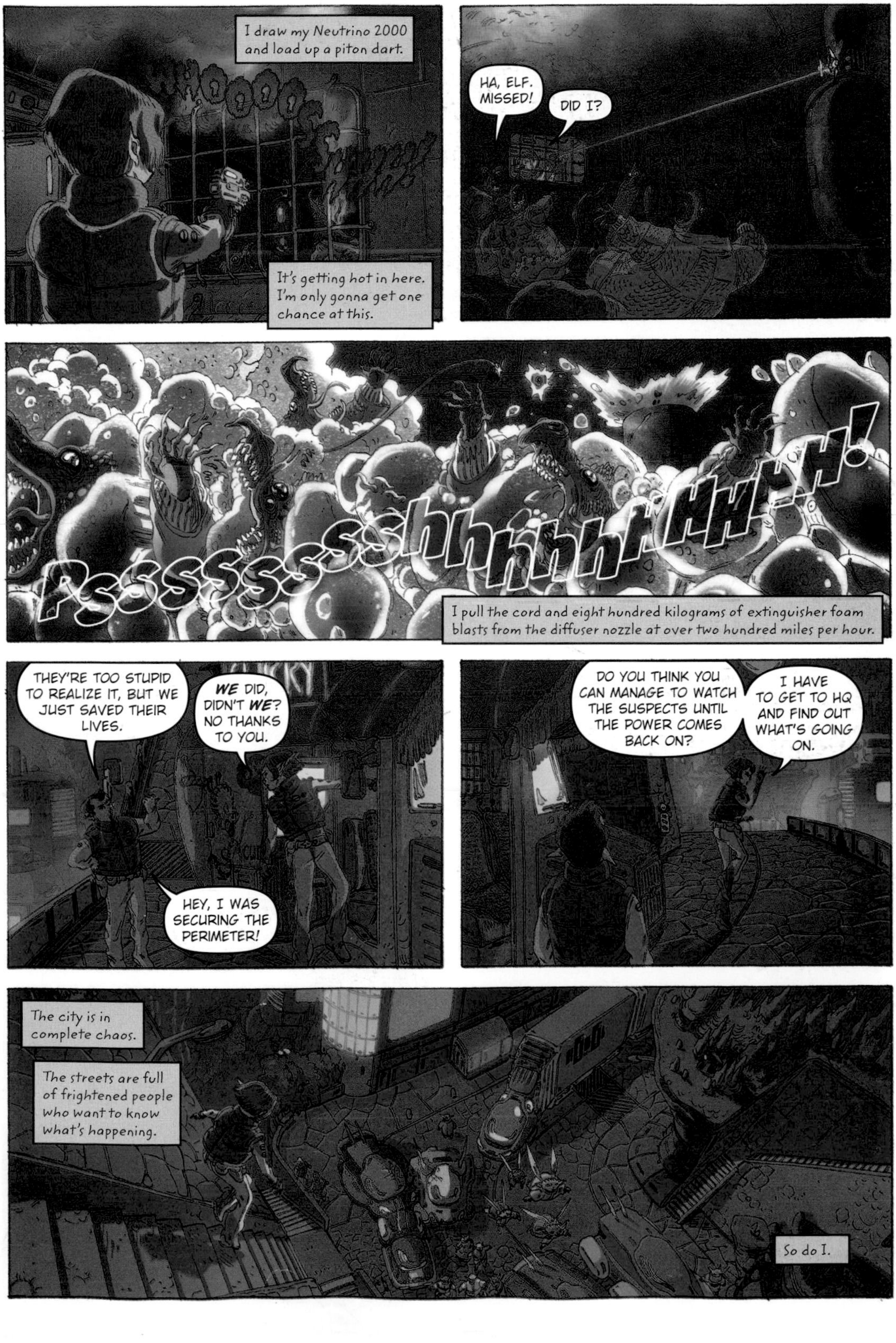
I draw my Neutrino 2000 and load up a piton dart.
It's getting hot in here. I'm only gonna get one chance at this.
HA, ELF. MISSED!
DID I?
I pull the cord and eight hundred kilograms of extinguisher foam blasts from the diffuser nozzle at over two hundred miles per hour.
THEY'RE TOO STUPID TO REALIZE IT, BUT WE JUST SAVED THEIR LIVES.
WE DID, DIDN'T WE? NO THANKS TO YOU.
HEY, I WAS SECURING THE PERIMETER!
DO YOU THINK YOU CAN MANAGE TO WATCH THE SUSPECTS UNTIL THE POWER COMES BACK ON?
I HAVE TO GET TO HQ AND FIND OUT WHAT'S GOING ON.
The city is in complete chaos.
The streets are full of frightened people who want to know what's happening.
So do I.

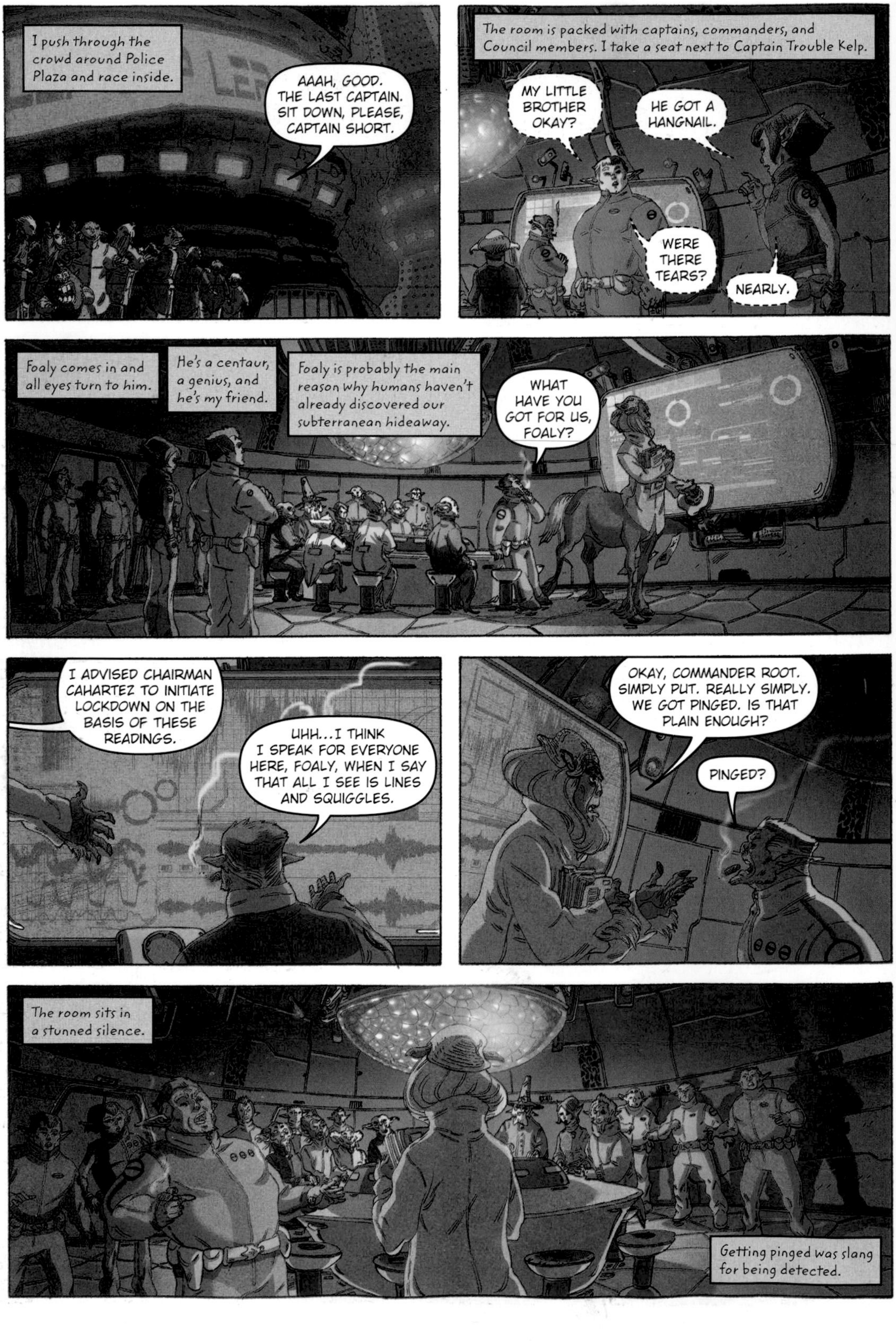
I push through the crowd around Police Plaza and race inside.
AAAH, GOOD. THE LAST CAPTAIN. SIT DOWN, PLEASE, CAPTAIN SHORT.
The room is packed with captains, commanders, and Council members. I take a seat next to Captain Trouble Kelp.
MY LITTLE BROTHER OKAY?
HE GOT A HANGNAIL.
WERE THERE TEARS?
NEARLY.
Foaly comes in and all eyes turn to him.
He's a centaur, a genius, and he's my friend.
Foaly is probably the main reason why humans haven't already discovered our subterranean hideaway.
WHAT HAVE YOU GOT FOR US, FOALY?
I ADVISED CHAIRMAN CAHARTEZ TO INITIATE LOCKDOWN ON THE BASIS OF THESE READINGS.
UHH...I THINK I SPEAK FOR EVERYONE HERE, FOALY, WHEN I SAY THAT ALL I SEE IS LINES AND SQUIGGLES.
OKAY, COMMANDER ROOT. SIMPLY PUT. REALLY SIMPLY. WE GOT PINGED. IS THAT PLAIN ENOUGH?
PINGED?
The room sits in a stunned silence.
Getting pinged was slang for being detected.

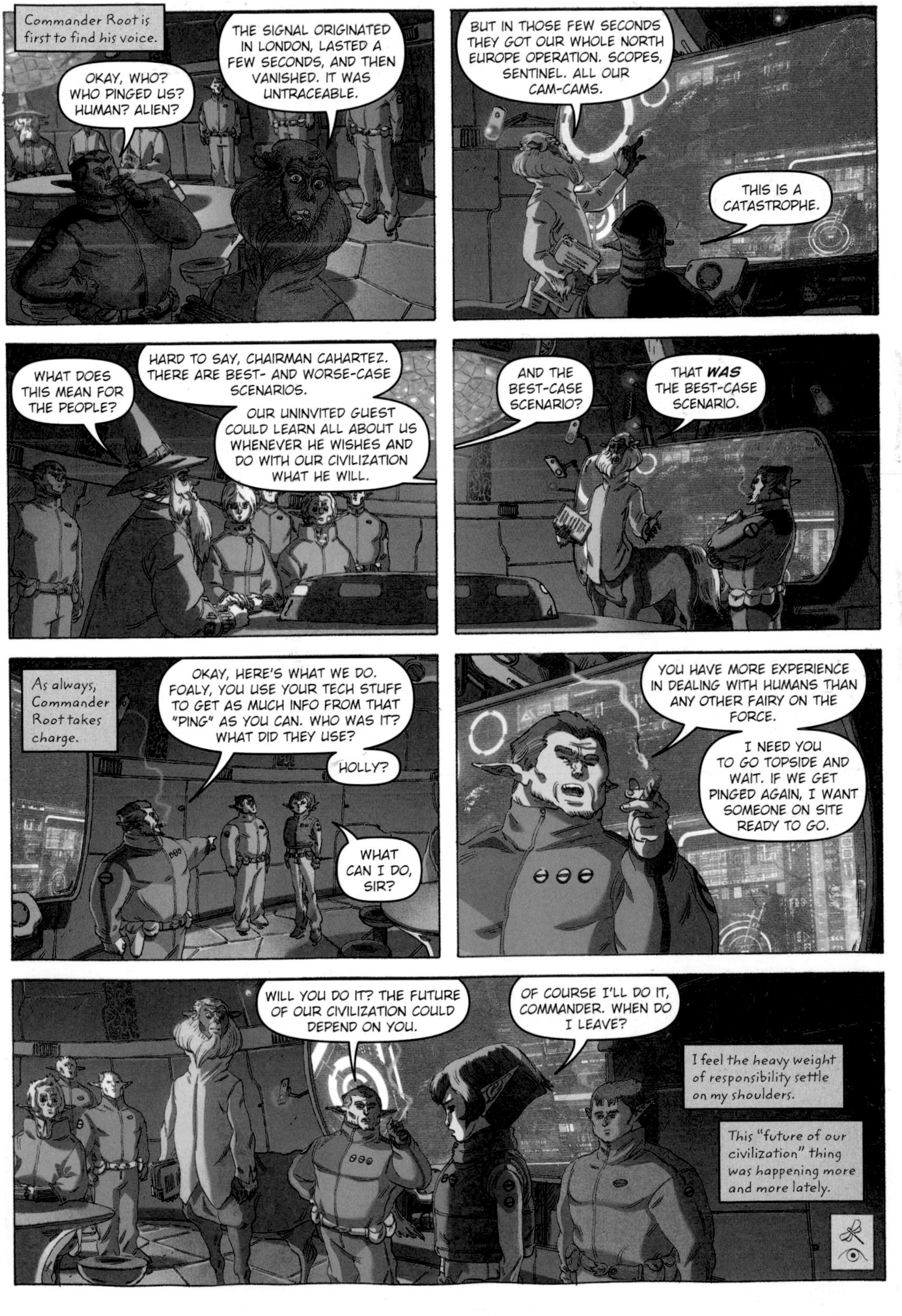
Commander Root is first to find his voice.
OKAY, WHO? WHO PINGED US? HUMAN? ALIEN?
THE SIGNAL ORIGINATED IN LONDON, LASTED A FEW SECONDS, AND THEN VANISHED. IT WAS UNTRACEABLE.
BUT IN THOSE FEW SECONDS THEY GOT OUR WHOLE NORTH EUROPE OPERATION. SCOPES, SENTINEL. ALL OUR CAM-CAMS.
THIS IS A CATASTROPHE.
WHAT DOES THIS MEAN FOR THE PEOPLE?
HARD TO SAY, CHAIRMAN CAHARTEZ. THERE ARE BEST- AND WORSE-CASE SCENARIOS.
OUR UNINVITED GUEST COULD LEARN ALL ABOUT US WHENEVER HE WISHES AND DO WITH OUR CIVILIZATION WHAT HE WILL.
AND THE BEST-CASE SCENARIO?
THAT **WAS** THE BEST-CASE SCENARIO.
As always, Commander Root takes charge.
OKAY, HERE'S WHAT WE DO. FOALY, YOU USE YOUR TECH STUFF TO GET AS MUCH INFO FROM THAT "PING" AS YOU CAN. WHO WAS IT? WHAT DID THEY USE?
HOLLY?
WHAT CAN I DO, SIR?
YOU HAVE MORE EXPERIENCE IN DEALING WITH HUMANS THAN ANY OTHER FAIRY ON THE FORCE.
I NEED YOU TO GO TOPSIDE AND WAIT. IF WE GET PINGED AGAIN, I WANT SOMEONE ON SITE READY TO GO.
WILL YOU DO IT? THE FUTURE OF OUR CIVILIZATION COULD DEPEND ON YOU.
OF COURSE I'LL DO IT, COMMANDER. WHEN DO I LEAVE?
I feel the heavy weight of responsibility settle on my shoulders.
This "future of our civilization" thing was happening more and more lately.

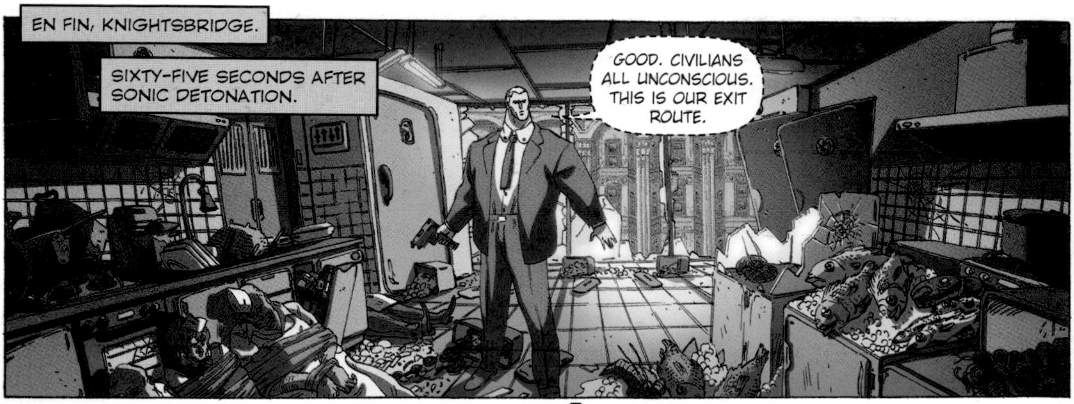
EN FIN, KNIGHTSBRIDGE.
SIXTY-FIVE SECONDS AFTER SONIC DETONATION.
GOOD. CIVILIANS ALL UNCONSCIOUS. THIS IS OUR EXIT ROUTE.

CHAPTER 3: ON ICE

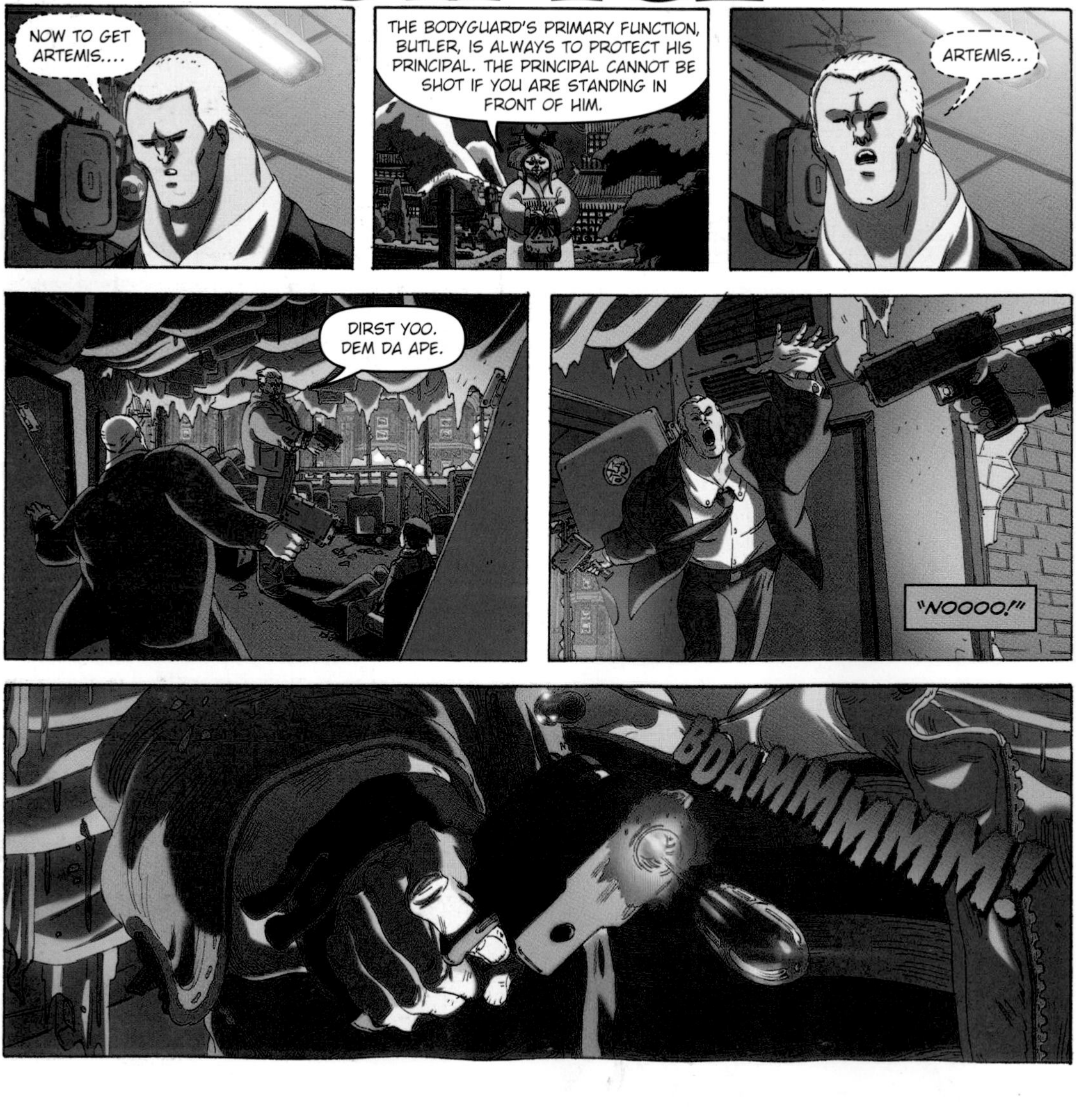
NOW TO GET ARTEMIS....
THE BODYGUARD'S PRIMARY FUNCTION, BUTLER, IS ALWAYS TO PROTECT HIS PRINCIPAL. THE PRINCIPAL CANNOT BE SHOT IF YOU ARE STANDING IN FRONT OF HIM.
ARTEMIS...
DIRST YOO. DEM DA APE.
"NOOOO!"
BDAMMMMMM!

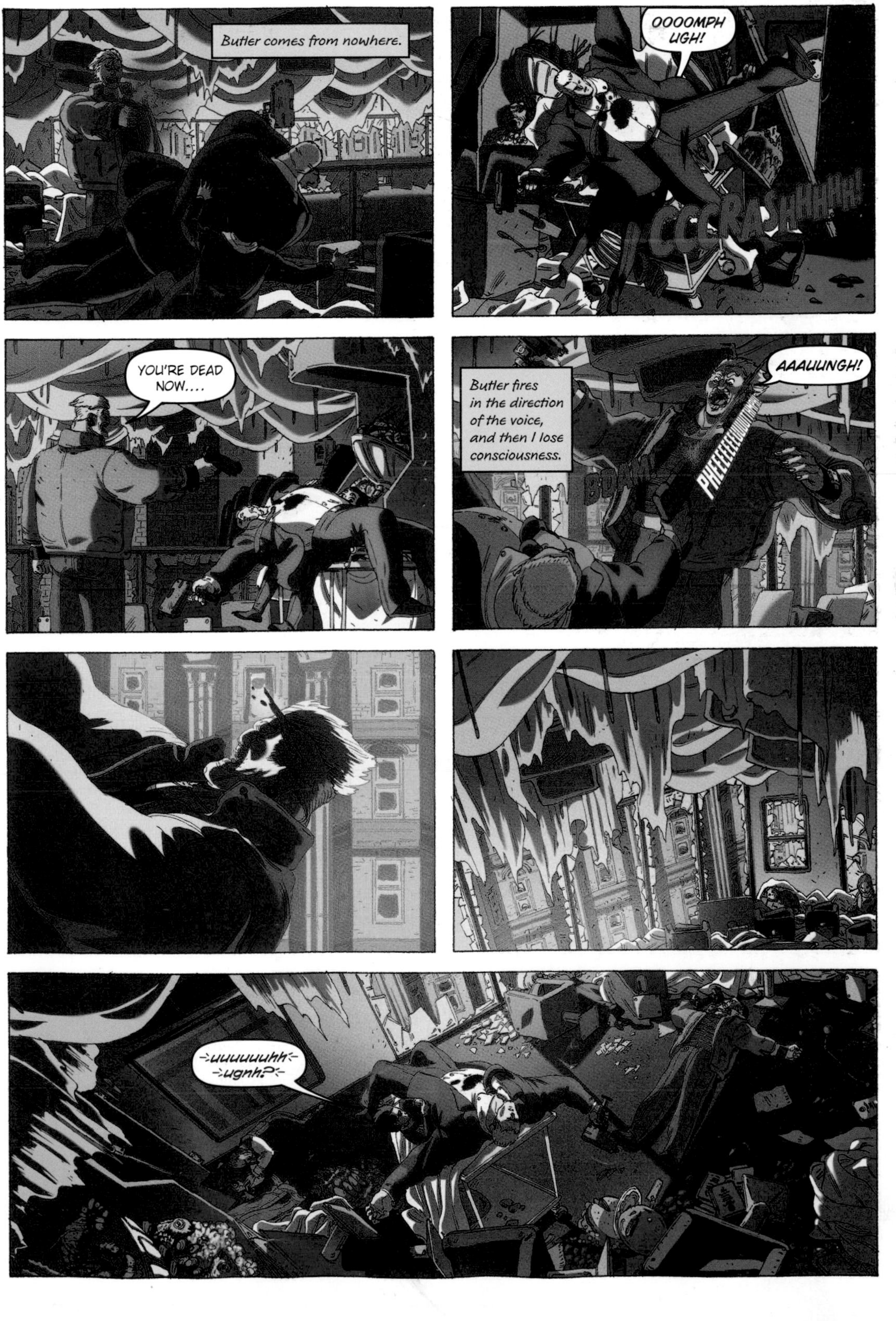
Butler comes from nowhere.
OOOOMPH UGH!
CCCRASHHHHH!
YOU'RE DEAD NOW....
Butler fires in the direction of the voice, and then I lose consciousness.
AAAUUNGH!
uuuuuuhh ugnh?

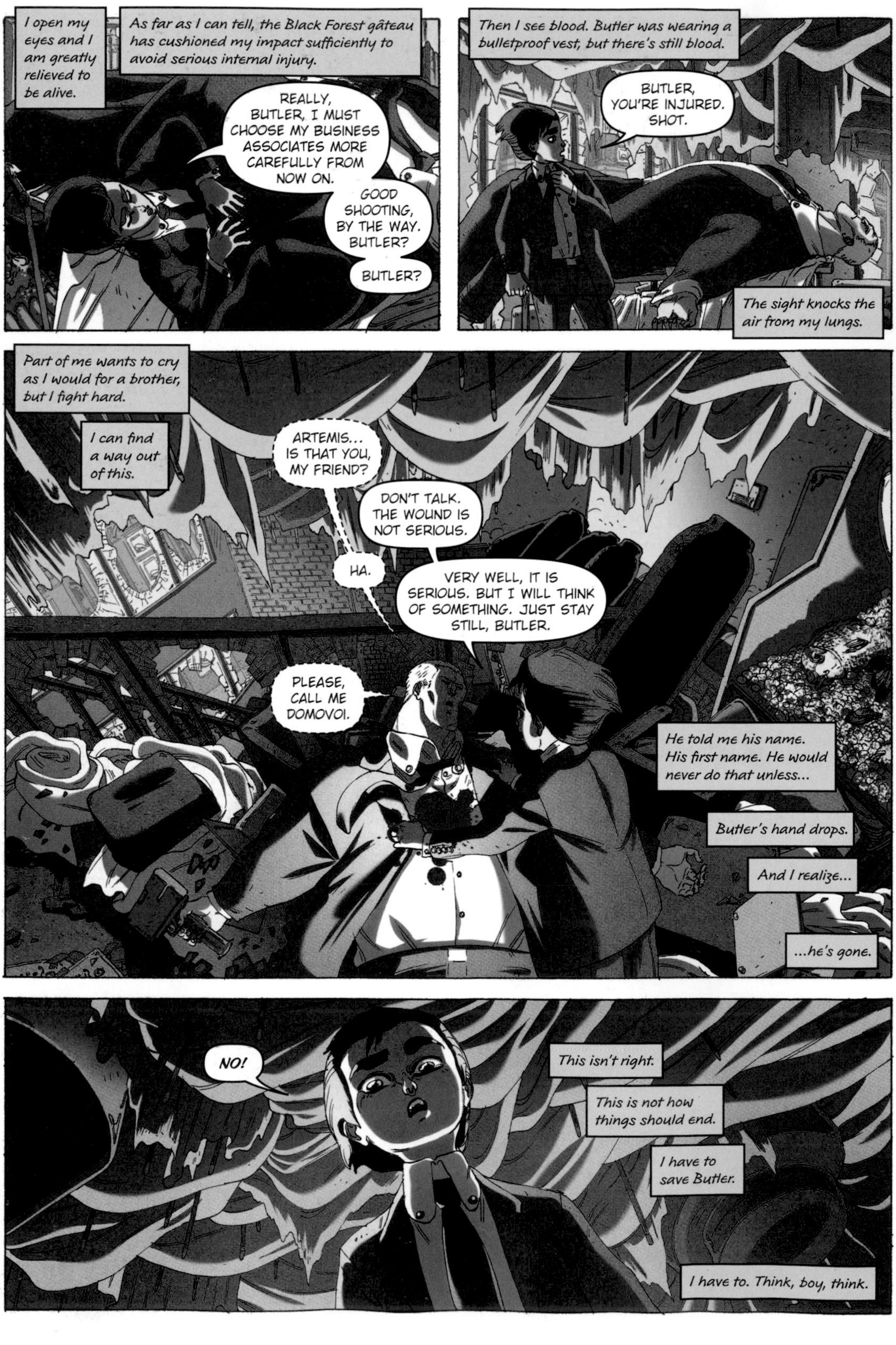
I open my eyes and I am greatly relieved to be alive.
As far as I can tell, the Black Forest gâteau has cushioned my impact sufficiently to avoid serious internal injury.
REALLY, BUTLER, I MUST CHOOSE MY BUSINESS ASSOCIATES MORE CAREFULLY FROM NOW ON.
GOOD SHOOTING, BY THE WAY. BUTLER?
BUTLER?
Then I see blood. Butler was wearing a bulletproof vest, but there's still blood.
BUTLER, YOU'RE INJURED. SHOT.
The sight knocks the air from my lungs.
Part of me wants to cry as I would for a brother, but I fight hard.
I can find a way out of this.
ARTEMIS... IS THAT YOU, MY FRIEND?
DON'T TALK. THE WOUND IS NOT SERIOUS.
HA.
VERY WELL, IT IS SERIOUS. BUT I WILL THINK OF SOMETHING. JUST STAY STILL, BUTLER.
PLEASE, CALL ME DOMOVOI.
He told me his name. His first name. He would never do that unless...
Butler's hand drops.
And I realize...
...he's gone.
NO!
This isn't right.
This is not how things should end.
I have to save Butler.
I have to. Think, boy, think.

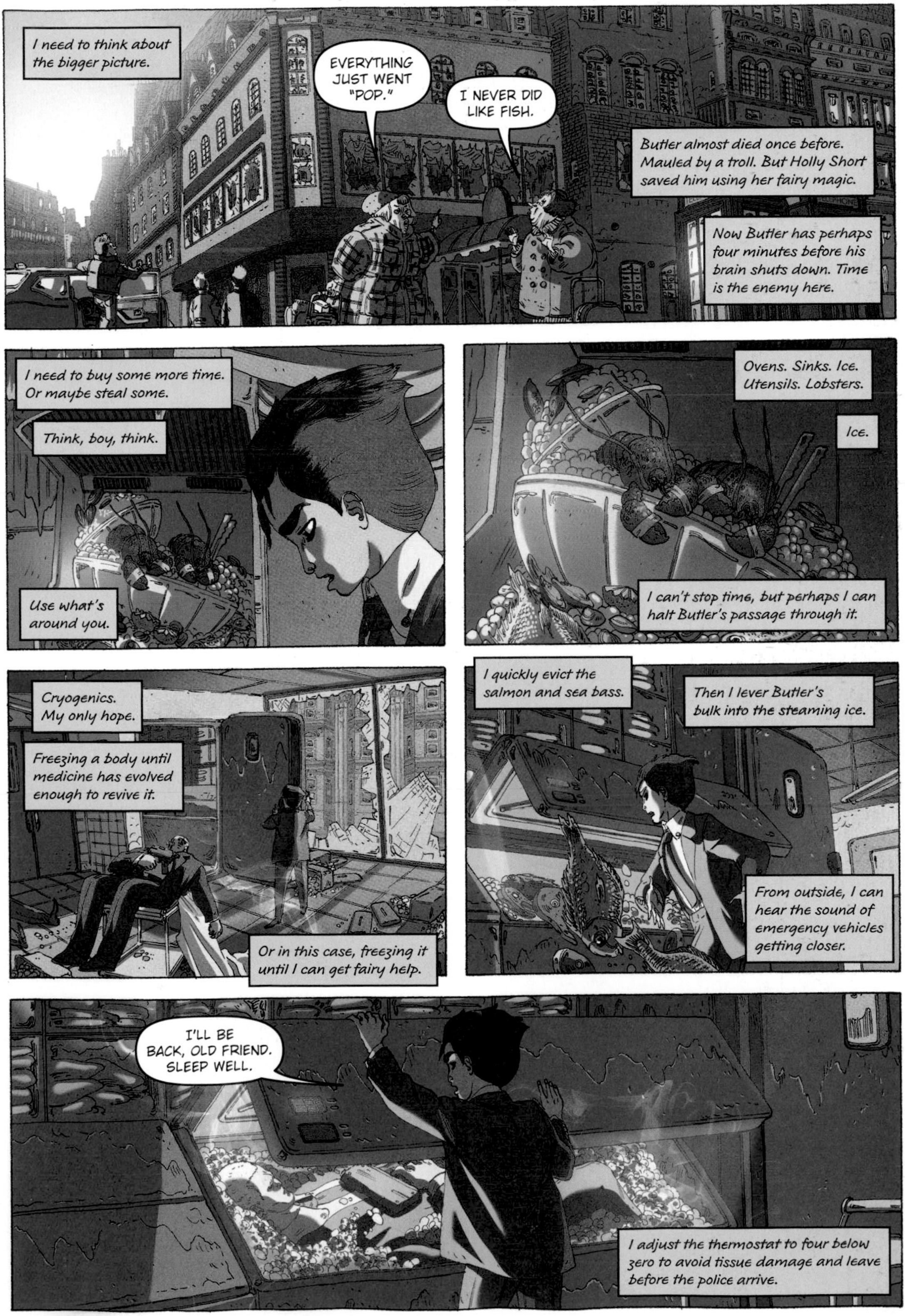
I need to think about the bigger picture.
EVERYTHING JUST WENT "POP."
I NEVER DID LIKE FISH.
Butler almost died once before. Mauled by a troll. But Holly Short saved him using her fairy magic.
Now Butler has perhaps four minutes before his brain shuts down. Time is the enemy here.
I need to buy some more time. Or maybe steal some.
Think, boy, think.
Use what's around you.
Ovens. Sinks. Ice. Utensils. Lobsters.
Ice.
I can't stop time, but perhaps I can halt Butler's passage through it.
Cryogenics. My only hope.
Freezing a body until medicine has evolved enough to revive it.
Or in this case, freezing it until I can get fairy help.
I quickly evict the salmon and sea bass.
Then I lever Butler's bulk into the steaming ice.
From outside, I can hear the sound of emergency vehicles getting closer.
I'LL BE BACK, OLD FRIEND. SLEEP WELL.
I adjust the thermostat to four below zero to avoid tissue damage and leave before the police arrive.

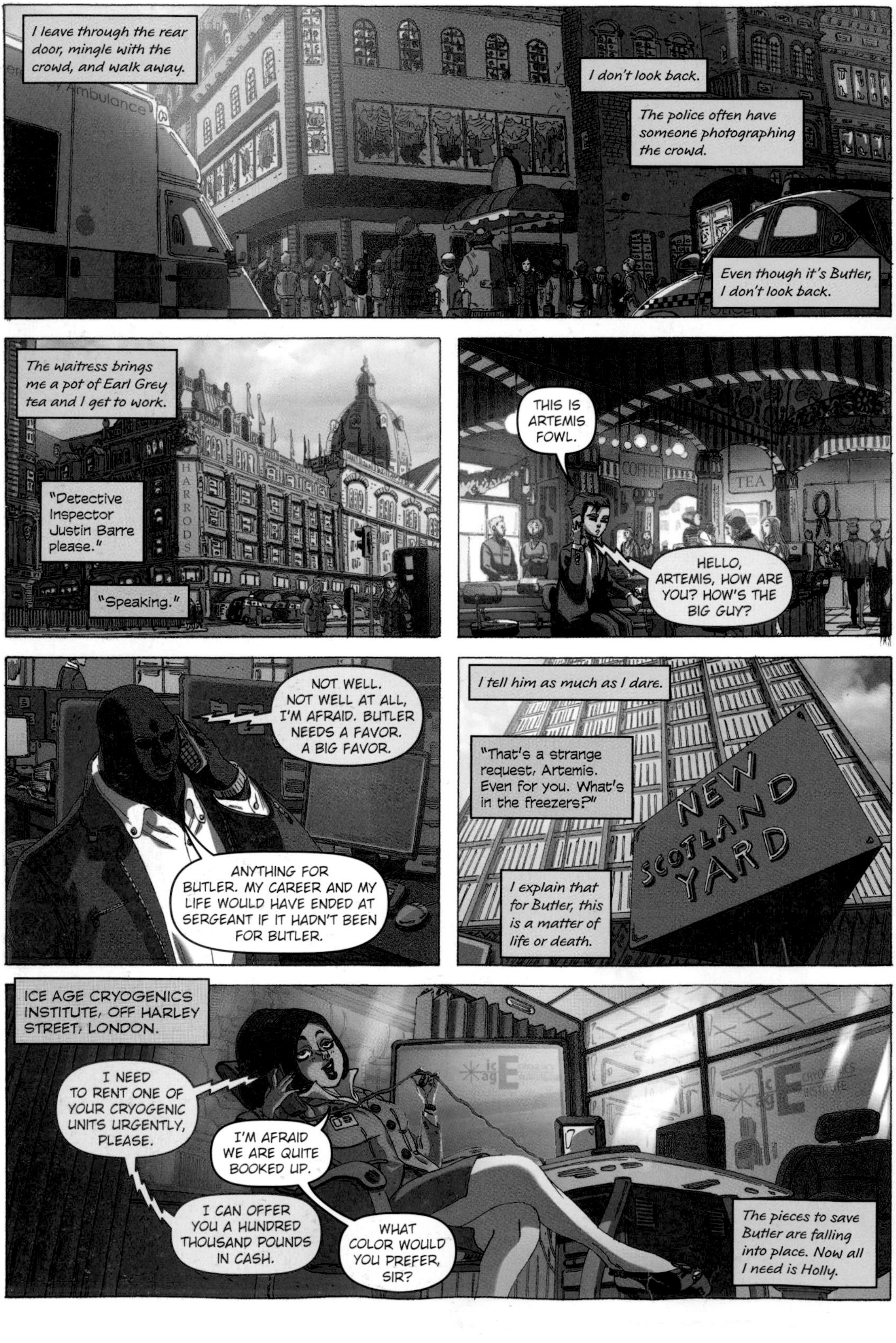
I leave through the rear door, mingle with the crowd, and walk away.
Ambulance
I don't look back.
The police often have someone photographing the crowd.
Even though it's Butler, I don't look back.
The waitress brings me a pot of Earl Grey tea and I get to work.
HARRODS
"Detective Inspector Justin Barre please."
"Speaking."
THIS IS ARTEMIS FOWL.
COFFEE
TEA
HELLO, ARTEMIS, HOW ARE YOU? HOW'S THE BIG GUY?
NOT WELL. NOT WELL AT ALL, I'M AFRAID. BUTLER NEEDS A FAVOR. A BIG FAVOR.
ANYTHING FOR BUTLER. MY CAREER AND MY LIFE WOULD HAVE ENDED AT SERGEANT IF IT HADN'T BEEN FOR BUTLER.
I tell him as much as I dare.
"That's a strange request, Artemis. Even for you. What's in the freezers?"
NEW SCOTLAND YARD
I explain that for Butler, this is a matter of life or death.
ICE AGE CRYOGENICS INSTITUTE, OFF HARLEY STREET, LONDON.
I NEED TO RENT ONE OF YOUR CRYOGENIC UNITS URGENTLY, PLEASE.
I'M AFRAID WE ARE QUITE BOOKED UP.
I CAN OFFER YOU A HUNDRED THOUSAND POUNDS IN CASH.
WHAT COLOR WOULD YOU PREFER, SIR?
CRYOGENICS INSTITUTE
The pieces to save Butler are falling into place. Now all I need is Holly.

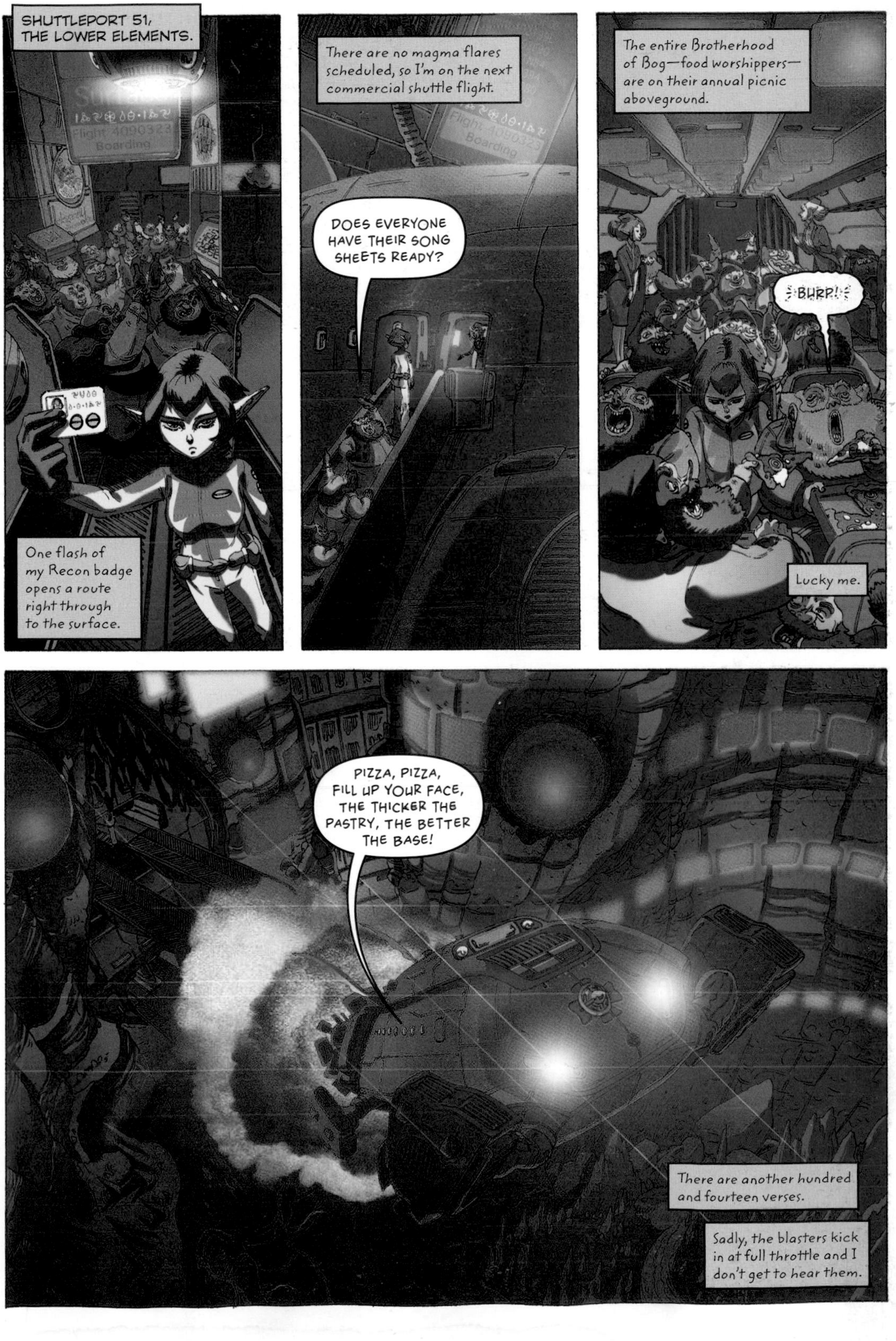
SHUTTLEPORT 51, THE LOWER ELEMENTS.
One flash of my Recon badge opens a route right through to the surface.
There are no magma flares scheduled, so I'm on the next commercial shuttle flight.
DOES EVERYONE HAVE THEIR SONG SHEETS READY?
The entire Brotherhood of Bog—food worshippers—are on their annual picnic aboveground.
BURP!
Lucky me.
PIZZA, PIZZA, FILL UP YOUR FACE, THE THICKER THE PASTRY, THE BETTER THE BASE!
There are another hundred and fourteen verses.
Sadly, the blasters kick in at full throttle and I don't get to hear them.

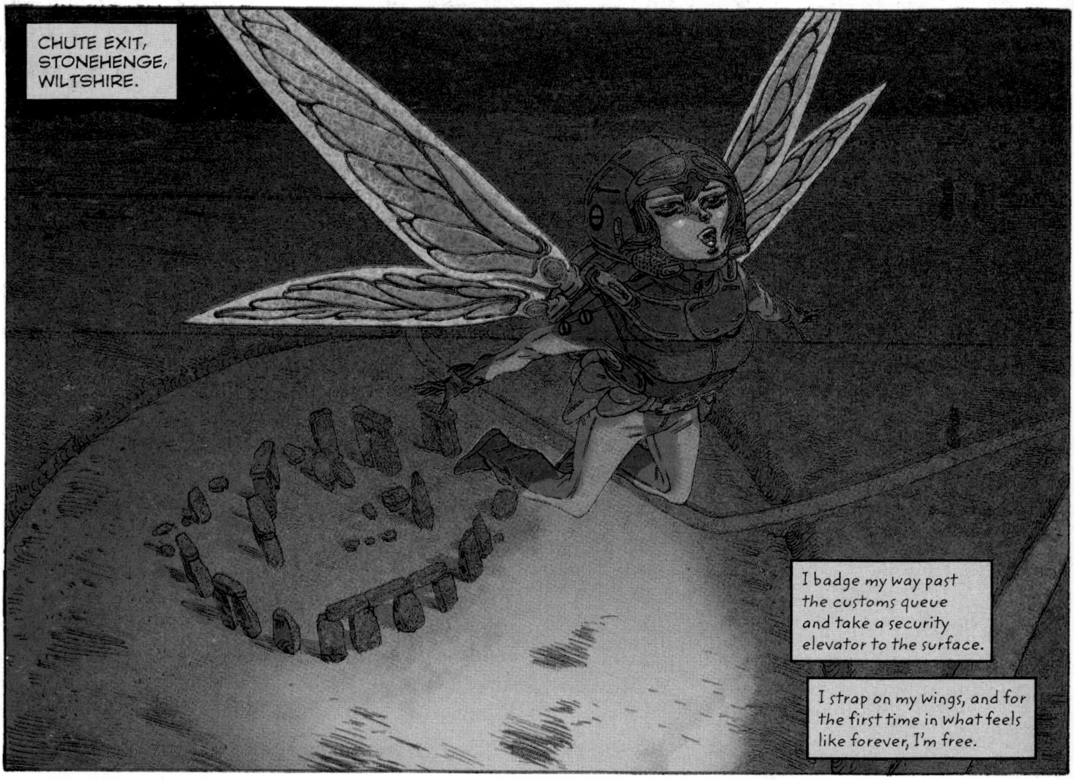
CHUTE EXIT, STONEHENGE, WILTSHIRE.
I badge my way past the customs queue and take a security elevator to the surface.
I strap on my wings, and for the first time in what feels like forever, I'm free.

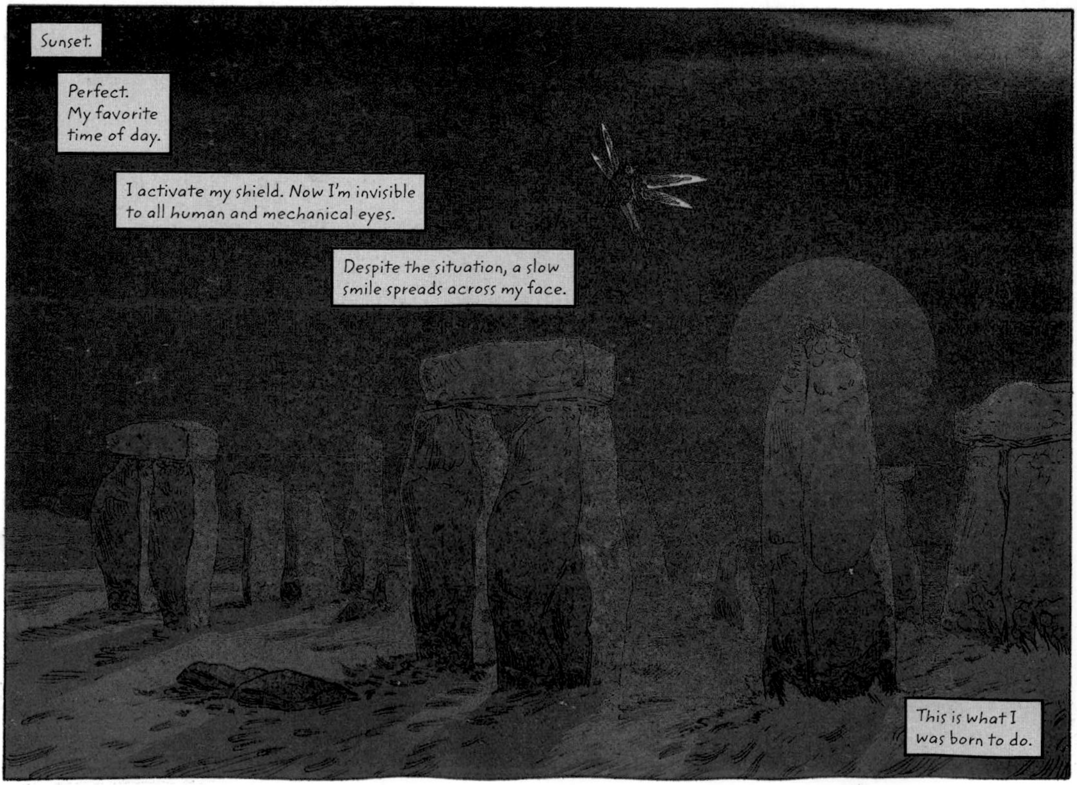
Sunset.
Perfect. My favorite time of day.
I activate my shield. Now I'm invisible to all human and mechanical eyes.
Despite the situation, a slow smile spreads across my face.
This is what I was born to do.

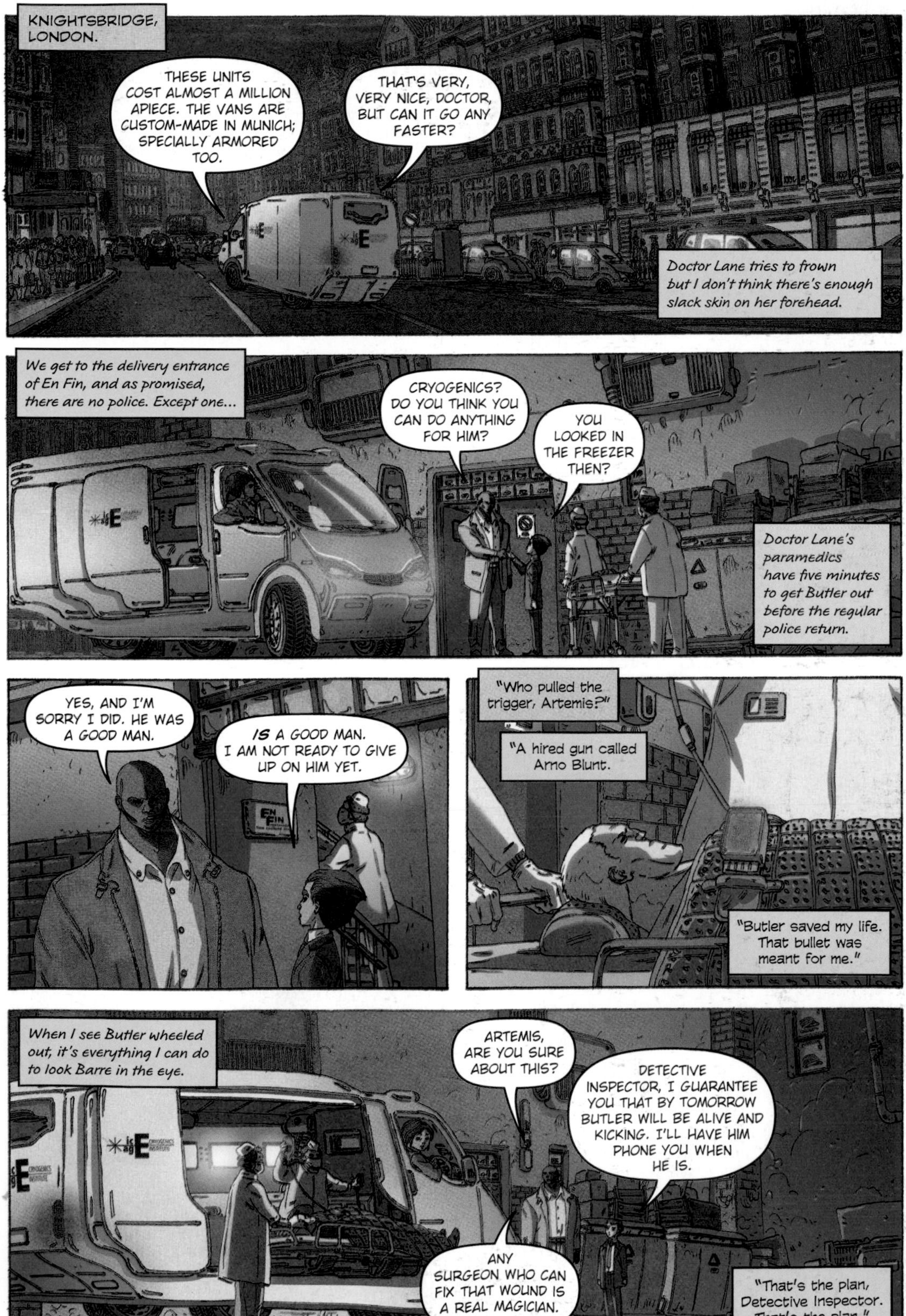

KNIGHTSBRIDGE, LONDON.
THESE UNITS COST ALMOST A MILLION APIECE. THE VANS ARE CUSTOM-MADE IN MUNICH; SPECIALLY ARMORED TOO.
THAT'S VERY, VERY NICE, DOCTOR, BUT CAN IT GO ANY FASTER?
Doctor Lane tries to frown but I don't think there's enough slack skin on her forehead.
We get to the delivery entrance of En Fin, and as promised, there are no police. Except one...
CRYOGENICS? DO YOU THINK YOU CAN DO ANYTHING FOR HIM?
YOU LOOKED IN THE FREEZER THEN?
Doctor Lane's paramedics have five minutes to get Butler out before the regular police return.
YES, AND I'M SORRY I DID. HE WAS A GOOD MAN.
IS A GOOD MAN. I AM NOT READY TO GIVE UP ON HIM YET.
"Who pulled the trigger, Artemis?"
"A hired gun called Arno Blunt.
"Butler saved my life. That bullet was meant for me."
When I see Butler wheeled out, it's everything I can do to look Barre in the eye.
ARTEMIS, ARE YOU SURE ABOUT THIS?
DETECTIVE INSPECTOR, I GUARANTEE YOU THAT BY TOMORROW BUTLER WILL BE ALIVE AND KICKING. I'LL HAVE HIM PHONE YOU WHEN HE IS.
ANY SURGEON WHO CAN FIX THAT WOUND IS A REAL MAGICIAN.
"That's the plan, Detective Inspector. That's the plan."

I head for London.

Doctor Lane prepares Butler.

I slip into Doctor Lane's office and make a very important phone call.

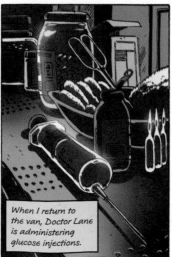
When I return to the van, Doctor Lane is administering glucose injections.

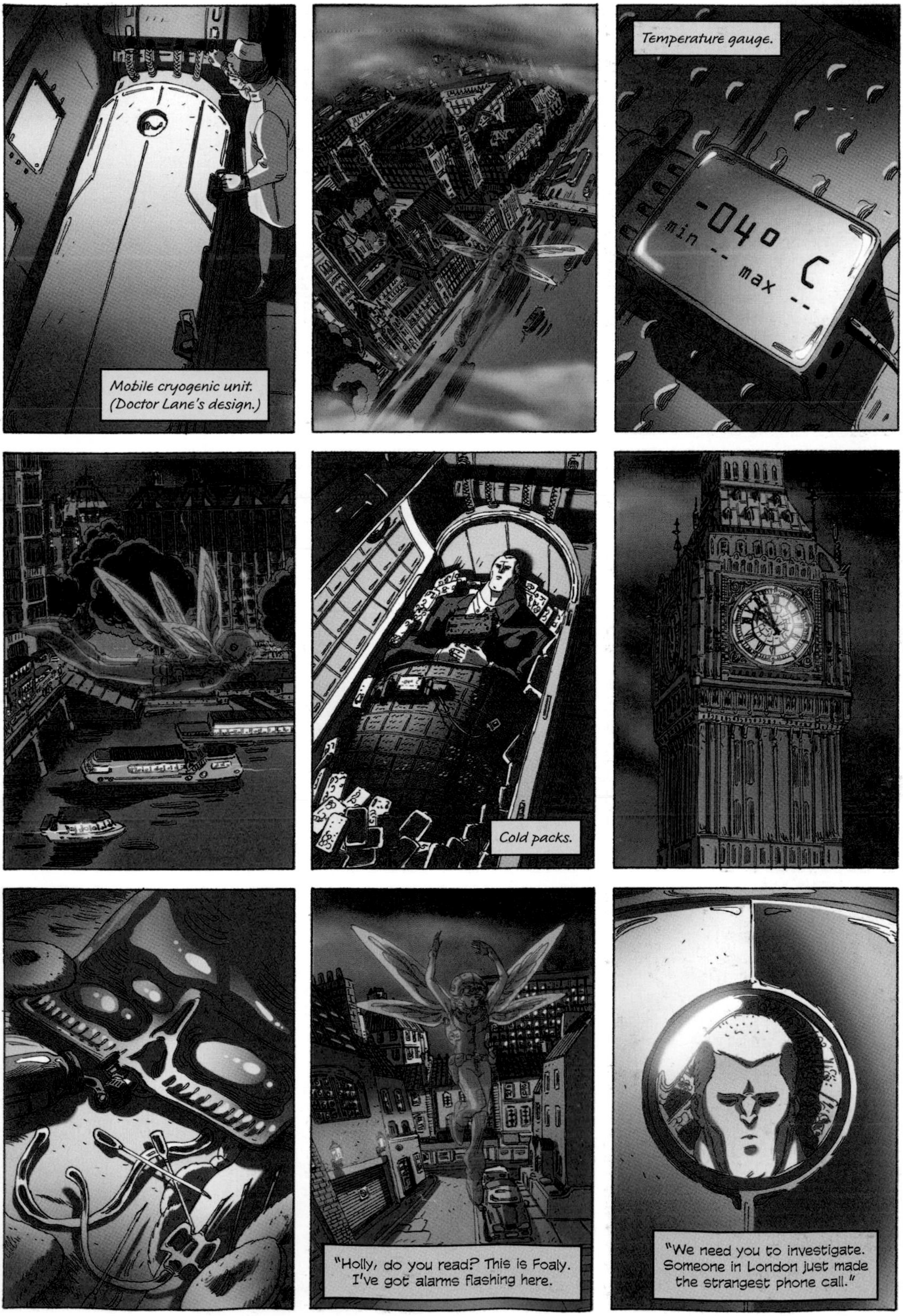
Mobile cryogenic unit.
(Doctor Lane's design.)
Temperature gauge.
-040 C
min -- max --
Cold packs.
"Holly, do you read? This is Foaly.
I've got alarms flashing here.
"We need you to investigate.
Someone in London just made
the strangest phone call."

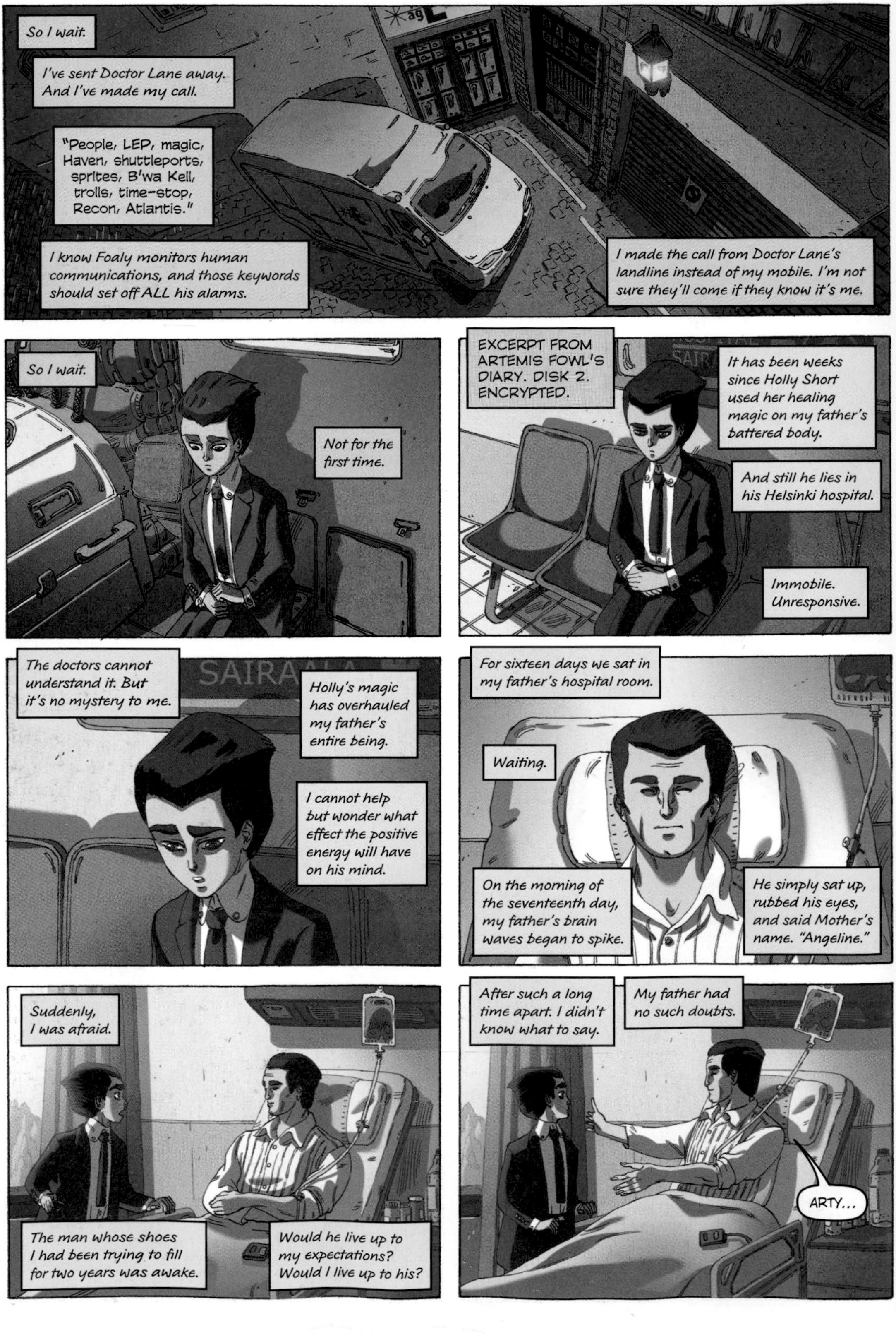
So I wait.
I've sent Doctor Lane away. And I've made my call.
"People, LEP, magic, Haven, shuttleports, sprites, B'wa Kell, trolls, time-stop, Recon, Atlantis."
I know Foaly monitors human communications, and those keywords should set off ALL his alarms.
I made the call from Doctor Lane's landline instead of my mobile. I'm not sure they'll come if they know it's me.
So I wait.
Not for the first time.
EXCERPT FROM ARTEMIS FOWL'S DIARY. DISK 2. ENCRYPTED.
It has been weeks since Holly Short used her healing magic on my father's battered body.
And still he lies in his Helsinki hospital.
Immobile. Unresponsive.
The doctors cannot understand it. But it's no mystery to me.
Holly's magic has overhauled my father's entire being.
I cannot help but wonder what effect the positive energy will have on his mind.
For sixteen days we sat in my father's hospital room.
Waiting.
On the morning of the seventeenth day, my father's brain waves began to spike.
He simply sat up, rubbed his eyes, and said Mother's name. "Angeline."
Suddenly, I was afraid.
The man whose shoes I had been trying to fill for two years was awake.
Would he live up to my expectations? Would I live up to his?
After such a long time apart. I didn't know what to say.
My father had no such doubts.
ARTY...

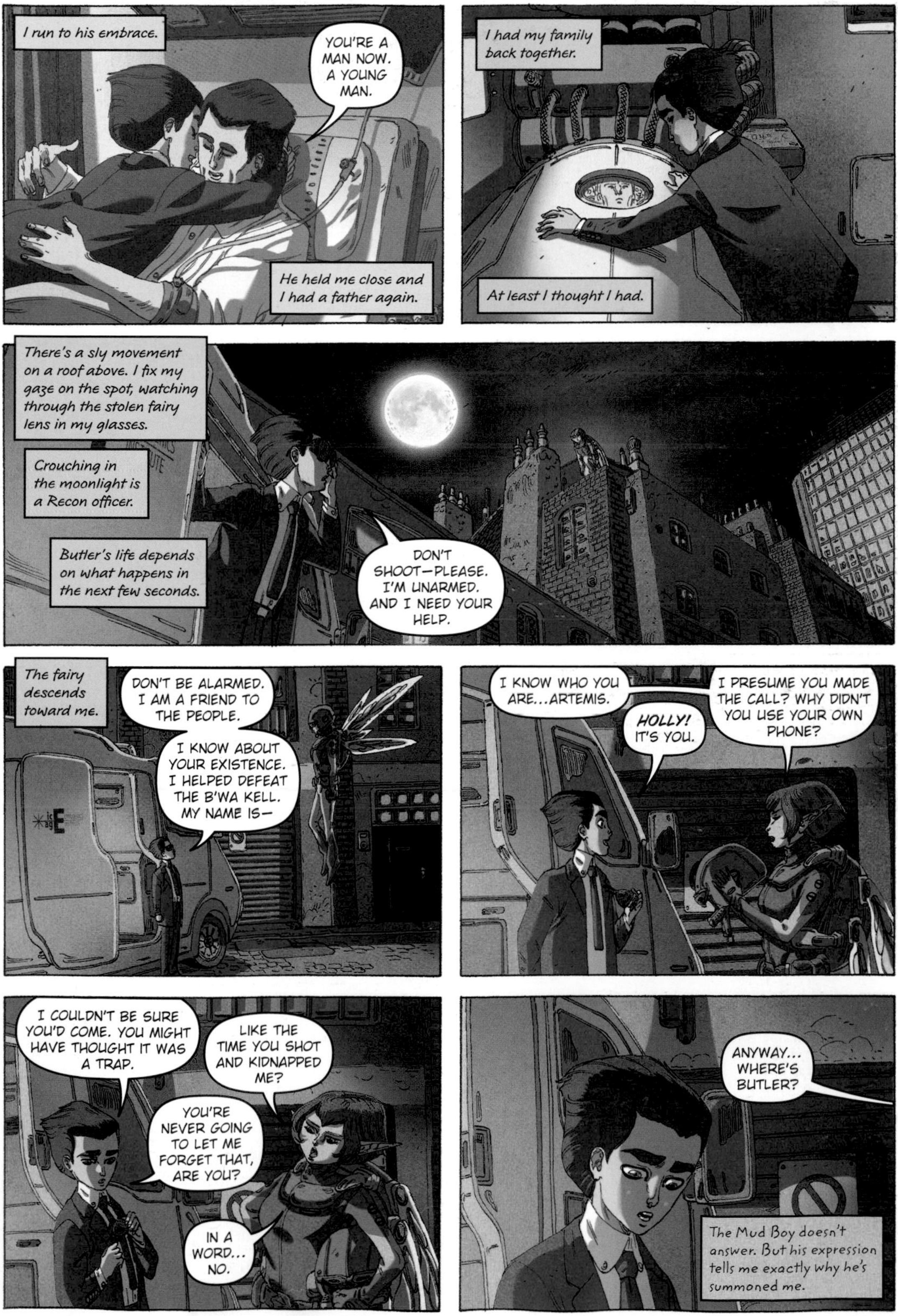
I run to his embrace.
YOU'RE A MAN NOW. A YOUNG MAN.
He held me close and I had a father again.
I had my family back together.
At least I thought I had.
There's a sly movement on a roof above. I fix my gaze on the spot, watching through the stolen fairy lens in my glasses.
Crouching in the moonlight is a Recon officer.
Butler's life depends on what happens in the next few seconds.
DON'T SHOOT—PLEASE. I'M UNARMED. AND I NEED YOUR HELP.
The fairy descends toward me.
DON'T BE ALARMED. I AM A FRIEND TO THE PEOPLE.
I KNOW ABOUT YOUR EXISTENCE. I HELPED DEFEAT THE B'WA KELL. MY NAME IS—
I KNOW WHO YOU ARE...ARTEMIS.
HOLLY! IT'S YOU.
I PRESUME YOU MADE THE CALL? WHY DIDN'T YOU USE YOUR OWN PHONE?
I COULDN'T BE SURE YOU'D COME. YOU MIGHT HAVE THOUGHT IT WAS A TRAP.
LIKE THE TIME YOU SHOT AND KIDNAPPED ME?
YOU'RE NEVER GOING TO LET ME FORGET THAT, ARE YOU?
IN A WORD... NO.
ANYWAY... WHERE'S BUTLER?
The Mud Boy doesn't answer. But his expression tells me exactly why he's summoned me.

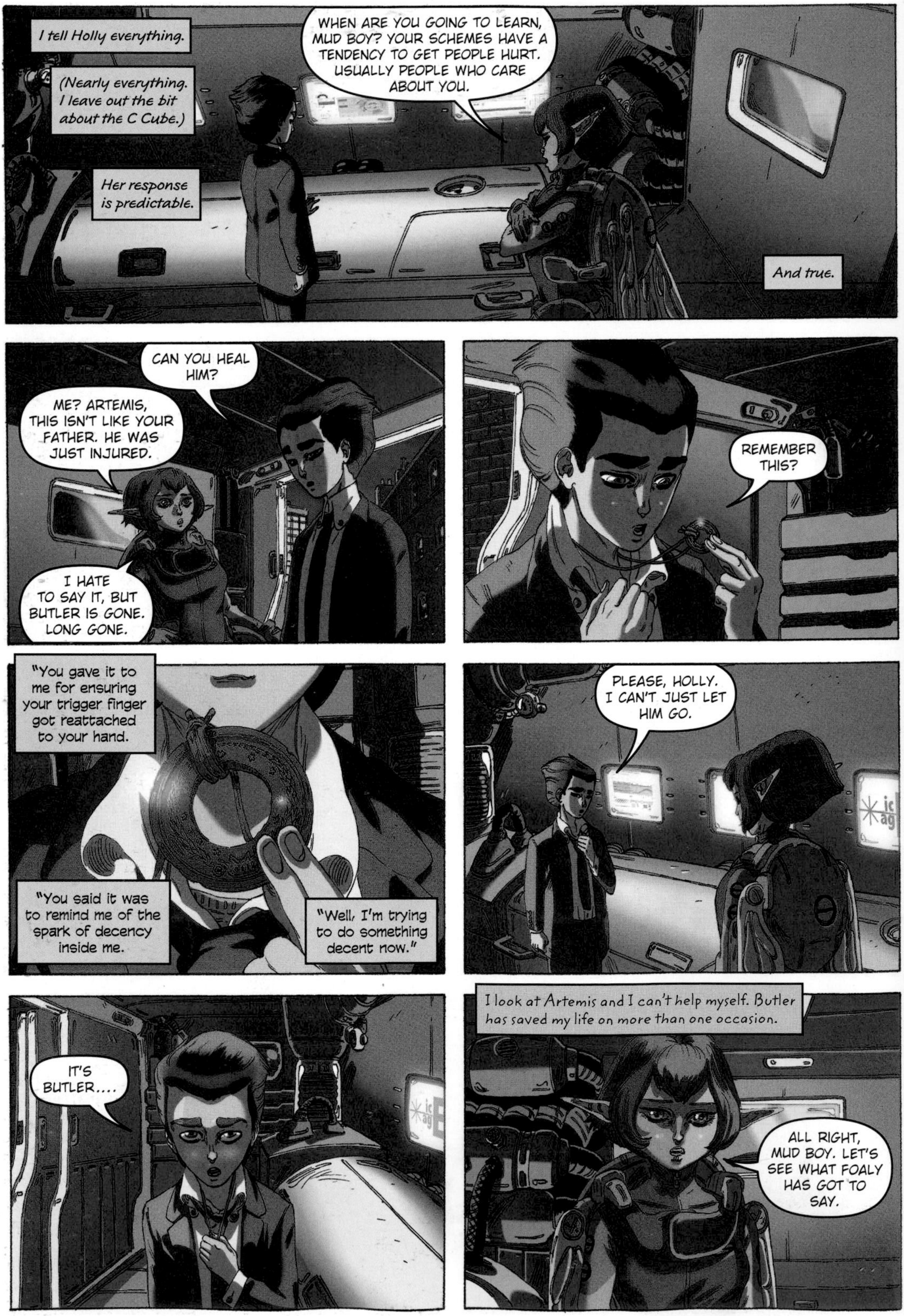
I tell Holly everything.
(Nearly everything. I leave out the bit about the C Cube.)
Her response is predictable.
WHEN ARE YOU GOING TO LEARN, MUD BOY? YOUR SCHEMES HAVE A TENDENCY TO GET PEOPLE HURT. USUALLY PEOPLE WHO CARE ABOUT YOU.
And true.
CAN YOU HEAL HIM?
ME? ARTEMIS, THIS ISN'T LIKE YOUR FATHER. HE WAS JUST INJURED.
I HATE TO SAY IT, BUT BUTLER IS GONE. LONG GONE.
REMEMBER THIS?
"You gave it to me for ensuring your trigger finger got reattached to your hand.
"You said it was to remind me of the spark of decency inside me.
"Well, I'm trying to do something decent now."
PLEASE, HOLLY. I CAN'T JUST LET HIM GO.
IT'S BUTLER....
I look at Artemis and I can't help myself. Butler has saved my life on more than one occasion.
ALL RIGHT, MUD BOY. LET'S SEE WHAT FOALY HAS GOT TO SAY.

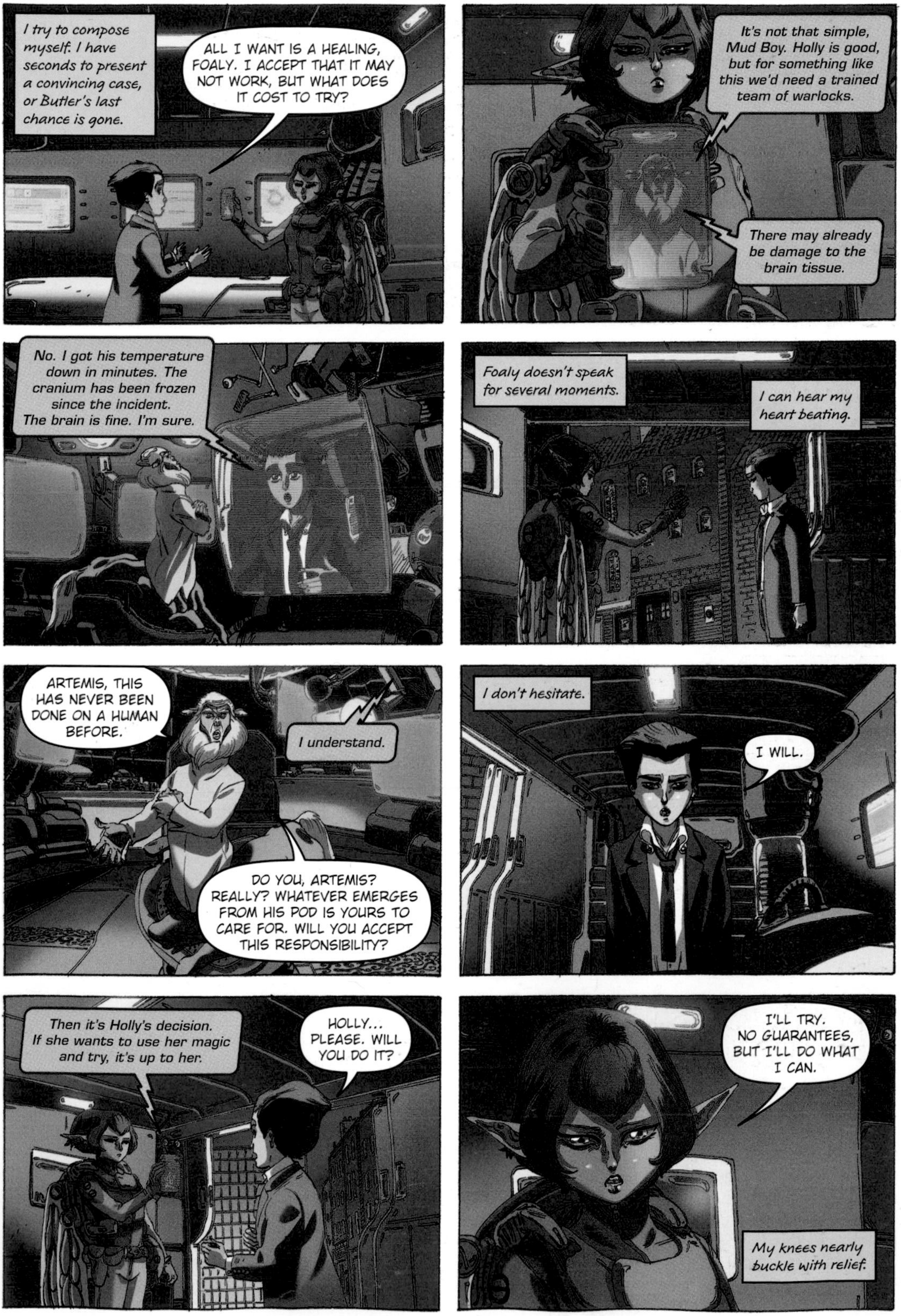
I try to compose myself. I have seconds to present a convincing case, or Butler's last chance is gone.
ALL I WANT IS A HEALING, FOALY. I ACCEPT THAT IT MAY NOT WORK, BUT WHAT DOES IT COST TO TRY?
It's not that simple, Mud Boy. Holly is good, but for something like this we'd need a trained team of warlocks.
There may already be damage to the brain tissue.
No. I got his temperature down in minutes. The cranium has been frozen since the incident. The brain is fine. I'm sure.
Foaly doesn't speak for several moments.
I can hear my heart beating.
ARTEMIS, THIS HAS NEVER BEEN DONE ON A HUMAN BEFORE.
I understand.
DO YOU, ARTEMIS? REALLY? WHATEVER EMERGES FROM HIS POD IS YOURS TO CARE FOR. WILL YOU ACCEPT THIS RESPONSIBILITY?
I don't hesitate.
I WILL.
Then it's Holly's decision. If she wants to use her magic and try, it's up to her.
HOLLY... PLEASE. WILL YOU DO IT?
I'LL TRY. NO GUARANTEES, BUT I'LL DO WHAT I CAN.
My knees nearly buckle with relief.

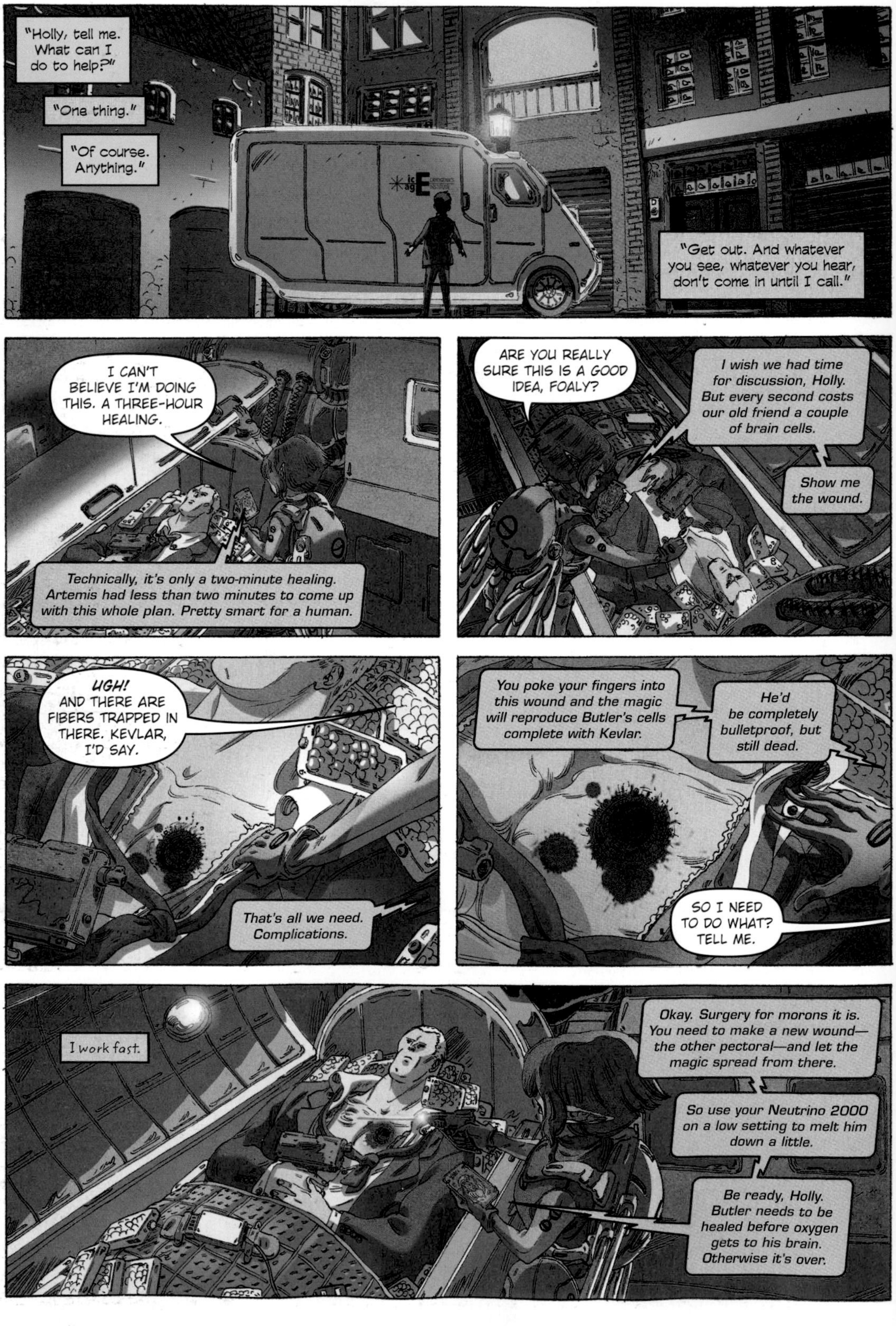
"Holly, tell me. What can I do to help?"
"One thing."
"Of course. Anything."
"Get out. And whatever you see, whatever you hear, don't come in until I call."
I CAN'T BELIEVE I'M DOING THIS. A THREE-HOUR HEALING.
Technically, it's only a two-minute healing. Artemis had less than two minutes to come up with this whole plan. Pretty smart for a human.
ARE YOU REALLY SURE THIS IS A GOOD IDEA, FOALY?
I wish we had time for discussion, Holly. But every second costs our old friend a couple of brain cells.
Show me the wound.
UGH! AND THERE ARE FIBERS TRAPPED IN THERE. KEVLAR, I'D SAY.
That's all we need. Complications.
You poke your fingers into this wound and the magic will reproduce Butler's cells complete with Kevlar.
He'd be completely bulletproof, but still dead.
SO I NEED TO DO WHAT? TELL ME.
I work fast.
Okay. Surgery for morons it is. You need to make a new wound—the other pectoral—and let the magic spread from there.
So use your Neutrino 2000 on a low setting to melt him down a little.
Be ready, Holly. Butler needs to be healed before oxygen gets to his brain. Otherwise it's over.

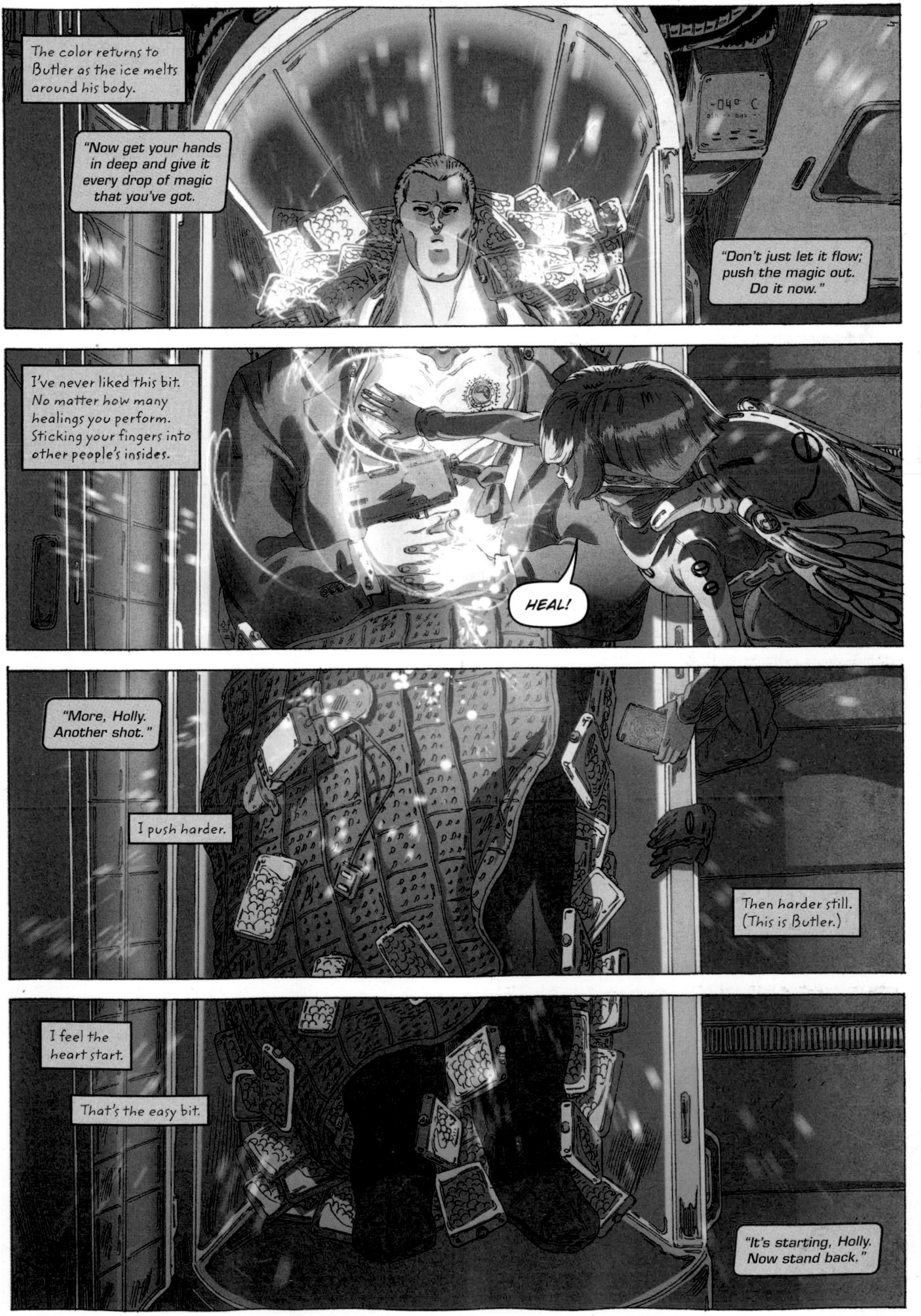
The color returns to Butler as the ice melts around his body.
"Now get your hands in deep and give it every drop of magic that you've got.
"Don't just let it flow; push the magic out. Do it now."
-04° C
I've never liked this bit. No matter how many healings you perform. Sticking your fingers into other people's insides.
HEAL!
"More, Holly. Another shot."
I push harder.
Then harder still. (This is Butler.)
I feel the heart start.
That's the easy bit.
"It's starting, Holly. Now stand back."

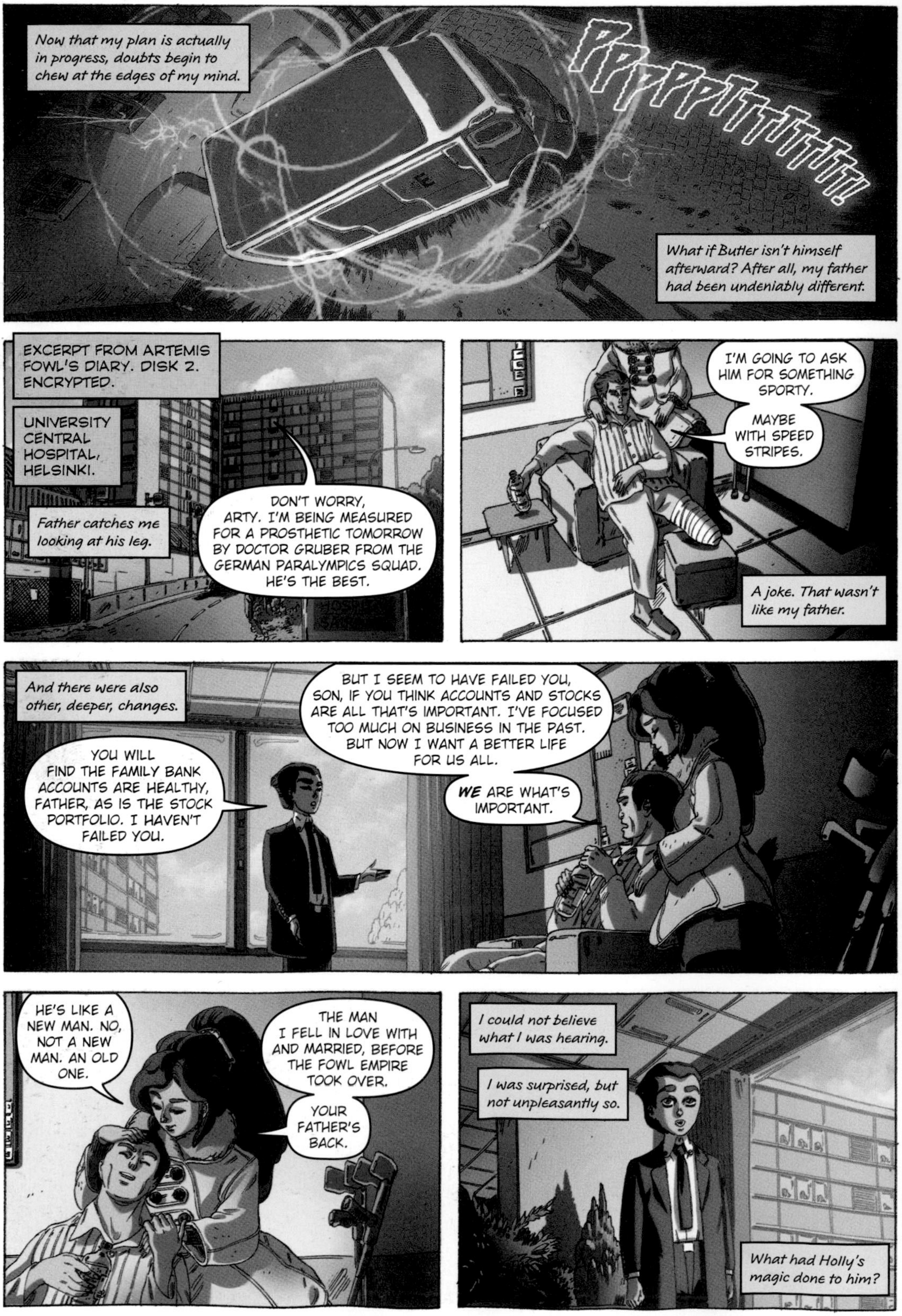

Now that my plan is actually in progress, doubts begin to chew at the edges of my mind.
PPPPPTTTTTTT!
What if Butler isn't himself afterward? After all, my father had been undeniably different.
EXCERPT FROM ARTEMIS FOWL'S DIARY. DISK 2. ENCRYPTED.
UNIVERSITY CENTRAL HOSPITAL, HELSINKI.
Father catches me looking at his leg.
DON'T WORRY, ARTY. I'M BEING MEASURED FOR A PROSTHETIC TOMORROW BY DOCTOR GRUBER FROM THE GERMAN PARALYMPICS SQUAD. HE'S THE BEST.
I'M GOING TO ASK HIM FOR SOMETHING SPORTY.
MAYBE WITH SPEED STRIPES.
A joke. That wasn't like my father.
And there were also other, deeper, changes.
YOU WILL FIND THE FAMILY BANK ACCOUNTS ARE HEALTHY, FATHER, AS IS THE STOCK PORTFOLIO. I HAVEN'T FAILED YOU.
BUT I SEEM TO HAVE FAILED YOU, SON, IF YOU THINK ACCOUNTS AND STOCKS ARE ALL THAT'S IMPORTANT. I'VE FOCUSED TOO MUCH ON BUSINESS IN THE PAST. BUT NOW I WANT A BETTER LIFE FOR US ALL.
WE ARE WHAT'S IMPORTANT.
HE'S LIKE A NEW MAN. NO, NOT A NEW MAN. AN OLD ONE.
THE MAN I FELL IN LOVE WITH AND MARRIED, BEFORE THE FOWL EMPIRE TOOK OVER.
YOUR FATHER'S BACK.
I could not believe what I was hearing.
I was surprised, but not unpleasantly so.
What had Holly's magic done to him?

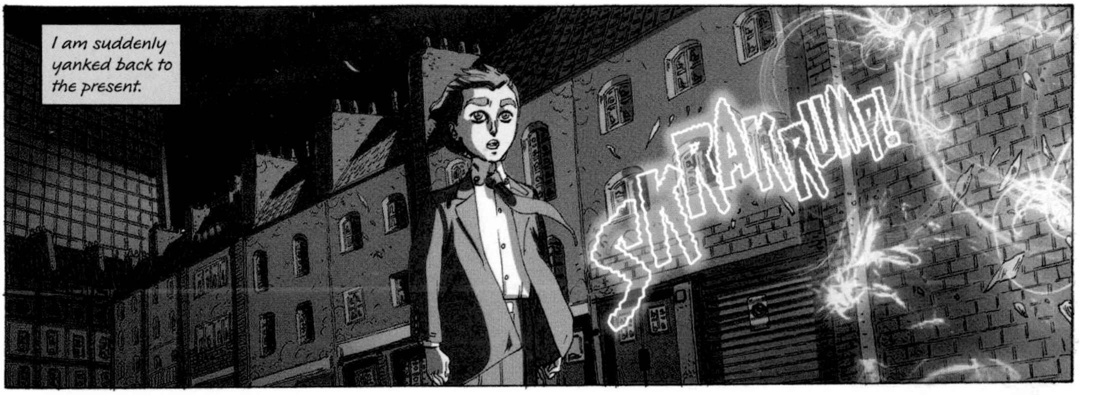
I am suddenly yanked back to the present.
SKRAKRUMP!

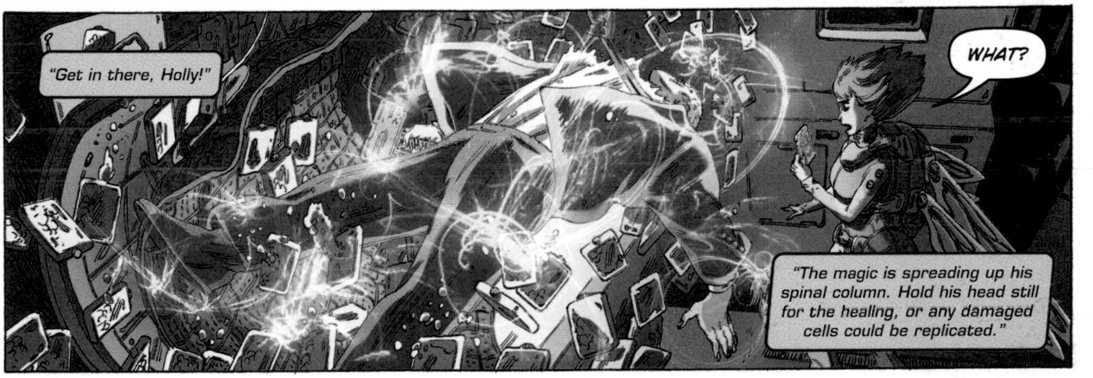
"Get in there, Holly!"
WHAT?
"The magic is spreading up his spinal column. Hold his head still for the healing, or any damaged cells could be replicated."

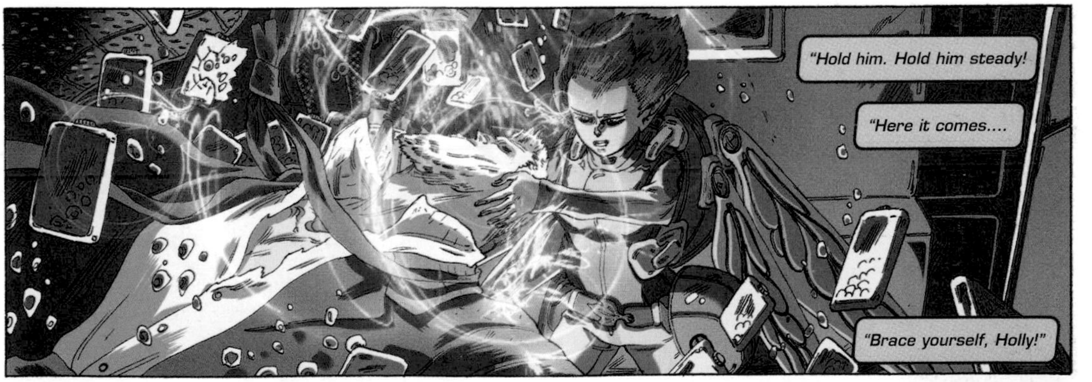
"Hold him. Hold him steady!
"Here it comes....
"Brace yourself, Holly!"

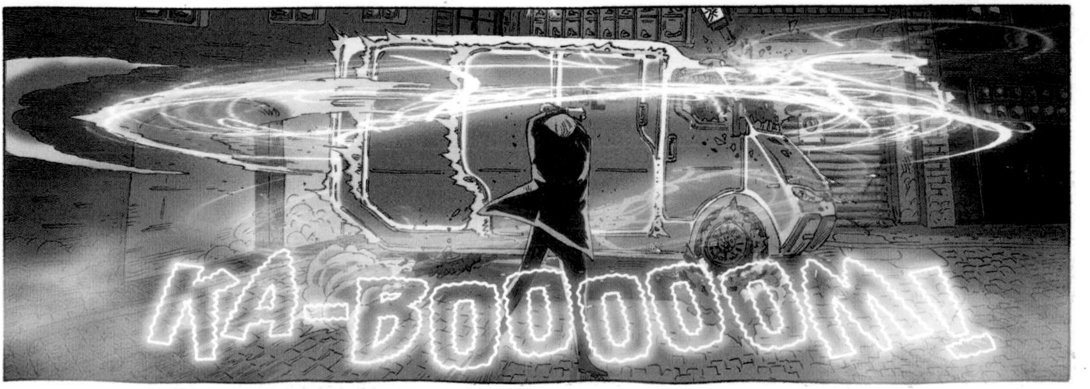
KA-BOOOOOOM!

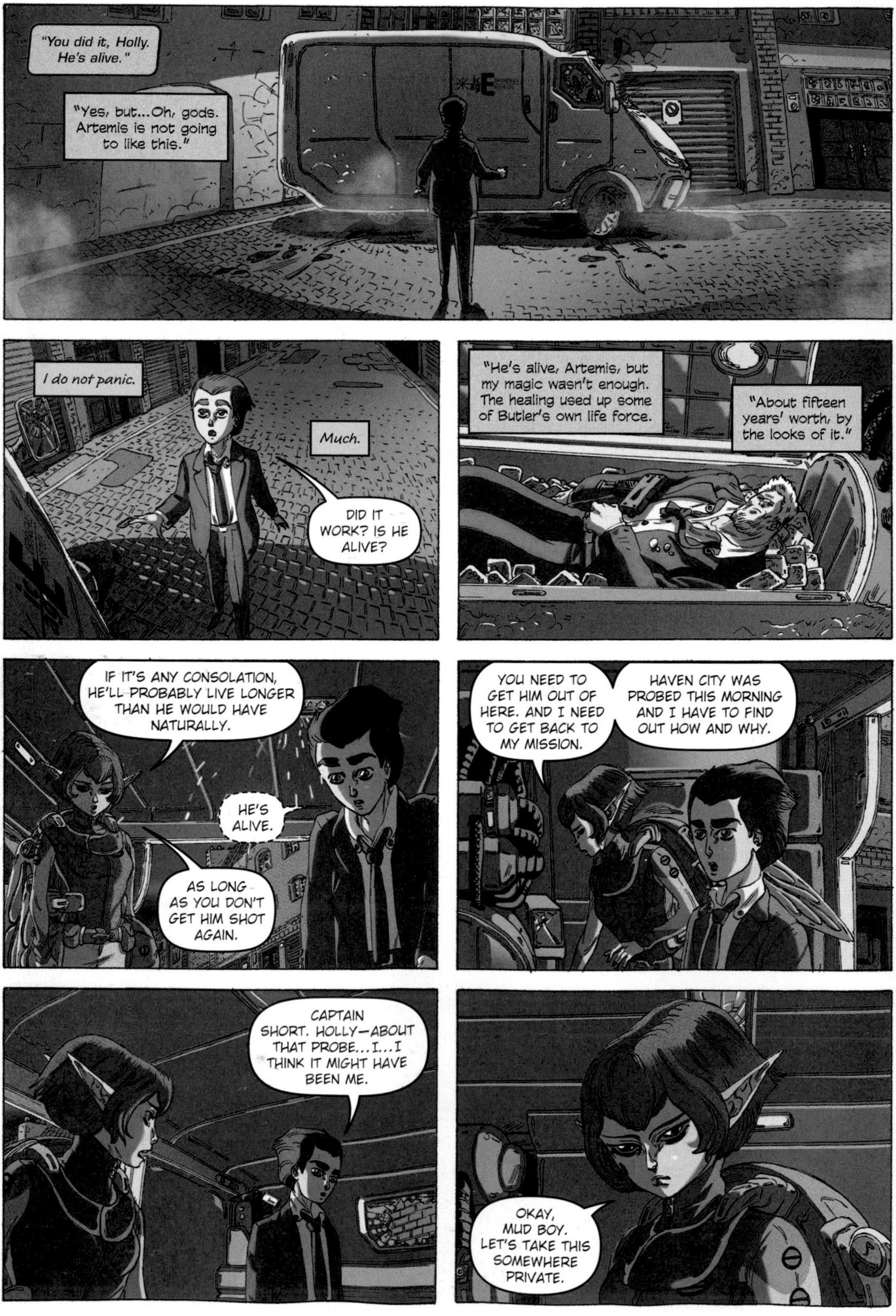
"You did it, Holly. He's alive."
"Yes, but...Oh, gods. Artemis is not going to like this."
I do not panic.
Much.
DID IT WORK? IS HE ALIVE?
"He's alive, Artemis, but my magic wasn't enough. The healing used up some of Butler's own life force.
"About fifteen years' worth, by the looks of it."
IF IT'S ANY CONSOLATION, HE'LL PROBABLY LIVE LONGER THAN HE WOULD HAVE NATURALLY.
HE'S ALIVE.
AS LONG AS YOU DON'T GET HIM SHOT AGAIN.
YOU NEED TO GET HIM OUT OF HERE. AND I NEED TO GET BACK TO MY MISSION.
HAVEN CITY WAS PROBED THIS MORNING AND I HAVE TO FIND OUT HOW AND WHY.
CAPTAIN SHORT. HOLLY—ABOUT THAT PROBE...I...I THINK IT MIGHT HAVE BEEN ME.
OKAY, MUD BOY. LET'S TAKE THIS SOMEWHERE PRIVATE.

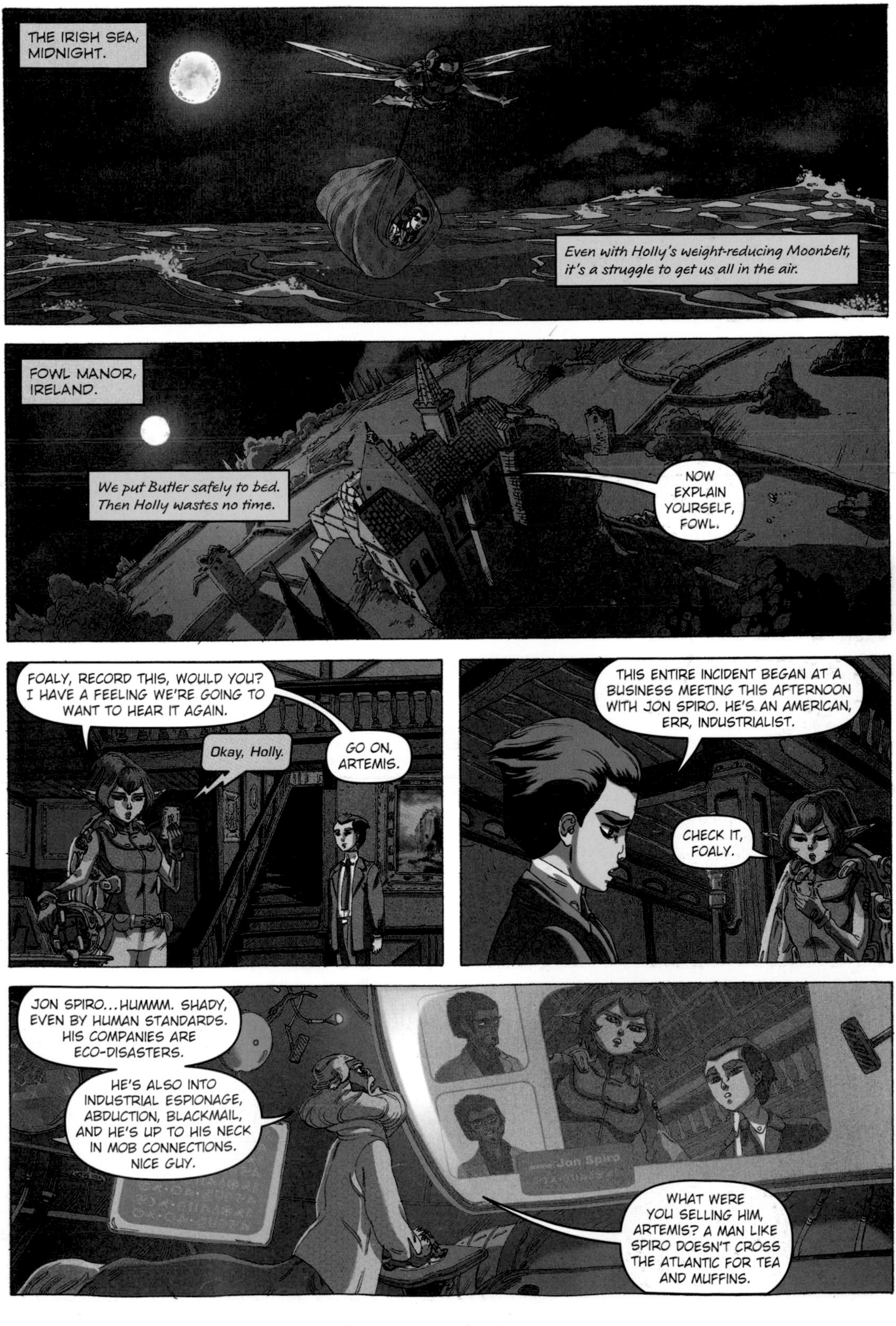
THE IRISH SEA, MIDNIGHT.
Even with Holly's weight-reducing Moonbelt, it's a struggle to get us all in the air.
FOWL MANOR, IRELAND.
We put Butler safely to bed. Then Holly wastes no time.
NOW EXPLAIN YOURSELF, FOWL.
FOALY, RECORD THIS, WOULD YOU? I HAVE A FEELING WE'RE GOING TO WANT TO HEAR IT AGAIN.
Okay, Holly.
GO ON, ARTEMIS.
THIS ENTIRE INCIDENT BEGAN AT A BUSINESS MEETING THIS AFTERNOON WITH JON SPIRO. HE'S AN AMERICAN, ERR, INDUSTRIALIST.
CHECK IT, FOALY.
JON SPIRO...HUMMM. SHADY, EVEN BY HUMAN STANDARDS. HIS COMPANIES ARE ECO-DISASTERS.
HE'S ALSO INTO INDUSTRIAL ESPIONAGE, ABDUCTION, BLACKMAIL, AND HE'S UP TO HIS NECK IN MOB CONNECTIONS. NICE GUY.
Jon Spiro
WHAT WERE YOU SELLING HIM, ARTEMIS? A MAN LIKE SPIRO DOESN'T CROSS THE ATLANTIC FOR TEA AND MUFFINS.

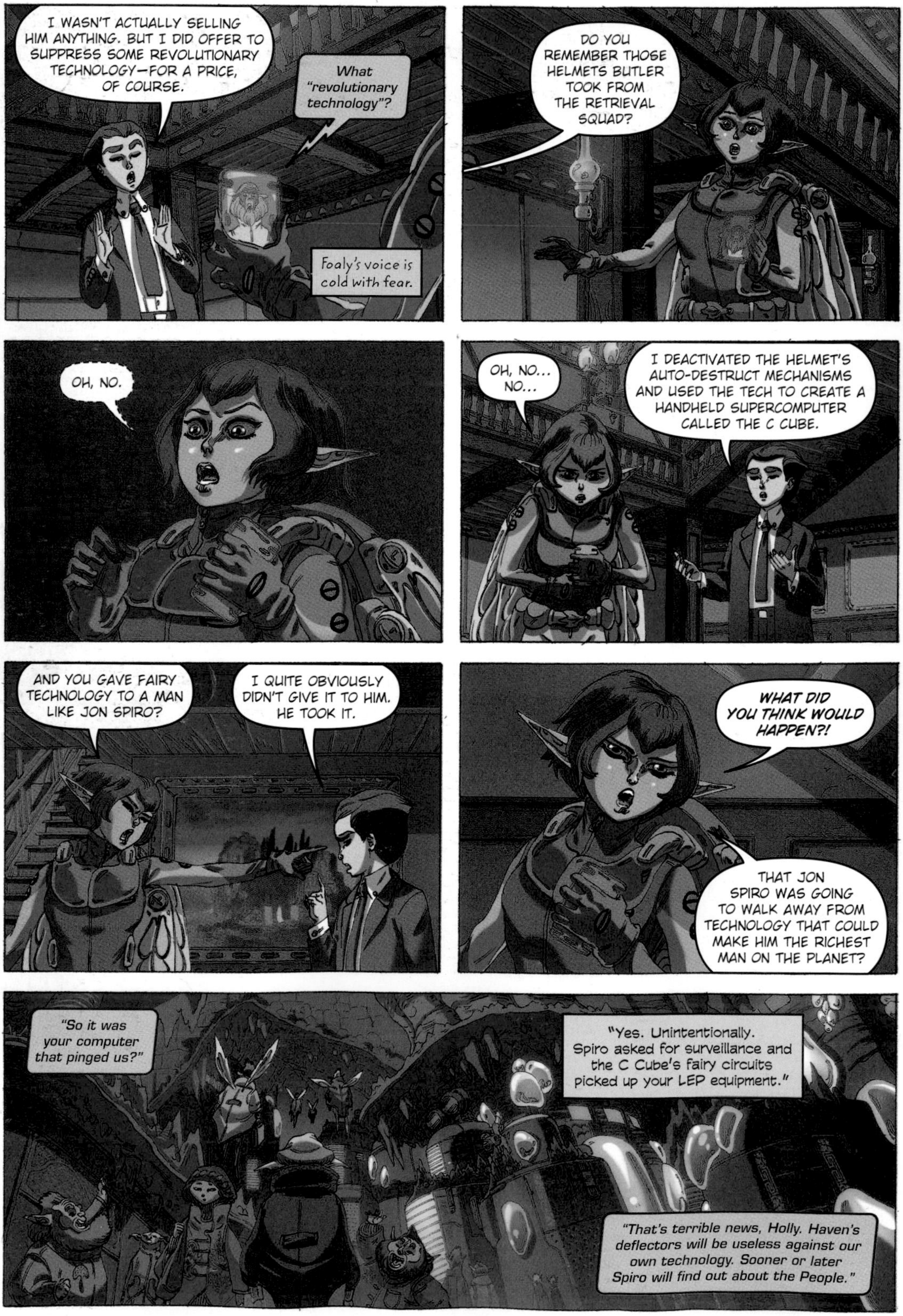
I WASN'T ACTUALLY SELLING HIM ANYTHING. BUT I DID OFFER TO SUPPRESS SOME REVOLUTIONARY TECHNOLOGY—FOR A PRICE, OF COURSE.
What "revolutionary technology"?
Foaly's voice is cold with fear.
DO YOU REMEMBER THOSE HELMETS BUTLER TOOK FROM THE RETRIEVAL SQUAD?
OH, NO.
OH, NO... NO...
I DEACTIVATED THE HELMET'S AUTO-DESTRUCT MECHANISMS AND USED THE TECH TO CREATE A HANDHELD SUPERCOMPUTER CALLED THE C CUBE.
AND YOU GAVE FAIRY TECHNOLOGY TO A MAN LIKE JON SPIRO?
I QUITE OBVIOUSLY DIDN'T GIVE IT TO HIM. HE TOOK IT.
WHAT DID YOU THINK WOULD HAPPEN?!
THAT JON SPIRO WAS GOING TO WALK AWAY FROM TECHNOLOGY THAT COULD MAKE HIM THE RICHEST MAN ON THE PLANET?
"So it was your computer that pinged us?"
"Yes. Unintentionally. Spiro asked for surveillance and the C Cube's fairy circuits picked up your LEP equipment."
"That's terrible news, Holly. Haven's deflectors will be useless against our own technology. Sooner or later Spiro will find out about the People."

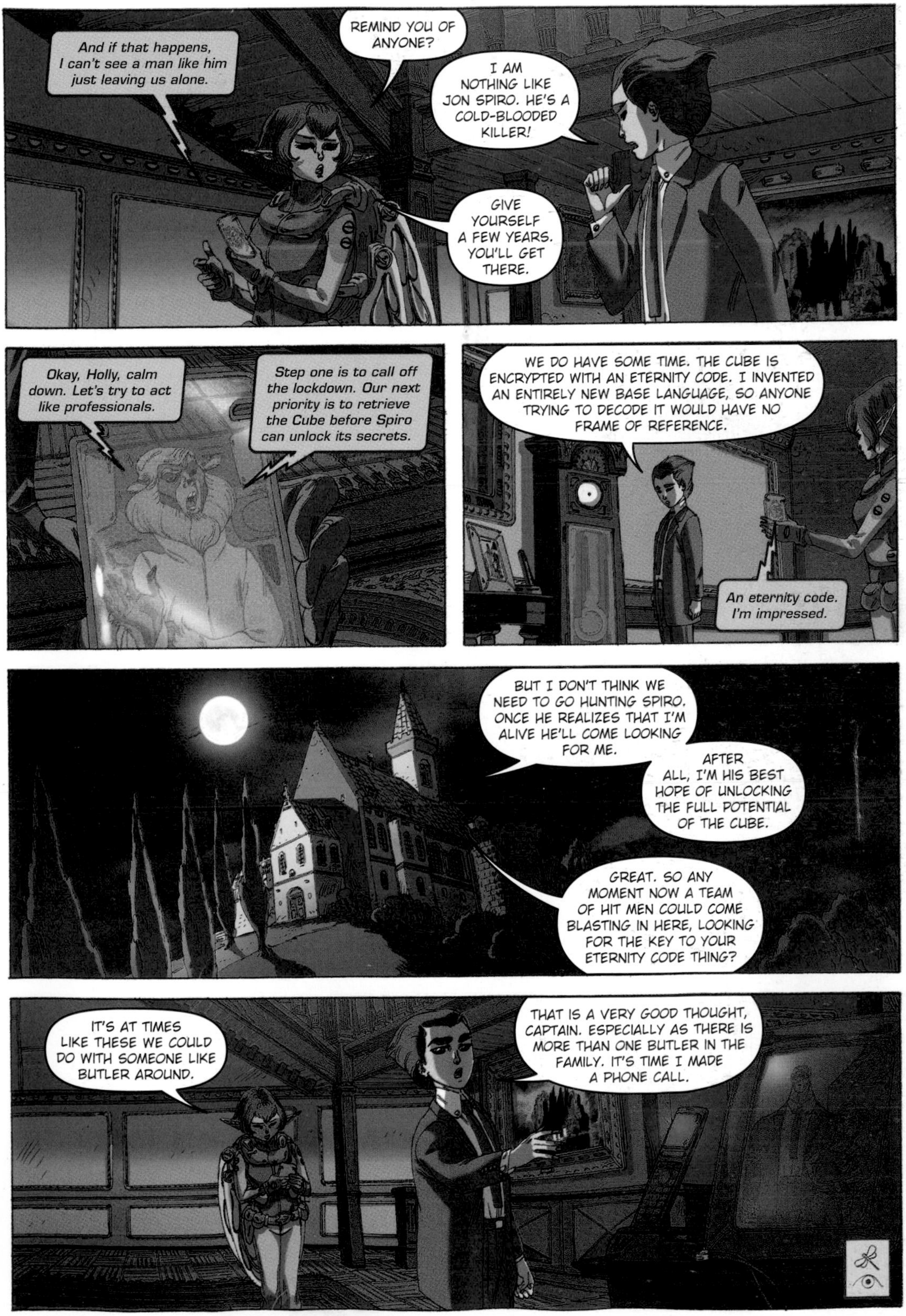
And if that happens, I can't see a man like him just leaving us alone.
REMIND YOU OF ANYONE?
I AM NOTHING LIKE JON SPIRO. HE'S A COLD-BLOODED KILLER!
GIVE YOURSELF A FEW YEARS. YOU'LL GET THERE.
Okay, Holly, calm down. Let's try to act like professionals.
Step one is to call off the lockdown. Our next priority is to retrieve the Cube before Spiro can unlock its secrets.
WE DO HAVE SOME TIME. THE CUBE IS ENCRYPTED WITH AN ETERNITY CODE. I INVENTED AN ENTIRELY NEW BASE LANGUAGE, SO ANYONE TRYING TO DECODE IT WOULD HAVE NO FRAME OF REFERENCE.
An eternity code. I'm impressed.
BUT I DON'T THINK WE NEED TO GO HUNTING SPIRO. ONCE HE REALIZES THAT I'M ALIVE HE'LL COME LOOKING FOR ME.
AFTER ALL, I'M HIS BEST HOPE OF UNLOCKING THE FULL POTENTIAL OF THE CUBE.
GREAT. SO ANY MOMENT NOW A TEAM OF HIT MEN COULD COME BLASTING IN HERE, LOOKING FOR THE KEY TO YOUR ETERNITY CODE THING?
IT'S AT TIMES LIKE THESE WE COULD DO WITH SOMEONE LIKE BUTLER AROUND.
THAT IS A VERY GOOD THOUGHT, CAPTAIN. ESPECIALLY AS THERE IS MORE THAN ONE BUTLER IN THE FAMILY. IT'S TIME I MADE A PHONE CALL.

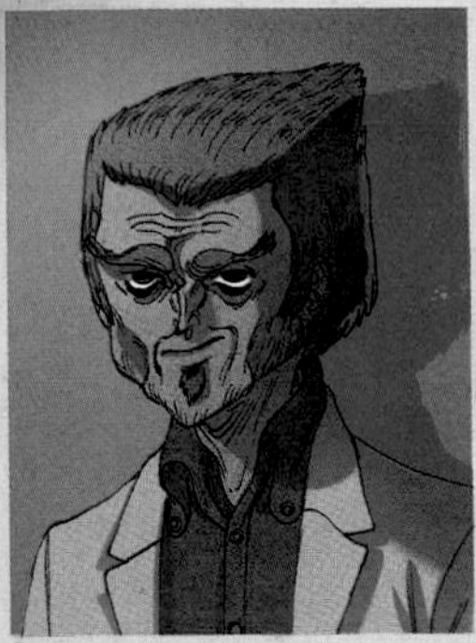

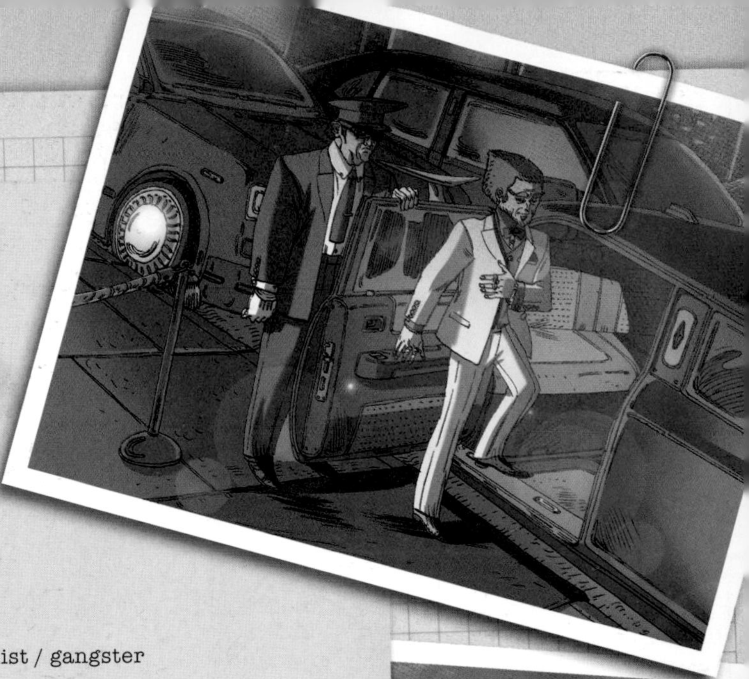

NAME: Jon Spiro

OCCUPATION: Industrialist / gangster

NUMBER OF PREVIOUS ARRESTS: 10

NUMBER OF PREVIOUS CONVICTIONS: None

LIKES: Money, dressing in white, gold jewelry, and more money.

DISLIKES: Rival company Phonetix, the FBI, the police, the CIA, the entire American justice system, etc., etc.

The Spiro Needle, a sliver of steel and glass rising eighty-six stories on the Chicago skyline. Spiro Industries is located on floors fifty through eighty-five. The eighty-sixth floor is Spiro's personal residence, accessible by either private elevator or heliport.

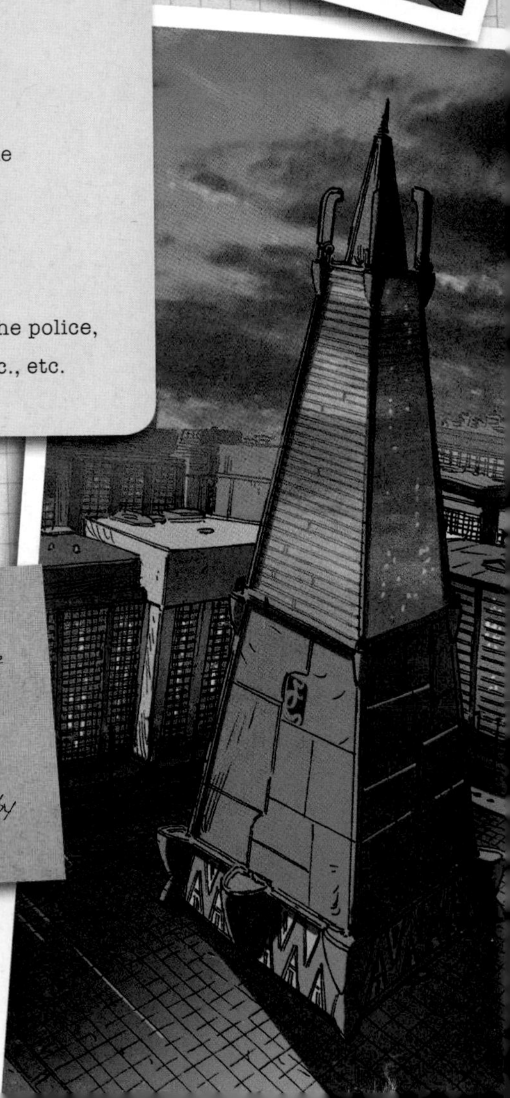

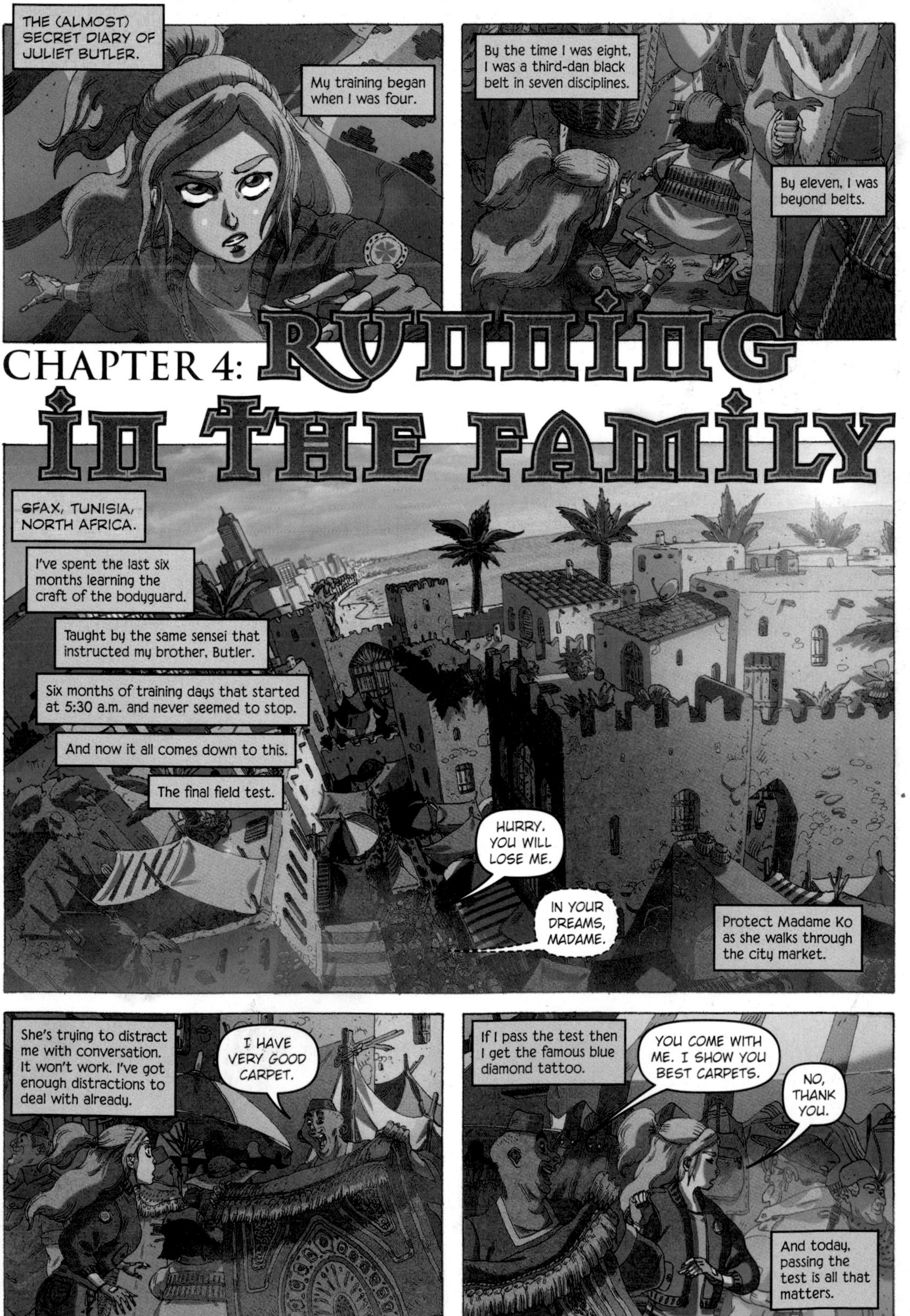

THE (ALMOST) SECRET DIARY OF JULIET BUTLER.
My training began when I was four.
By the time I was eight, I was a third-dan black belt in seven disciplines.
By eleven, I was beyond belts.
CHAPTER 4: RUNNING IN THE FAMILY
SFAX, TUNISIA, NORTH AFRICA.
I've spent the last six months learning the craft of the bodyguard.
Taught by the same sensei that instructed my brother, Butler.
Six months of training days that started at 5:30 a.m. and never seemed to stop.
And now it all comes down to this.
The final field test.
HURRY. YOU WILL LOSE ME.
IN YOUR DREAMS, MADAME.
Protect Madame Ko as she walks through the city market.
She's trying to distract me with conversation. It won't work. I've got enough distractions to deal with already.
I HAVE VERY GOOD CARPET.
If I pass the test then I get the famous blue diamond tattoo.
YOU COME WITH ME. I SHOW YOU BEST CARPETS.
NO, THANK YOU.
And today, passing the test is all that matters.

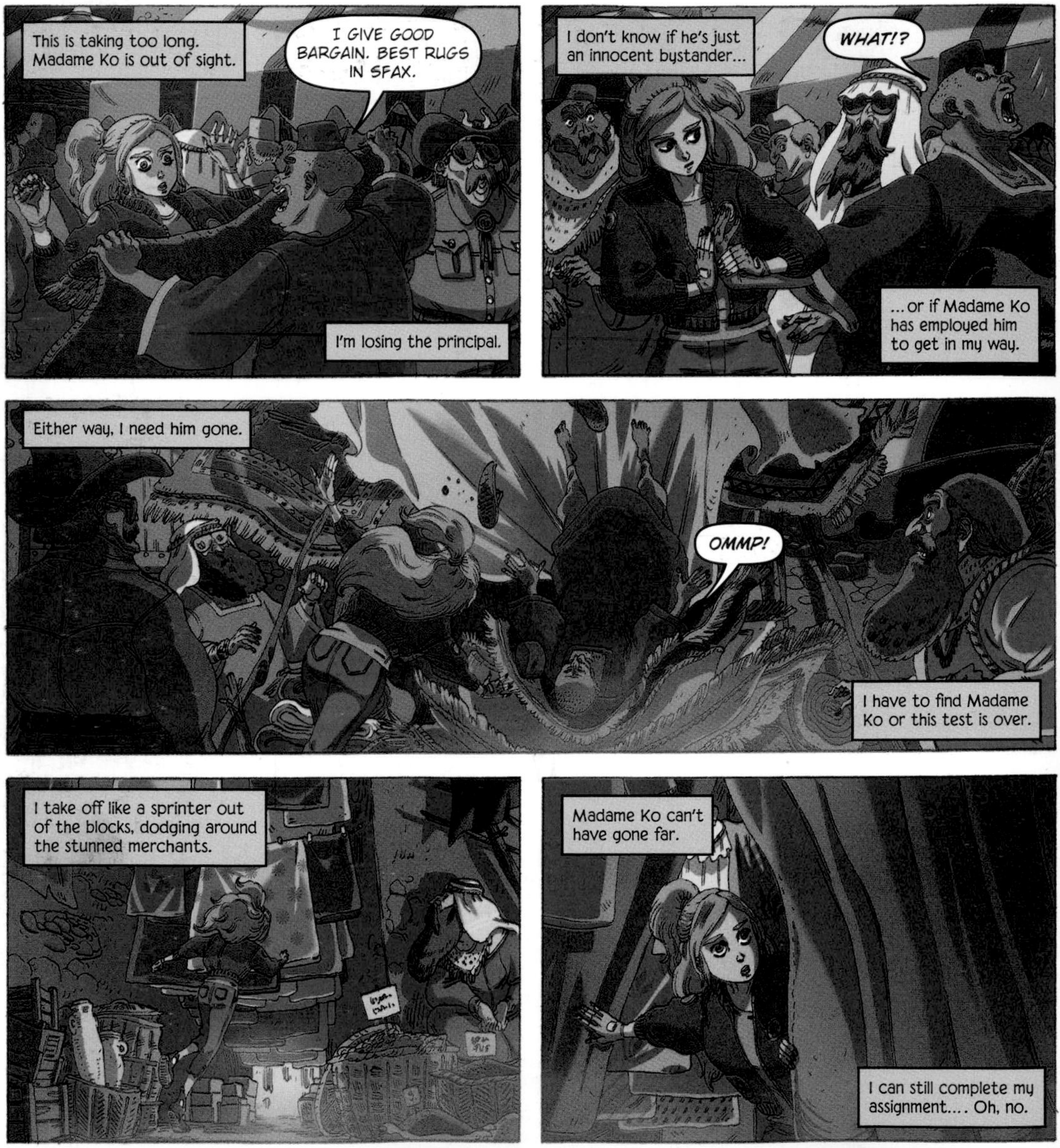
This is taking too long. Madame Ko is out of sight.
I GIVE GOOD BARGAIN. BEST RUGS IN SFAX.
I'm losing the principal.
I don't know if he's just an innocent bystander...
WHAT!?
...or if Madame Ko has employed him to get in my way.
Either way, I need him gone.
OMMP!
I have to find Madame Ko or this test is over.
I take off like a sprinter out of the blocks, dodging around the stunned merchants.
Madame Ko can't have gone far.
I can still complete my assignment.... Oh, no.
These aren't merchants.
This is no test.
These men are trying to kill my sensei.

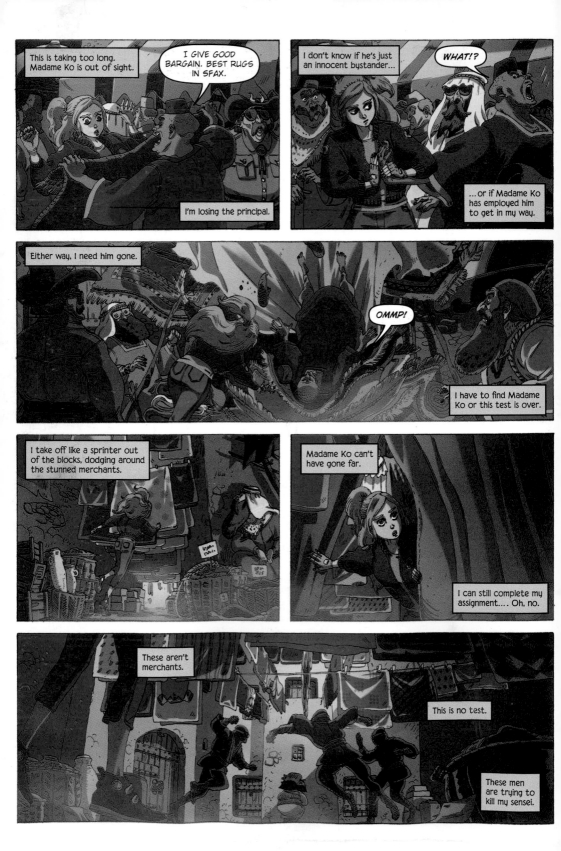

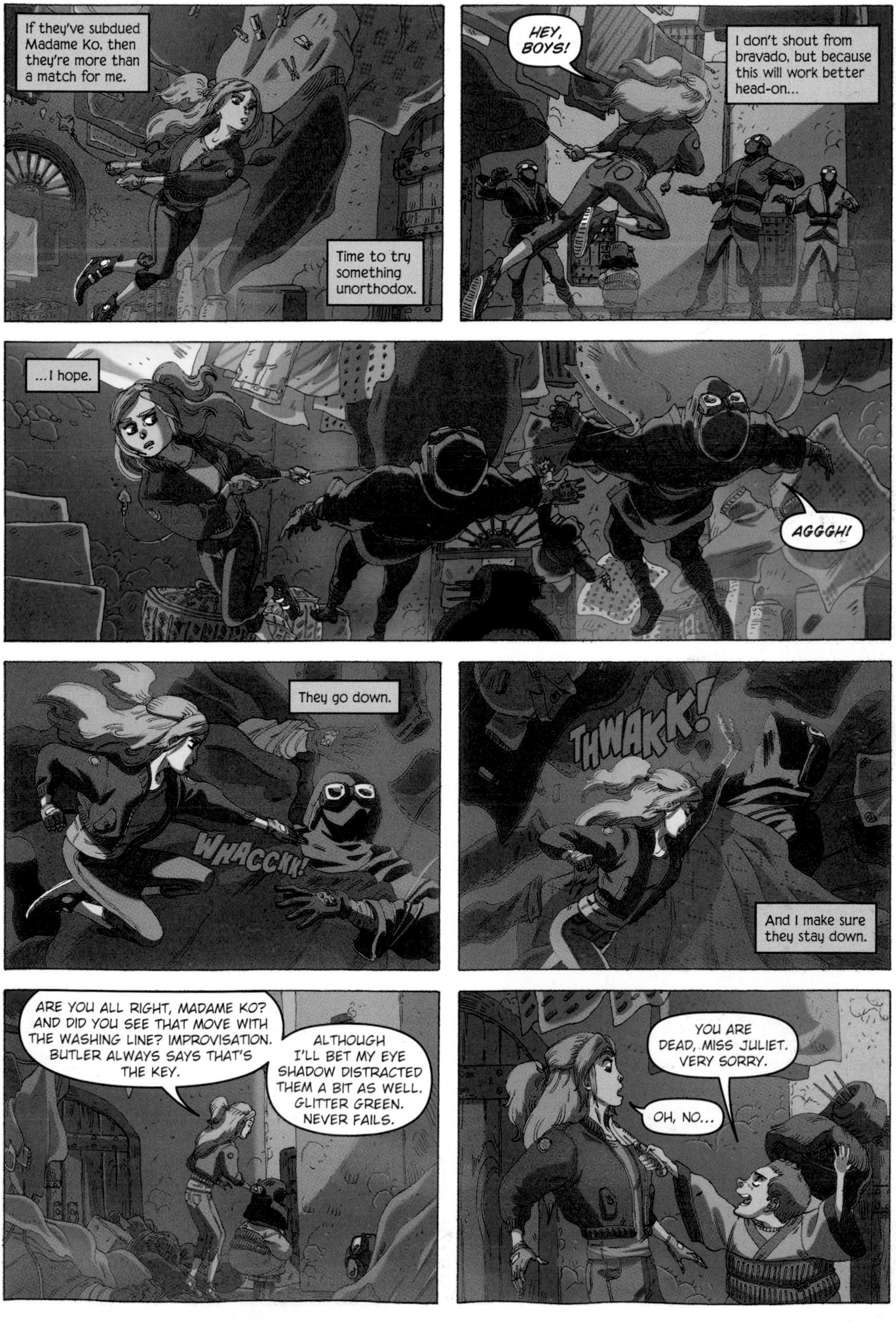

If they've subdued Madame Ko, then they're more than a match for me.
Time to try something unorthodox.
HEY, BOYS!
I don't shout from bravado, but because this will work better head-on...
...I hope.
AGGGH!
They go down.
WHACCKK!
THWAKK!
And I make sure they stay down.
ARE YOU ALL RIGHT, MADAME KO? AND DID YOU SEE THAT MOVE WITH THE WASHING LINE? IMPROVISATION. BUTLER ALWAYS SAYS THAT'S THE KEY.
ALTHOUGH I'LL BET MY EYE SHADOW DISTRACTED THEM A BIT AS WELL. GLITTER GREEN. NEVER FAILS.
YOU ARE DEAD, MISS JULIET. VERY SORRY.
OH, NO...

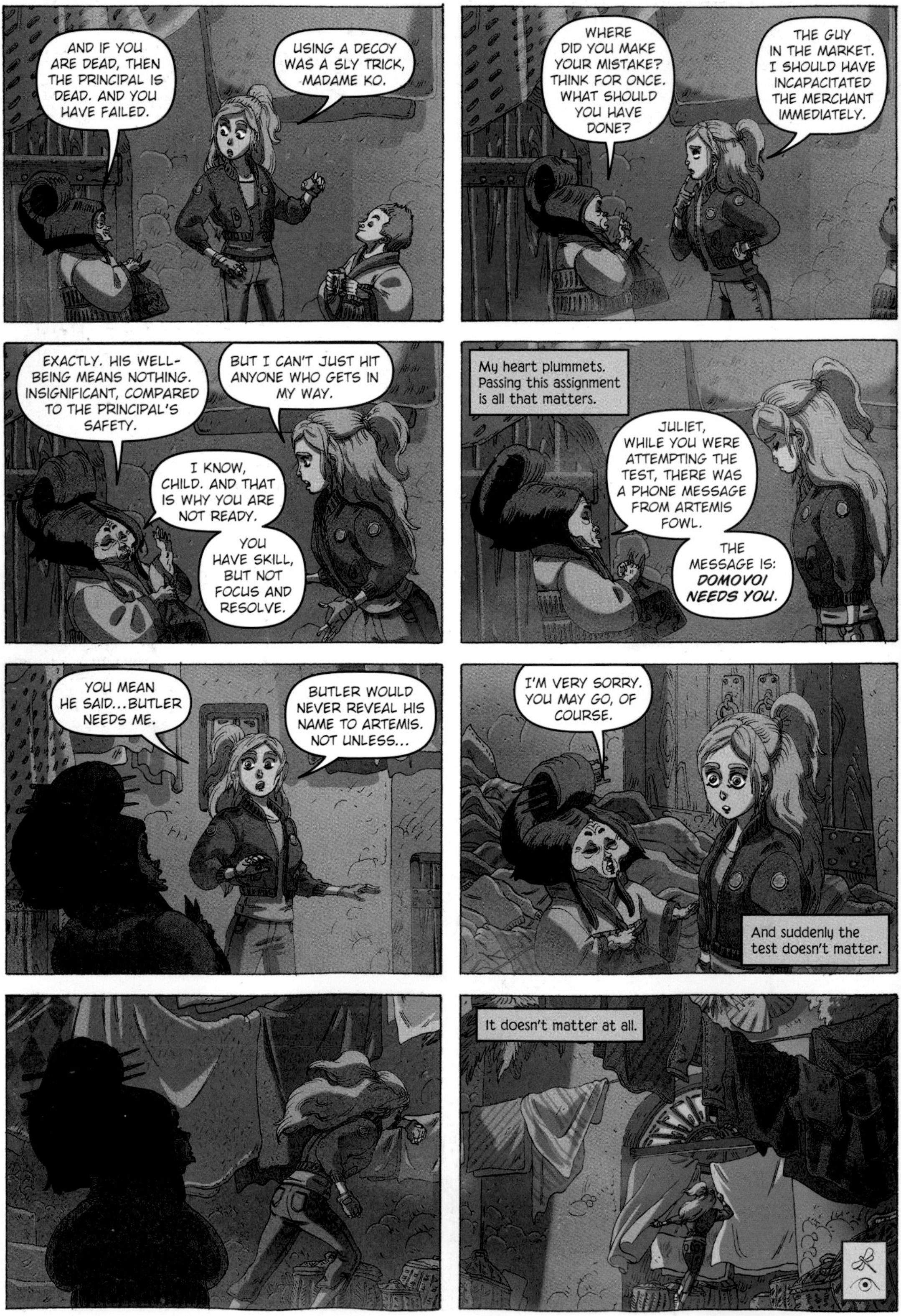
AND IF YOU ARE DEAD, THEN THE PRINCIPAL IS DEAD. AND YOU HAVE FAILED.
USING A DECOY WAS A SLY TRICK, MADAME KO.
WHERE DID YOU MAKE YOUR MISTAKE? THINK FOR ONCE. WHAT SHOULD YOU HAVE DONE?
THE GUY IN THE MARKET. I SHOULD HAVE INCAPACITATED THE MERCHANT IMMEDIATELY.
EXACTLY. HIS WELL-BEING MEANS NOTHING. INSIGNIFICANT, COMPARED TO THE PRINCIPAL'S SAFETY.
BUT I CAN'T JUST HIT ANYONE WHO GETS IN MY WAY.
I KNOW, CHILD. AND THAT IS WHY YOU ARE NOT READY.
YOU HAVE SKILL, BUT NOT FOCUS AND RESOLVE.
My heart plummets. Passing this assignment is all that matters.
JULIET, WHILE YOU WERE ATTEMPTING THE TEST, THERE WAS A PHONE MESSAGE FROM ARTEMIS FOWL.
THE MESSAGE IS: ***DOMOVOI NEEDS YOU***.
YOU MEAN HE SAID...BUTLER NEEDS ME.
BUTLER WOULD NEVER REVEAL HIS NAME TO ARTEMIS. NOT UNLESS...
I'M VERY SORRY. YOU MAY GO, OF COURSE.
And suddenly the test doesn't matter.
It doesn't matter at all.

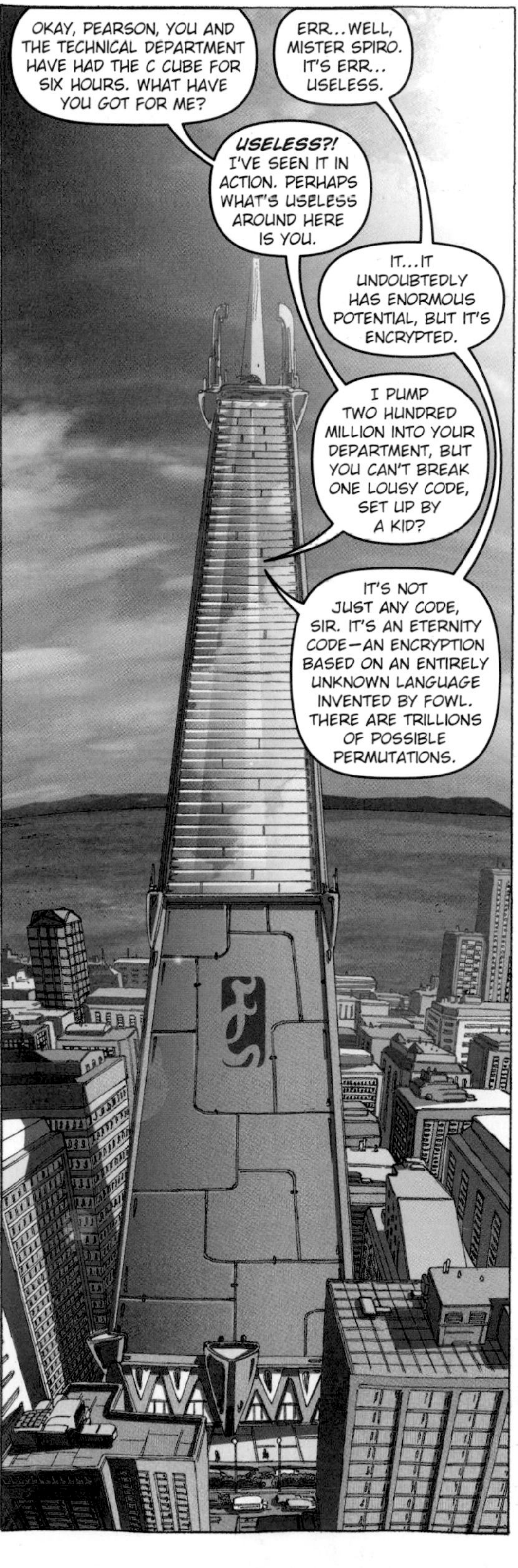
OKAY, PEARSON, YOU AND THE TECHNICAL DEPARTMENT HAVE HAD THE C CUBE FOR SIX HOURS. WHAT HAVE YOU GOT FOR ME?
ERR...WELL, MISTER SPIRO. IT'S ERR... USELESS.
USELESS?! I'VE SEEN IT IN ACTION. PERHAPS WHAT'S USELESS AROUND HERE IS YOU.
IT...IT UNDOUBTEDLY HAS ENORMOUS POTENTIAL, BUT IT'S ENCRYPTED.
I PUMP TWO HUNDRED MILLION INTO YOUR DEPARTMENT, BUT YOU CAN'T BREAK ONE LOUSY CODE, SET UP BY A KID?
IT'S NOT JUST ANY CODE, SIR. IT'S AN ETERNITY CODE—AN ENCRYPTION BASED ON AN ENTIRELY UNKNOWN LANGUAGE INVENTED BY FOWL. THERE ARE TRILLIONS OF POSSIBLE PERMUTATIONS.

CHAPTER 5: THE METAL MAN AND THE MONKEY

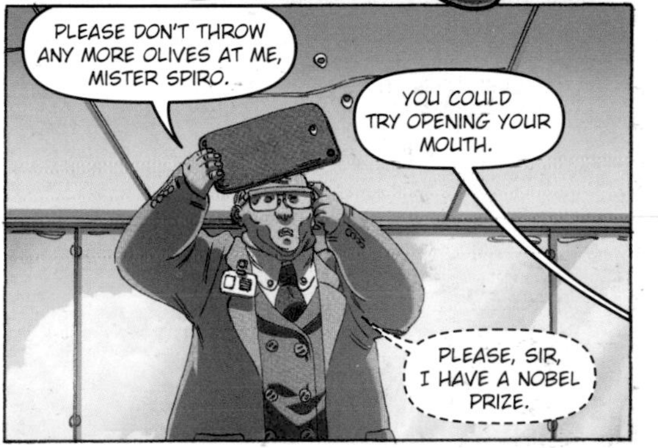
PLEASE DON'T THROW ANY MORE OLIVES AT ME, MISTER SPIRO.
YOU COULD TRY OPENING YOUR MOUTH.
PLEASE, SIR, I HAVE A NOBEL PRIZE.

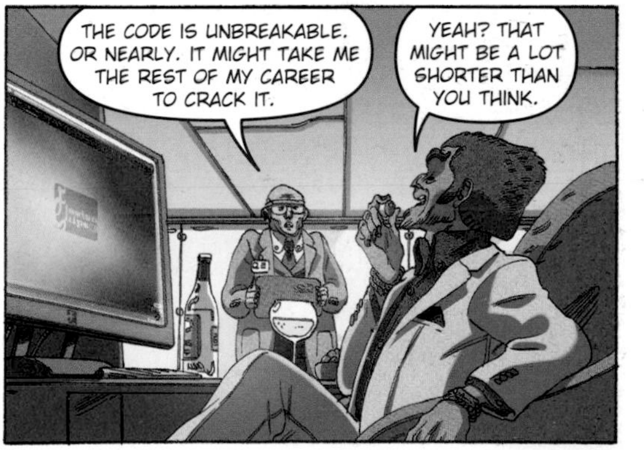
THE CODE IS UNBREAKABLE. OR NEARLY. IT MIGHT TAKE ME THE REST OF MY CAREER TO CRACK IT.
YEAH? THAT MIGHT BE A LOT SHORTER THAN YOU THINK.

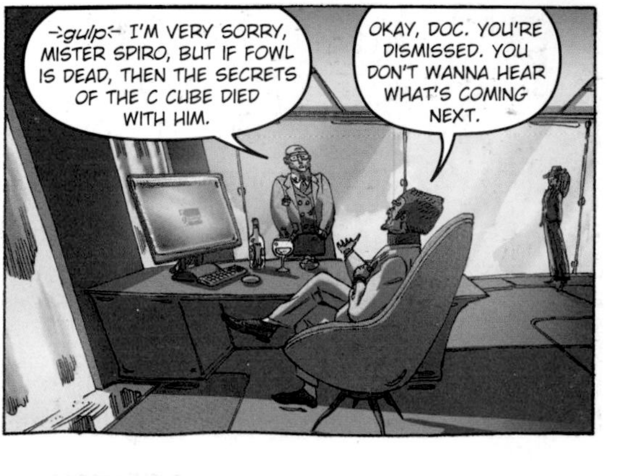
-gulp- I'M VERY SORRY, MISTER SPIRO, BUT IF FOWL IS DEAD, THEN THE SECRETS OF THE C CUBE DIED WITH HIM.
OKAY, DOC. YOU'RE DISMISSED. YOU DON'T WANNA HEAR WHAT'S COMING NEXT.

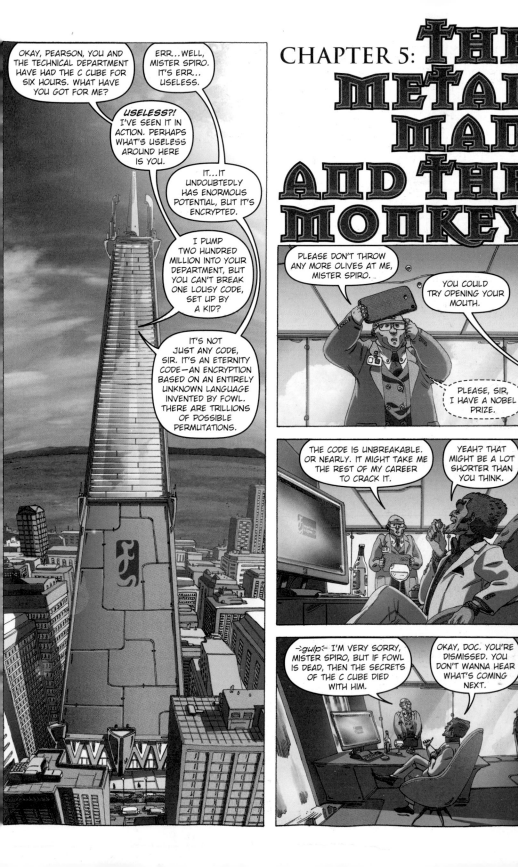

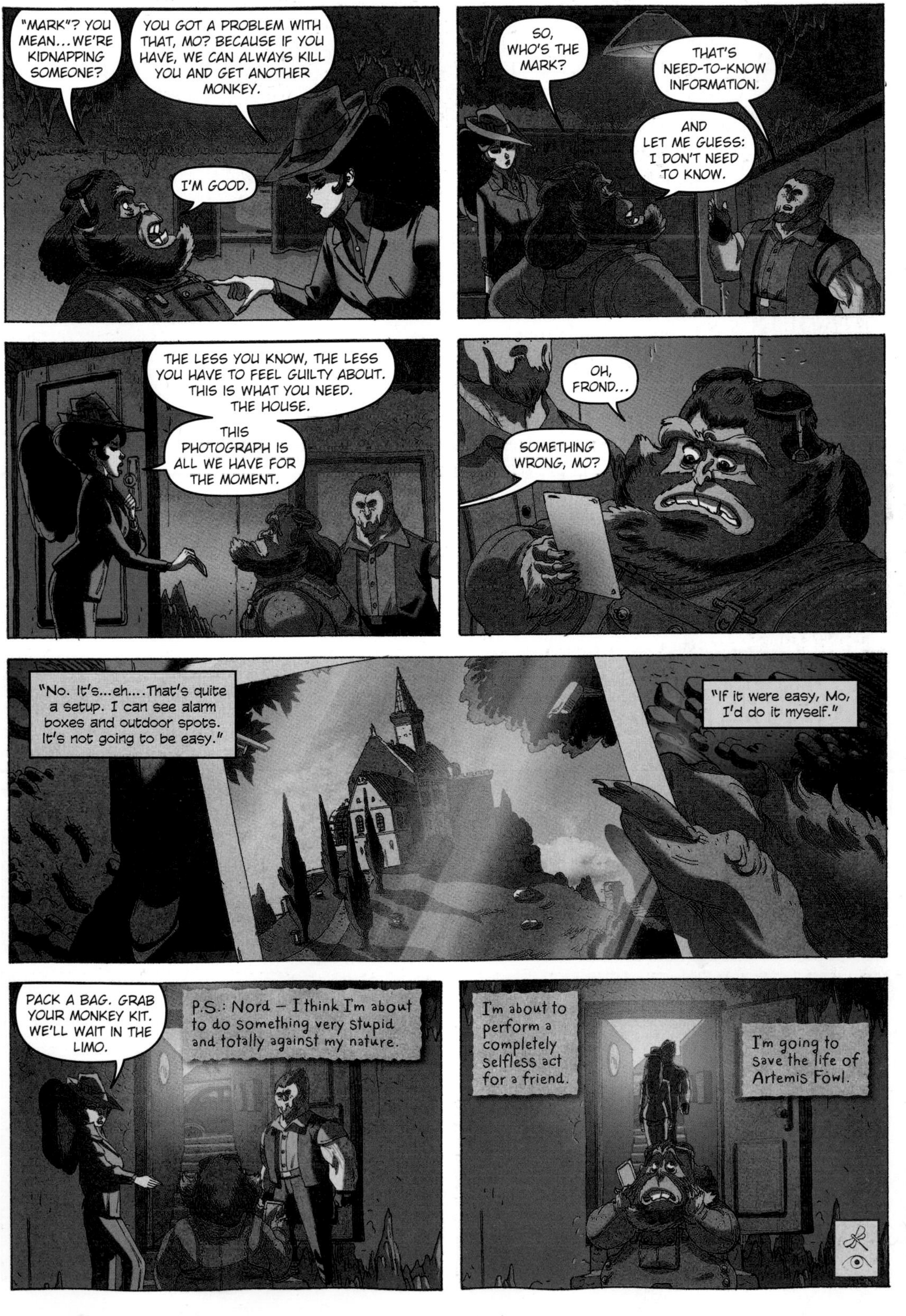
"MARK"? YOU MEAN...WE'RE KIDNAPPING SOMEONE?
YOU GOT A PROBLEM WITH THAT, MO? BECAUSE IF YOU HAVE, WE CAN ALWAYS KILL YOU AND GET ANOTHER MONKEY.
I'M GOOD.
SO, WHO'S THE MARK?
THAT'S NEED-TO-KNOW INFORMATION.
AND LET ME GUESS: I DON'T NEED TO KNOW.
THE LESS YOU KNOW, THE LESS YOU HAVE TO FEEL GUILTY ABOUT. THIS IS WHAT YOU NEED. THE HOUSE.
THIS PHOTOGRAPH IS ALL WE HAVE FOR THE MOMENT.
OH, FROND...
SOMETHING WRONG, MO?
"No. It's...eh....That's quite a setup. I can see alarm boxes and outdoor spots. It's not going to be easy."
"If it were easy, Mo, I'd do it myself."
PACK A BAG. GRAB YOUR MONKEY KIT. WE'LL WAIT IN THE LIMO.
P.S.: Nord – I think I'm about to do something very stupid and totally against my nature.
I'm about to perform a completely selfless act for a friend.
I'm going to save the life of Artemis Fowl.

CHAPTER 6: ASSAULT ON FOWL MANOR

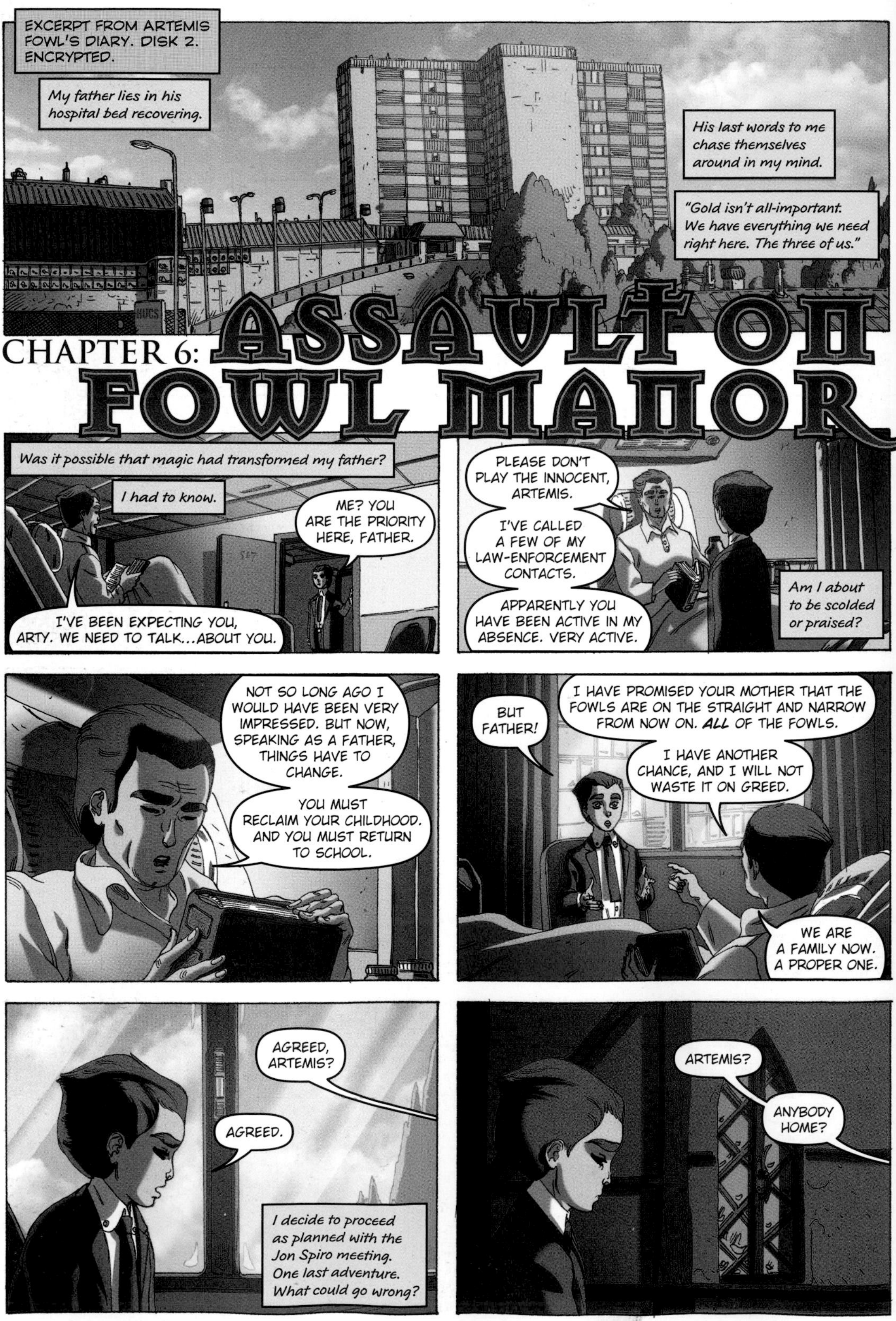

EXCERPT FROM ARTEMIS FOWL'S DIARY. DISK 2. ENCRYPTED.
My father lies in his hospital bed recovering.
His last words to me chase themselves around in my mind.
"Gold isn't all-important. We have everything we need right here. The three of us."
Was it possible that magic had transformed my father?
I had to know.
ME? YOU ARE THE PRIORITY HERE, FATHER.
I'VE BEEN EXPECTING YOU, ARTY. WE NEED TO TALK...ABOUT YOU.
PLEASE DON'T PLAY THE INNOCENT, ARTEMIS.
I'VE CALLED A FEW OF MY LAW-ENFORCEMENT CONTACTS.
APPARENTLY YOU HAVE BEEN ACTIVE IN MY ABSENCE. VERY ACTIVE.
Am I about to be scolded or praised?
NOT SO LONG AGO I WOULD HAVE BEEN VERY IMPRESSED. BUT NOW, SPEAKING AS A FATHER, THINGS HAVE TO CHANGE.
YOU MUST RECLAIM YOUR CHILDHOOD. AND YOU MUST RETURN TO SCHOOL.
BUT FATHER!
I HAVE PROMISED YOUR MOTHER THAT THE FOWLS ARE ON THE STRAIGHT AND NARROW FROM NOW ON. ***ALL*** OF THE FOWLS.
I HAVE ANOTHER CHANCE, AND I WILL NOT WASTE IT ON GREED.
WE ARE A FAMILY NOW. A PROPER ONE.
AGREED, ARTEMIS?
AGREED.
I decide to proceed as planned with the Jon Spiro meeting. One last adventure. What could go wrong?
ARTEMIS?
ANYBODY HOME?

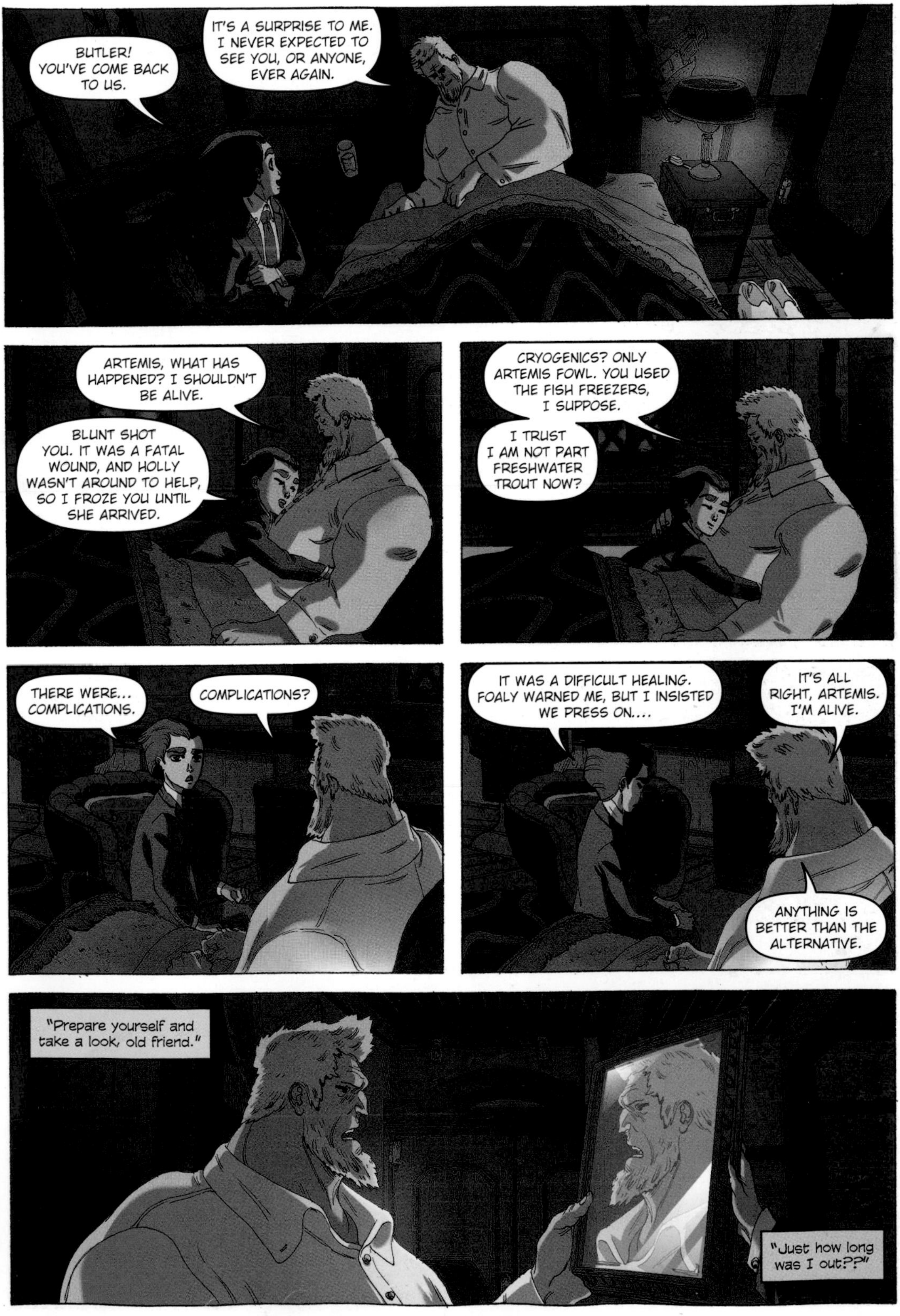
BUTLER! YOU'VE COME BACK TO US.
IT'S A SURPRISE TO ME. I NEVER EXPECTED TO SEE YOU, OR ANYONE, EVER AGAIN.
ARTEMIS, WHAT HAS HAPPENED? I SHOULDN'T BE ALIVE.
BLUNT SHOT YOU. IT WAS A FATAL WOUND, AND HOLLY WASN'T AROUND TO HELP, SO I FROZE YOU UNTIL SHE ARRIVED.
CRYOGENICS? ONLY ARTEMIS FOWL. YOU USED THE FISH FREEZERS, I SUPPOSE.
I TRUST I AM NOT PART FRESHWATER TROUT NOW?
THERE WERE... COMPLICATIONS.
COMPLICATIONS?
IT WAS A DIFFICULT HEALING. FOALY WARNED ME, BUT I INSISTED WE PRESS ON....
IT'S ALL RIGHT, ARTEMIS. I'M ALIVE.
ANYTHING IS BETTER THAN THE ALTERNATIVE.
"Prepare yourself and take a look, old friend."
"Just how long was I out??"

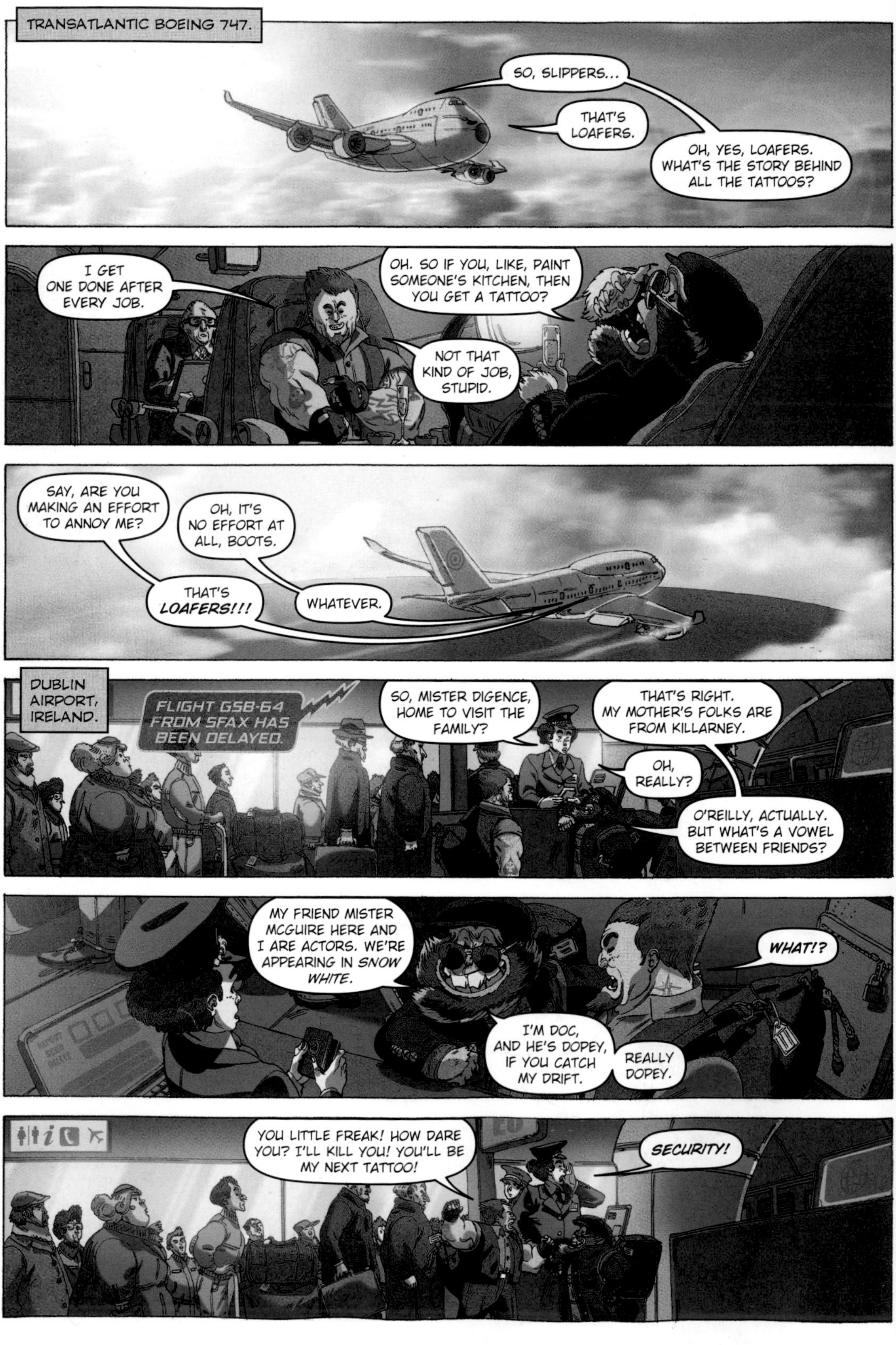
TRANSATLANTIC BOEING 747.
SO, SLIPPERS...
THAT'S LOAFERS.
OH, YES, LOAFERS. WHAT'S THE STORY BEHIND ALL THE TATTOOS?
I GET ONE DONE AFTER EVERY JOB.
OH. SO IF YOU, LIKE, PAINT SOMEONE'S KITCHEN, THEN YOU GET A TATTOO?
NOT THAT KIND OF JOB, STUPID.
SAY, ARE YOU MAKING AN EFFORT TO ANNOY ME?
OH, IT'S NO EFFORT AT ALL, BOOTS.
THAT'S *LOAFERS!!!*
WHATEVER.
DUBLIN AIRPORT, IRELAND.
FLIGHT GSB-64 FROM SFAX HAS BEEN DELAYED.
SO, MISTER DIGENCE, HOME TO VISIT THE FAMILY?
THAT'S RIGHT. MY MOTHER'S FOLKS ARE FROM KILLARNEY.
OH, REALLY?
O'REILLY, ACTUALLY. BUT WHAT'S A VOWEL BETWEEN FRIENDS?
MY FRIEND MISTER MCGUIRE HERE AND I ARE ACTORS. WE'RE APPEARING IN *SNOW WHITE*.
WHAT!?
I'M DOC, AND HE'S DOPEY, IF YOU CATCH MY DRIFT.
REALLY DOPEY.
YOU LITTLE FREAK! HOW DARE YOU? I'LL KILL YOU! YOU'LL BE MY NEXT TATTOO!
SECURITY!

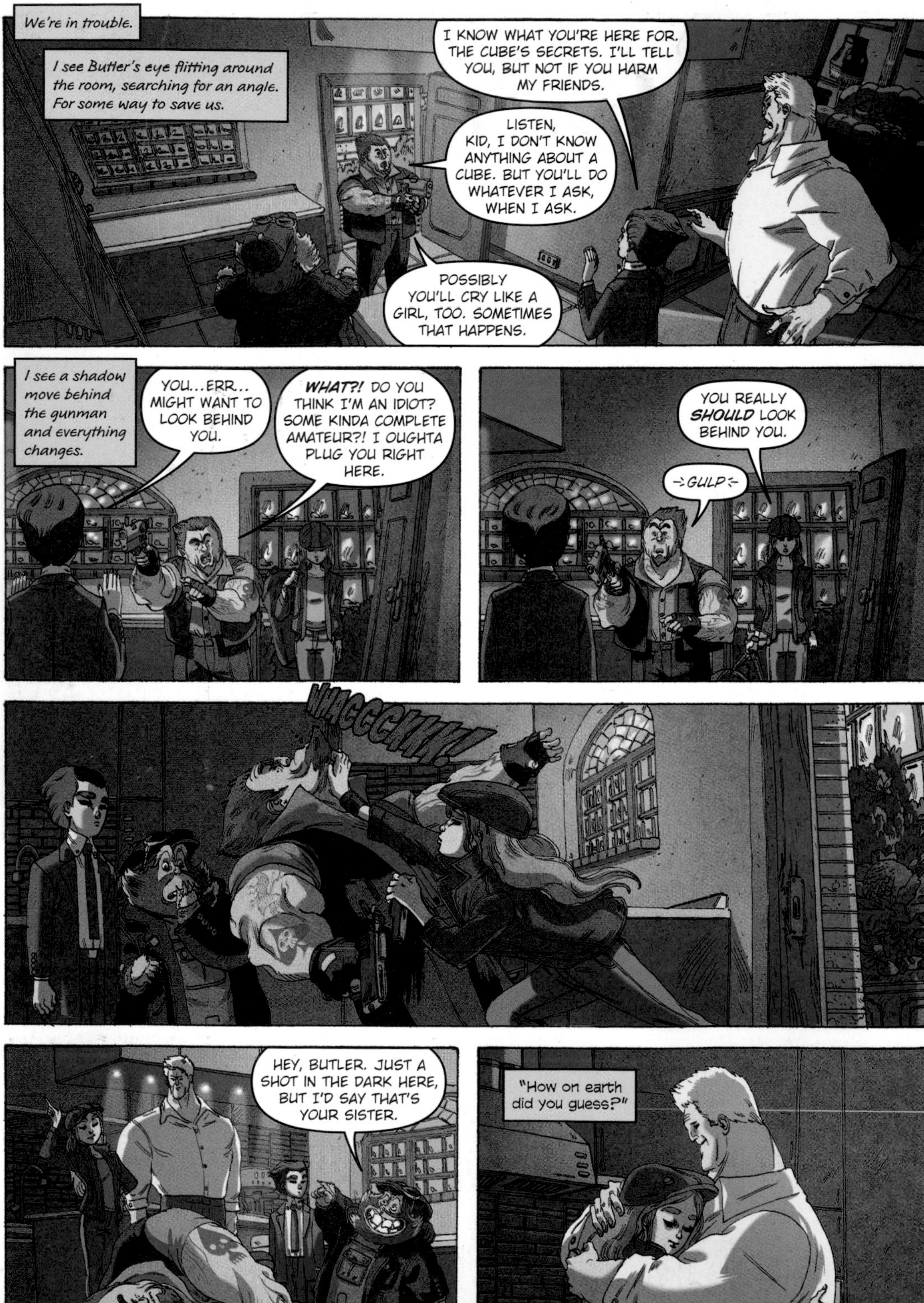
We're in trouble.
I see Butler's eye flitting around the room, searching for an angle. For some way to save us.
I KNOW WHAT YOU'RE HERE FOR. THE CUBE'S SECRETS. I'LL TELL YOU, BUT NOT IF YOU HARM MY FRIENDS.
LISTEN, KID, I DON'T KNOW ANYTHING ABOUT A CUBE. BUT YOU'LL DO WHATEVER I ASK, WHEN I ASK.
POSSIBLY YOU'LL CRY LIKE A GIRL, TOO. SOMETIMES THAT HAPPENS.
I see a shadow move behind the gunman and everything changes.
YOU...ERR... MIGHT WANT TO LOOK BEHIND YOU.
WHAT?! DO YOU THINK I'M AN IDIOT? SOME KINDA COMPLETE AMATEUR?! I OUGHTA PLUG YOU RIGHT HERE.
YOU REALLY SHOULD LOOK BEHIND YOU.
GULP
WHACCCKKK!!
HEY, BUTLER. JUST A SHOT IN THE DARK HERE, BUT I'D SAY THAT'S YOUR SISTER.
"How on earth did you guess?"

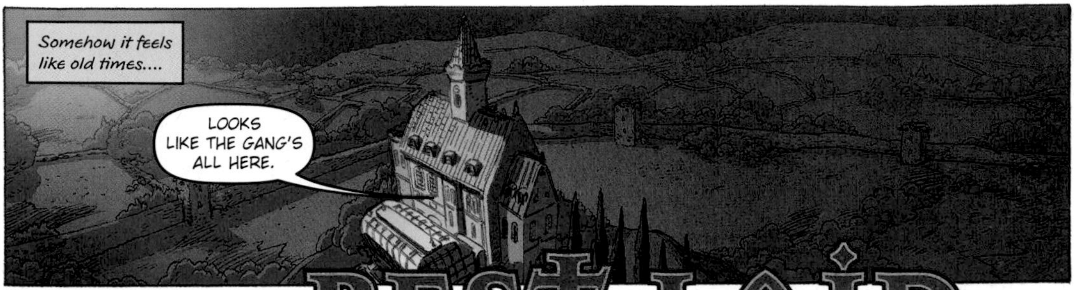
Somehow it feels like old times....
LOOKS LIKE THE GANG'S ALL HERE.

CHAPTER 7: BEST-LAID PLANS

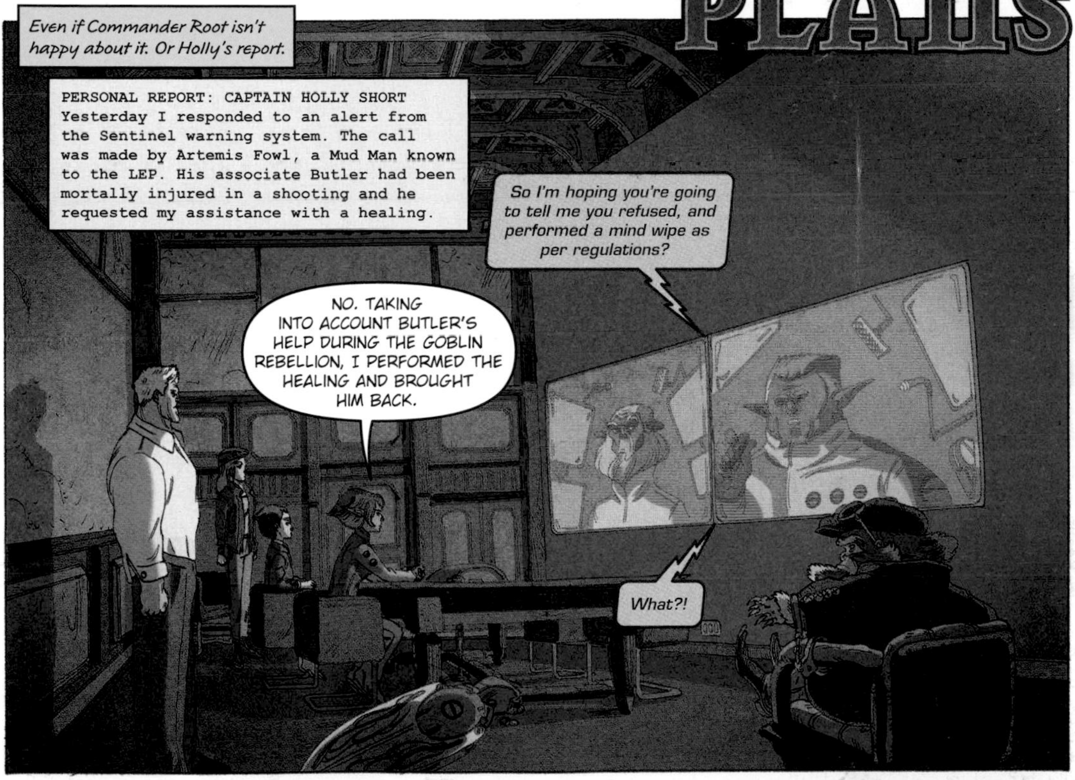
Even if Commander Root isn't happy about it. Or Holly's report.
PERSONAL REPORT: CAPTAIN HOLLY SHORT Yesterday I responded to an alert from the Sentinel warning system. The call was made by Artemis Fowl, a Mud Man known to the LEP. His associate Butler had been mortally injured in a shooting and he requested my assistance with a healing.
So I'm hoping you're going to tell me you refused, and performed a mind wipe as per regulations?
NO. TAKING INTO ACCOUNT BUTLER'S HELP DURING THE GOBLIN REBELLION, I PERFORMED THE HEALING AND BROUGHT HIM BACK.
What?!

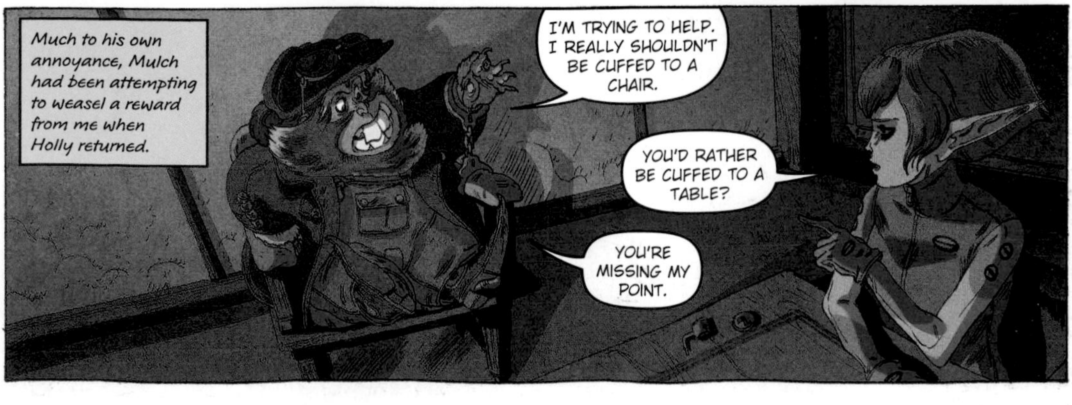
Much to his own annoyance, Mulch had been attempting to weasel a reward from me when Holly returned.
I'M TRYING TO HELP. I REALLY SHOULDN'T BE CUFFED TO A CHAIR.
YOU'D RATHER BE CUFFED TO A TABLE?
YOU'RE MISSING MY POINT.

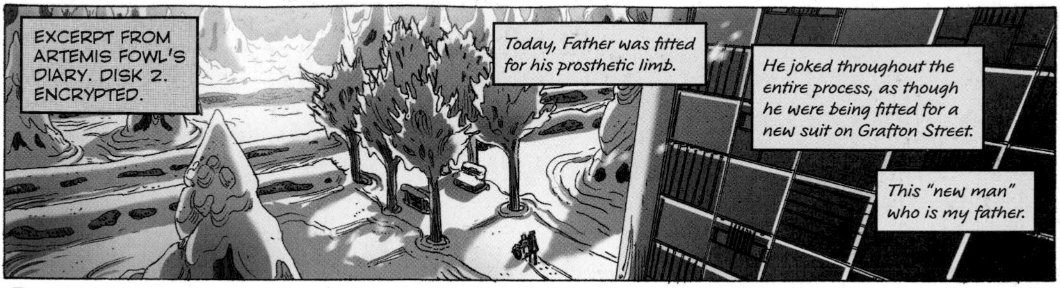
EXCERPT FROM ARTEMIS FOWL'S DIARY. DISK 2. ENCRYPTED.
Today, Father was fitted for his prosthetic limb.
He joked throughout the entire process, as though he were being fitted for a new suit on Grafton Street.
This "new man" who is my father.

CHAPTER 8: HOOKS, LINES, AND SINKERS

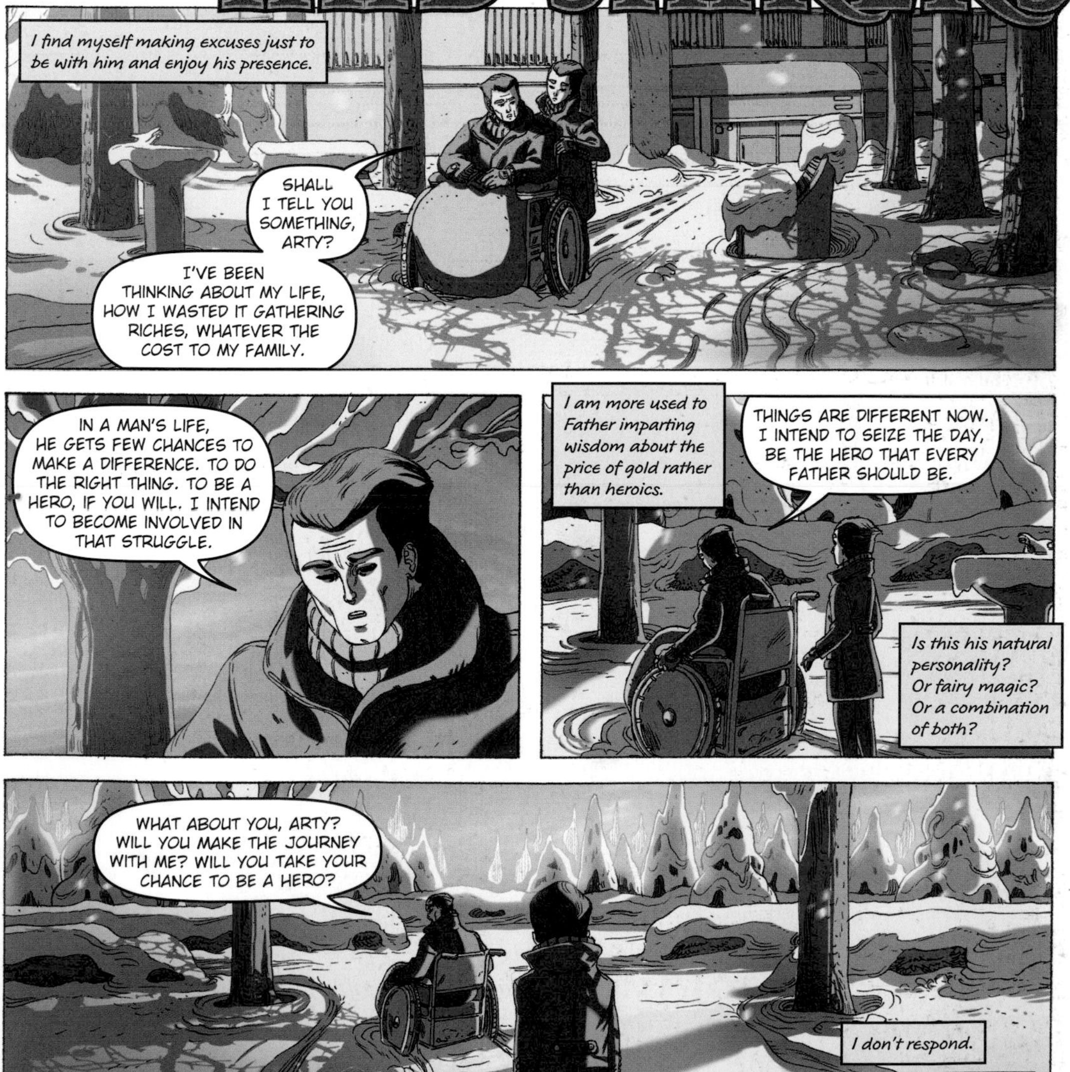
I find myself making excuses just to be with him and enjoy his presence.
SHALL I TELL YOU SOMETHING, ARTY?
I'VE BEEN THINKING ABOUT MY LIFE, HOW I WASTED IT GATHERING RICHES, WHATEVER THE COST TO MY FAMILY.
IN A MAN'S LIFE, HE GETS FEW CHANCES TO MAKE A DIFFERENCE. TO DO THE RIGHT THING. TO BE A HERO, IF YOU WILL. I INTEND TO BECOME INVOLVED IN THAT STRUGGLE.
I am more used to Father imparting wisdom about the price of gold rather than heroics.
THINGS ARE DIFFERENT NOW. I INTEND TO SEIZE THE DAY, BE THE HERO THAT EVERY FATHER SHOULD BE.
Is this his natural personality? Or fairy magic? Or a combination of both?
WHAT ABOUT YOU, ARTY? WILL YOU MAKE THE JOURNEY WITH ME? WILL YOU TAKE YOUR CHANCE TO BE A HERO?
I don't respond.
I don't know the answer.

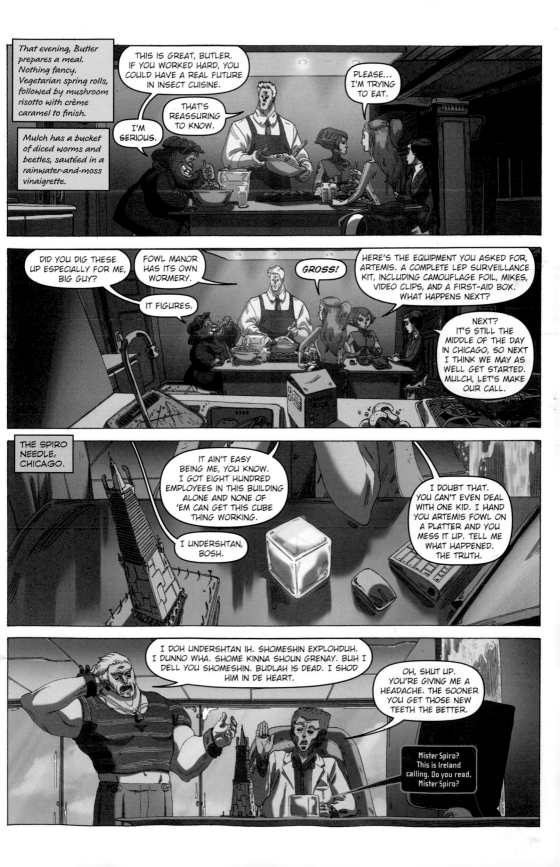

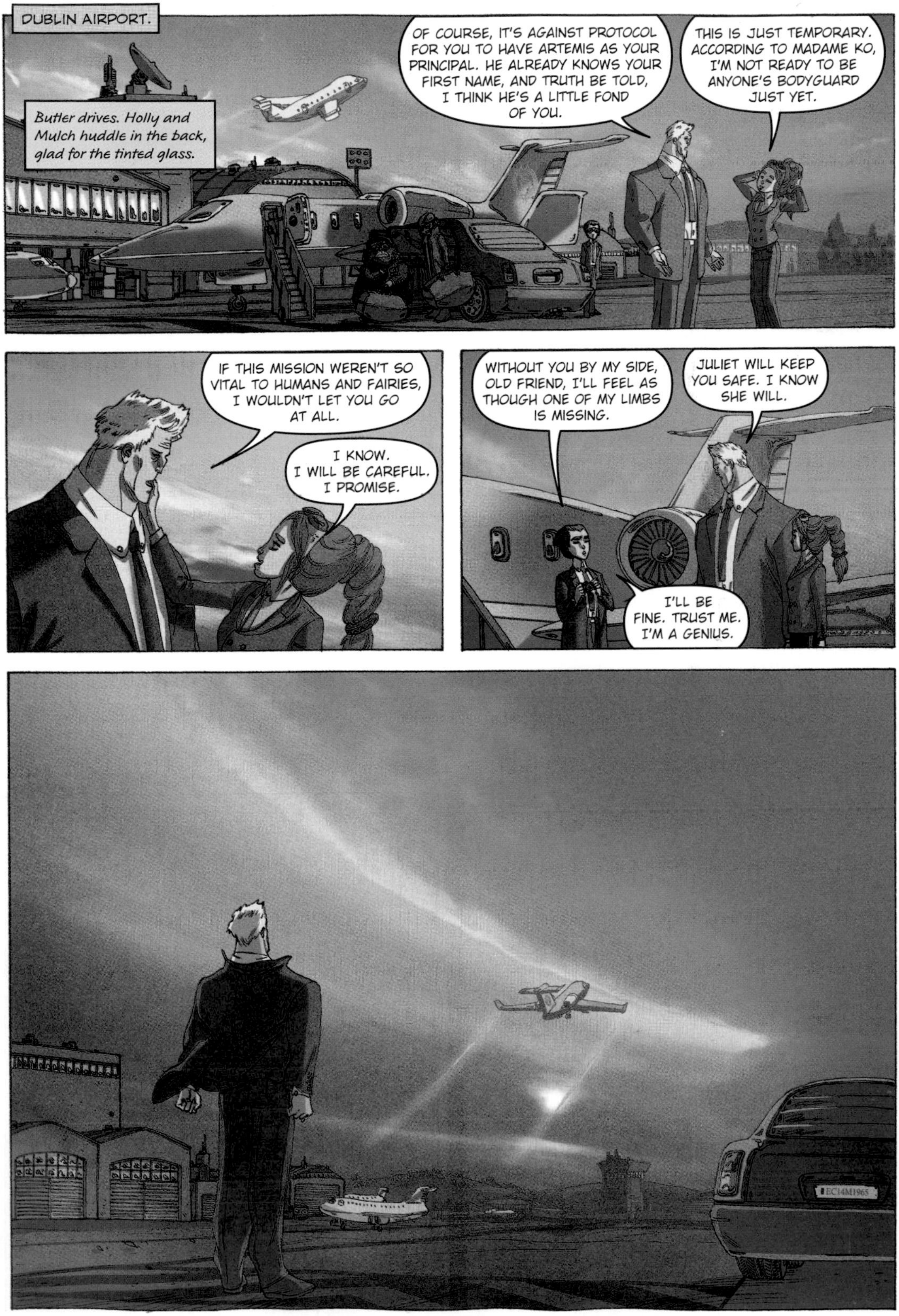
DUBLIN AIRPORT.
Butler drives. Holly and Mulch huddle in the back, glad for the tinted glass.
OF COURSE, IT'S AGAINST PROTOCOL FOR YOU TO HAVE ARTEMIS AS YOUR PRINCIPAL. HE ALREADY KNOWS YOUR FIRST NAME, AND TRUTH BE TOLD, I THINK HE'S A LITTLE FOND OF YOU.
THIS IS JUST TEMPORARY. ACCORDING TO MADAME KO, I'M NOT READY TO BE ANYONE'S BODYGUARD JUST YET.
IF THIS MISSION WEREN'T SO VITAL TO HUMANS AND FAIRIES, I WOULDN'T LET YOU GO AT ALL.
I KNOW. I WILL BE CAREFUL. I PROMISE.
WITHOUT YOU BY MY SIDE, OLD FRIEND, I'LL FEEL AS THOUGH ONE OF MY LIMBS IS MISSING.
JULIET WILL KEEP YOU SAFE. I KNOW SHE WILL.
I'LL BE FINE. TRUST ME. I'M A GENIUS.
EC14M1965

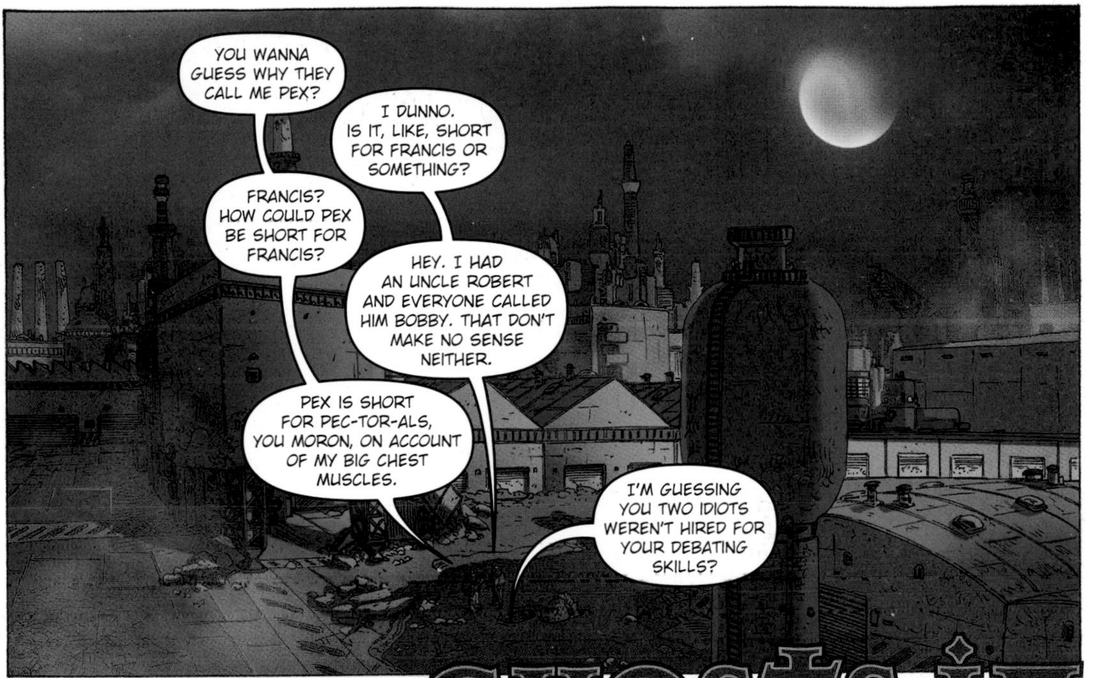
YOU WANNA GUESS WHY THEY CALL ME PEX?
I DUNNO. IS IT, LIKE, SHORT FOR FRANCIS OR SOMETHING?
FRANCIS? HOW COULD PEX BE SHORT FOR FRANCIS?
HEY. I HAD AN UNCLE ROBERT AND EVERYONE CALLED HIM BOBBY. THAT DON'T MAKE NO SENSE NEITHER.
PEX IS SHORT FOR PEC-TOR-ALS, YOU MORON, ON ACCOUNT OF MY BIG CHEST MUSCLES.
I'M GUESSING YOU TWO IDIOTS WEREN'T HIRED FOR YOUR DEBATING SKILLS?

CHAPTER 9: GHOSTS IN THE MACHINE

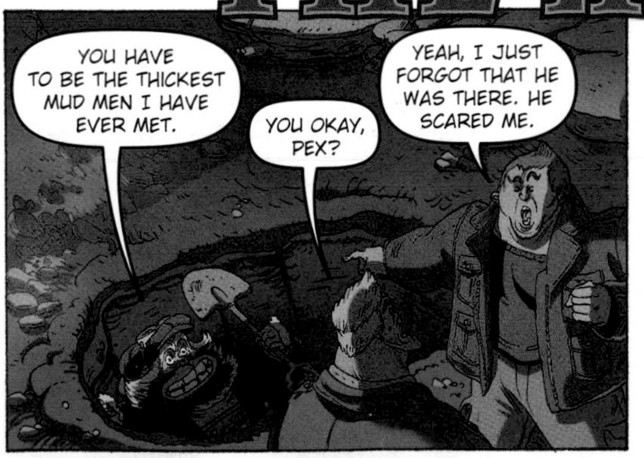
YOU HAVE TO BE THE THICKEST MUD MEN I HAVE EVER MET.
YOU OKAY, PEX?
YEAH, I JUST FORGOT THAT HE WAS THERE. HE SCARED ME.

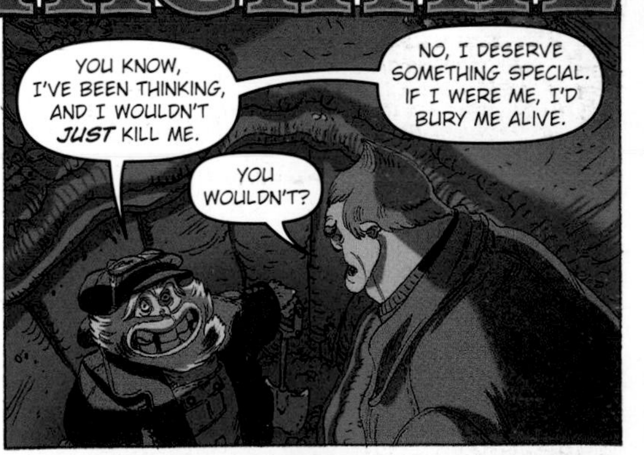
YOU KNOW, I'VE BEEN THINKING, AND I WOULDN'T *JUST* KILL ME.
NO, I DESERVE SOMETHING SPECIAL. IF I WERE ME, I'D BURY ME ALIVE.
YOU WOULDN'T?

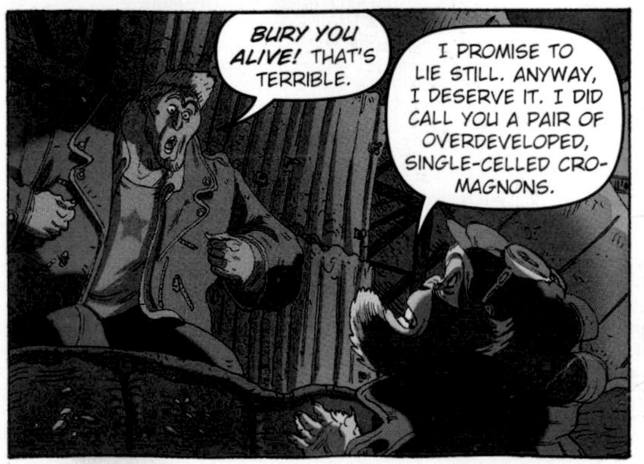
BURY YOU ALIVE! THAT'S TERRIBLE.
I PROMISE TO LIE STILL. ANYWAY, I DESERVE IT. I DID CALL YOU A PAIR OF OVERDEVELOPED, SINGLE-CELLED CRO-MAGNONS.

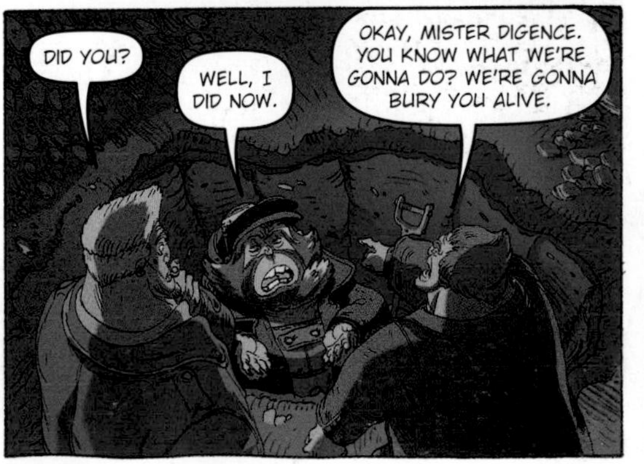
DID YOU?
WELL, I DID NOW.
OKAY, MISTER DIGENCE. YOU KNOW WHAT WE'RE GONNA DO? WE'RE GONNA BURY YOU ALIVE.

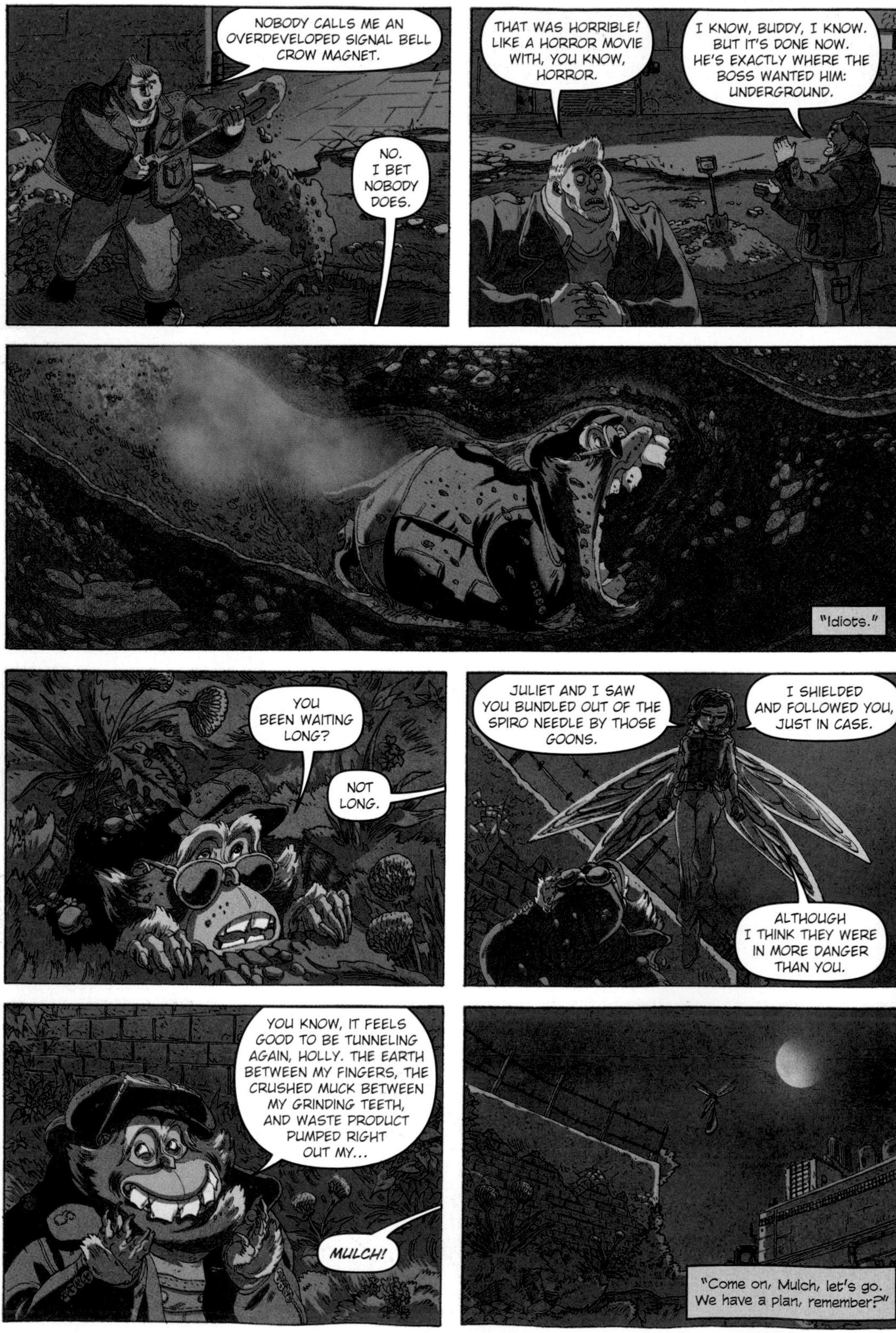
NOBODY CALLS ME AN OVERDEVELOPED SIGNAL BELL CROW MAGNET.
NO. I BET NOBODY DOES.
THAT WAS HORRIBLE! LIKE A HORROR MOVIE WITH, YOU KNOW, HORROR.
I KNOW, BUDDY, I KNOW. BUT IT'S DONE NOW. HE'S EXACTLY WHERE THE BOSS WANTED HIM: UNDERGROUND.
"Idiots."
YOU BEEN WAITING LONG?
NOT LONG.
JULIET AND I SAW YOU BUNDLED OUT OF THE SPIRO NEEDLE BY THOSE GOONS.
I SHIELDED AND FOLLOWED YOU, JUST IN CASE.
ALTHOUGH I THINK THEY WERE IN MORE DANGER THAN YOU.
YOU KNOW, IT FEELS GOOD TO BE TUNNELING AGAIN, HOLLY. THE EARTH BETWEEN MY FINGERS, THE CRUSHED MUCK BETWEEN MY GRINDING TEETH, AND WASTE PRODUCT PUMPED RIGHT OUT MY...
MULCH!
"Come on, Mulch, let's go. We have a plan, remember?"

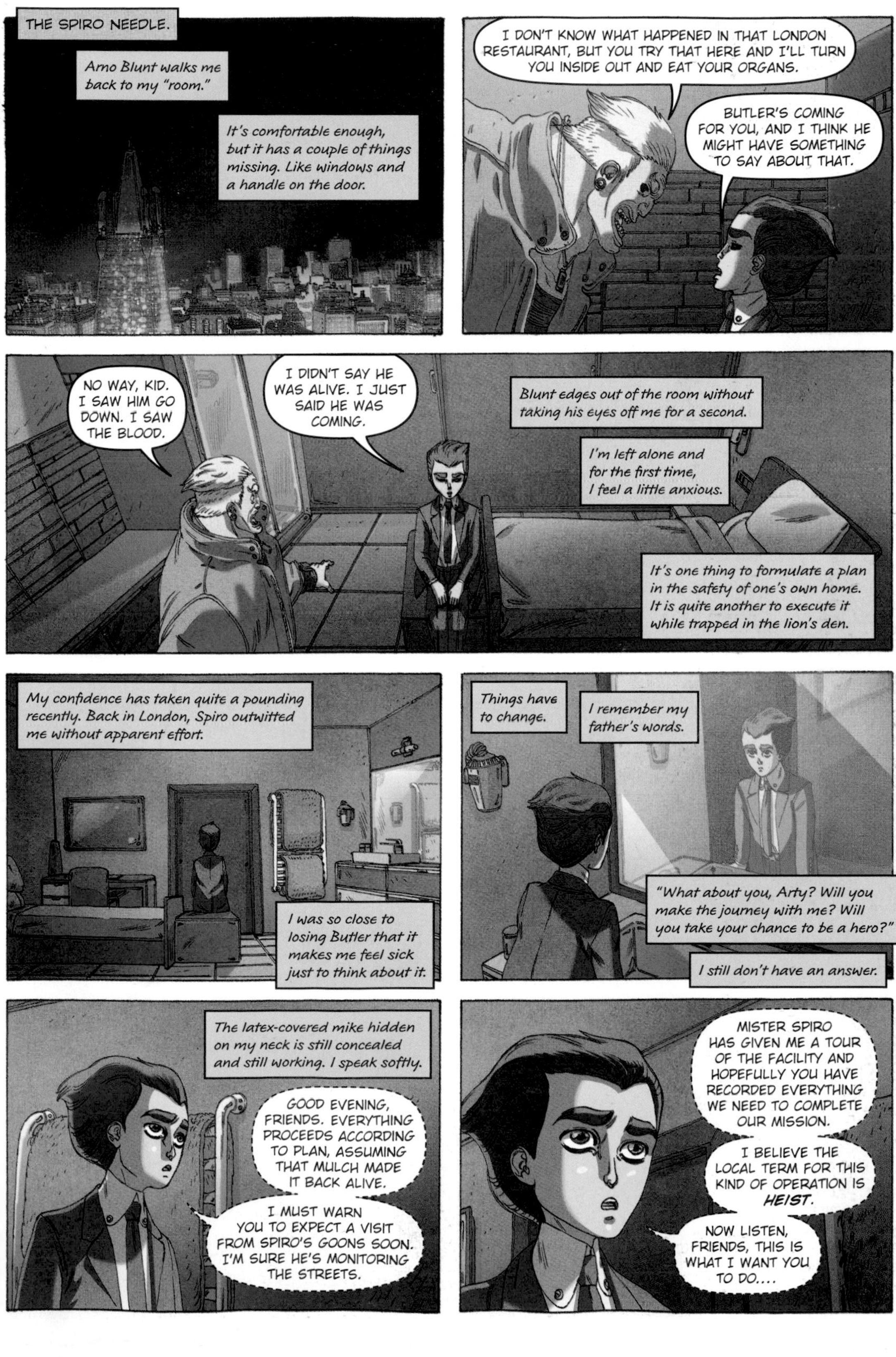
THE SPIRO NEEDLE.
Arno Blunt walks me back to my "room."
It's comfortable enough, but it has a couple of things missing. Like windows and a handle on the door.
I DON'T KNOW WHAT HAPPENED IN THAT LONDON RESTAURANT, BUT YOU TRY THAT HERE AND I'LL TURN YOU INSIDE OUT AND EAT YOUR ORGANS.
BUTLER'S COMING FOR YOU, AND I THINK HE MIGHT HAVE SOMETHING TO SAY ABOUT THAT.
NO WAY, KID. I SAW HIM GO DOWN. I SAW THE BLOOD.
I DIDN'T SAY HE WAS ALIVE. I JUST SAID HE WAS COMING.
Blunt edges out of the room without taking his eyes off me for a second.
I'm left alone and for the first time, I feel a little anxious.
It's one thing to formulate a plan in the safety of one's own home. It is quite another to execute it while trapped in the lion's den.
My confidence has taken quite a pounding recently. Back in London, Spiro outwitted me without apparent effort.
I was so close to losing Butler that it makes me feel sick just to think about it.
Things have to change.
I remember my father's words.
"What about you, Arty? Will you make the journey with me? Will you take your chance to be a hero?"
I still don't have an answer.
The latex-covered mike hidden on my neck is still concealed and still working. I speak softly.
GOOD EVENING, FRIENDS. EVERYTHING PROCEEDS ACCORDING TO PLAN, ASSUMING THAT MULCH MADE IT BACK ALIVE.
I MUST WARN YOU TO EXPECT A VISIT FROM SPIRO'S GOONS SOON. I'M SURE HE'S MONITORING THE STREETS.
MISTER SPIRO HAS GIVEN ME A TOUR OF THE FACILITY AND HOPEFULLY YOU HAVE RECORDED EVERYTHING WE NEED TO COMPLETE OUR MISSION.
I BELIEVE THE LOCAL TERM FOR THIS KIND OF OPERATION IS ***HEIST***.
NOW LISTEN, FRIENDS, THIS IS WHAT I WANT YOU TO DO....

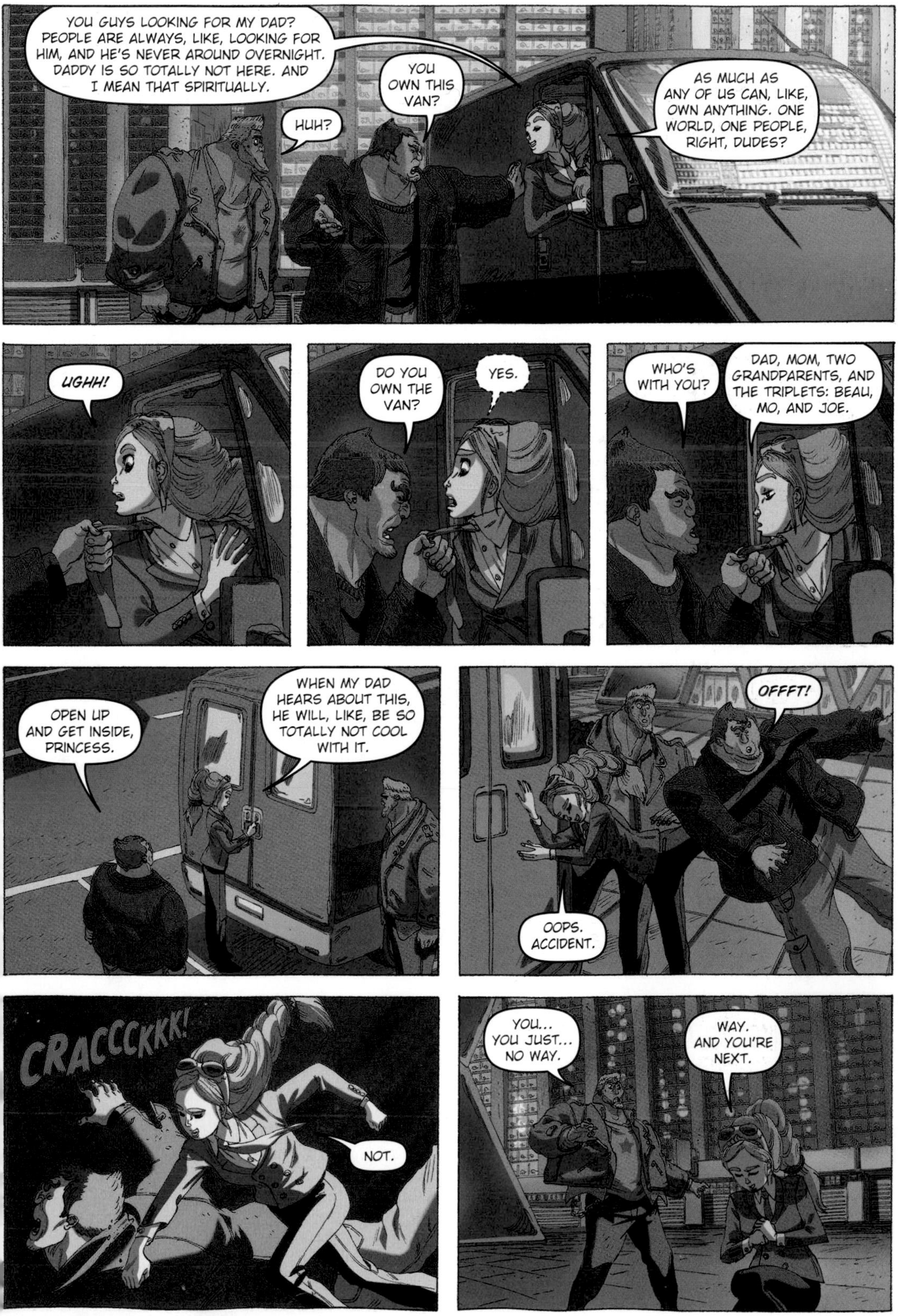
YOU GUYS LOOKING FOR MY DAD? PEOPLE ARE ALWAYS, LIKE, LOOKING FOR HIM, AND HE'S NEVER AROUND OVERNIGHT. DADDY IS SO TOTALLY NOT HERE. AND I MEAN THAT SPIRITUALLY.
HUH?
YOU OWN THIS VAN?
AS MUCH AS ANY OF US CAN, LIKE, OWN ANYTHING. ONE WORLD, ONE PEOPLE, RIGHT, DUDES?
UGHH!
DO YOU OWN THE VAN?
YES.
WHO'S WITH YOU?
DAD, MOM, TWO GRANDPARENTS, AND THE TRIPLETS: BEAU, MO, AND JOE.
OPEN UP AND GET INSIDE, PRINCESS.
WHEN MY DAD HEARS ABOUT THIS, HE WILL, LIKE, BE SO TOTALLY NOT COOL WITH IT.
OFFFT!
OOPS. ACCIDENT.
CRACCCKKK!
NOT.
YOU... YOU JUST... NO WAY.
WAY. AND YOU'RE NEXT.

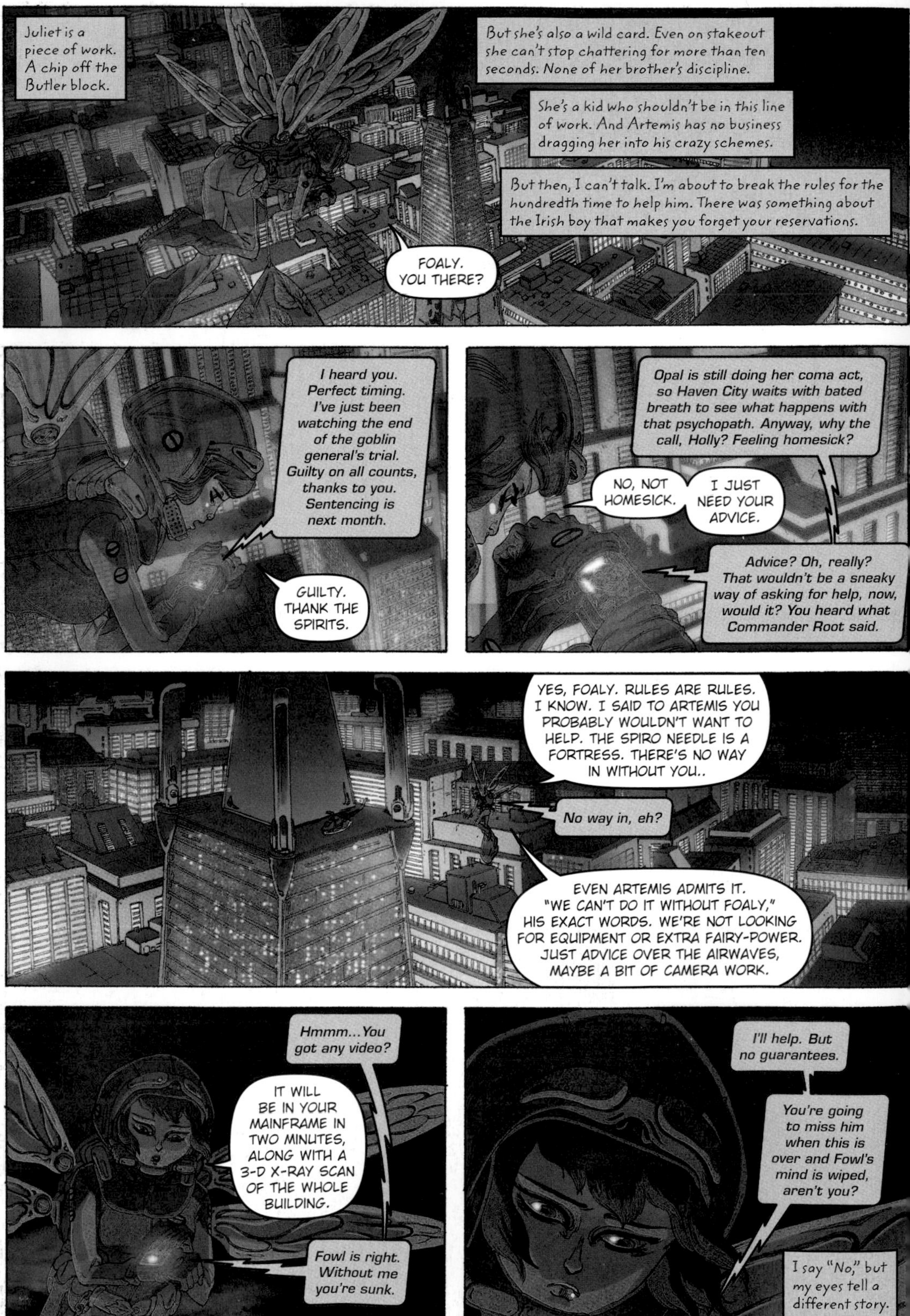
Juliet is a piece of work. A chip off the Butler block.
But she's also a wild card. Even on stakeout she can't stop chattering for more than ten seconds. None of her brother's discipline.
She's a kid who shouldn't be in this line of work. And Artemis has no business dragging her into his crazy schemes.
But then, I can't talk. I'm about to break the rules for the hundredth time to help him. There was something about the Irish boy that makes you forget your reservations.
FOALY. YOU THERE?
I heard you. Perfect timing. I've just been watching the end of the goblin general's trial. Guilty on all counts, thanks to you. Sentencing is next month.
GUILTY. THANK THE SPIRITS.
Opal is still doing her coma act, so Haven City waits with bated breath to see what happens with that psychopath. Anyway, why the call, Holly? Feeling homesick?
NO, NOT HOMESICK.
I JUST NEED YOUR ADVICE.
Advice? Oh, really? That wouldn't be a sneaky way of asking for help, now, would it? You heard what Commander Root said.
YES, FOALY. RULES ARE RULES. I KNOW. I SAID TO ARTEMIS YOU PROBABLY WOULDN'T WANT TO HELP. THE SPIRO NEEDLE IS A FORTRESS. THERE'S NO WAY IN WITHOUT YOU..
No way in, eh?
EVEN ARTEMIS ADMITS IT. "WE CAN'T DO IT WITHOUT FOALY," HIS EXACT WORDS. WE'RE NOT LOOKING FOR EQUIPMENT OR EXTRA FAIRY-POWER. JUST ADVICE OVER THE AIRWAVES, MAYBE A BIT OF CAMERA WORK.
Hmmm...You got any video?
IT WILL BE IN YOUR MAINFRAME IN TWO MINUTES, ALONG WITH A 3-D X-RAY SCAN OF THE WHOLE BUILDING.
Fowl is right. Without me you're sunk.
I'll help. But no guarantees.
You're going to miss him when this is over and Fowl's mind is wiped, aren't you?
I say "No," but my eyes tell a different story.

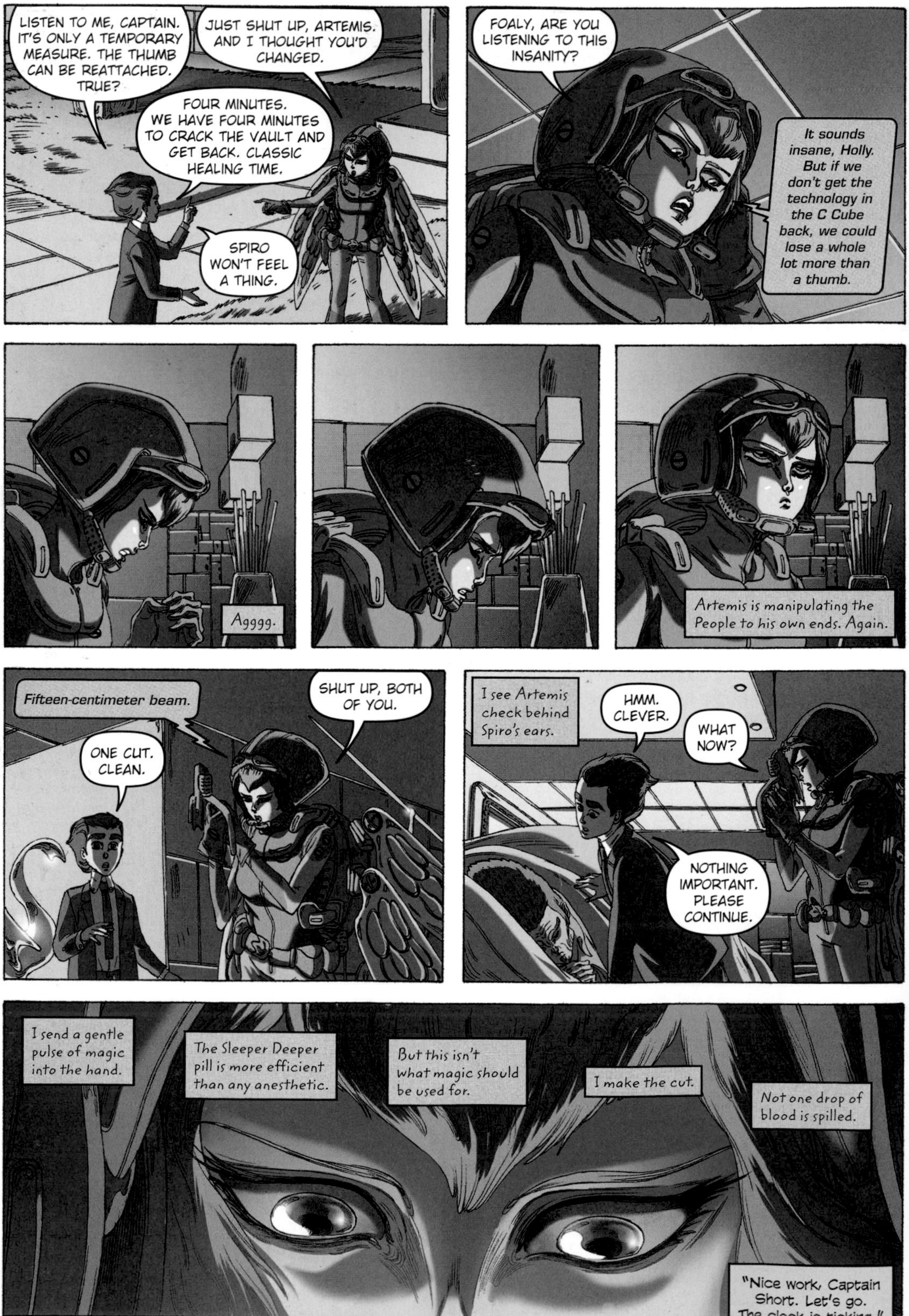

LISTEN TO ME, CAPTAIN. IT'S ONLY A TEMPORARY MEASURE. THE THUMB CAN BE REATTACHED. TRUE?
JUST SHUT UP, ARTEMIS. AND I THOUGHT YOU'D CHANGED.
FOUR MINUTES. WE HAVE FOUR MINUTES TO CRACK THE VAULT AND GET BACK. CLASSIC HEALING TIME.
SPIRO WON'T FEEL A THING.
FOALY, ARE YOU LISTENING TO THIS INSANITY?
It sounds insane, Holly. But if we don't get the technology in the C Cube back, we could lose a whole lot more than a thumb.
Agggg.
Artemis is manipulating the People to his own ends. Again.
Fifteen-centimeter beam.
SHUT UP, BOTH OF YOU.
ONE CUT. CLEAN.
I see Artemis check behind Spiro's ears.
HMM. CLEVER.
WHAT NOW?
NOTHING IMPORTANT. PLEASE CONTINUE.
I send a gentle pulse of magic into the hand.
The Sleeper Deeper pill is more efficient than any anesthetic.
But this isn't what magic should be used for.
I make the cut.
Not one drop of blood is spilled.
"Nice work, Captain Short. Let's go. The clock is ticking."

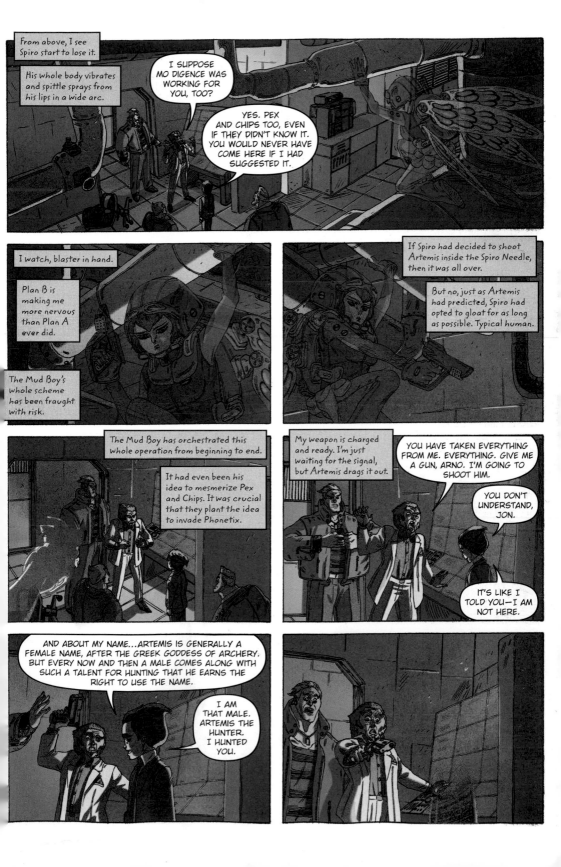

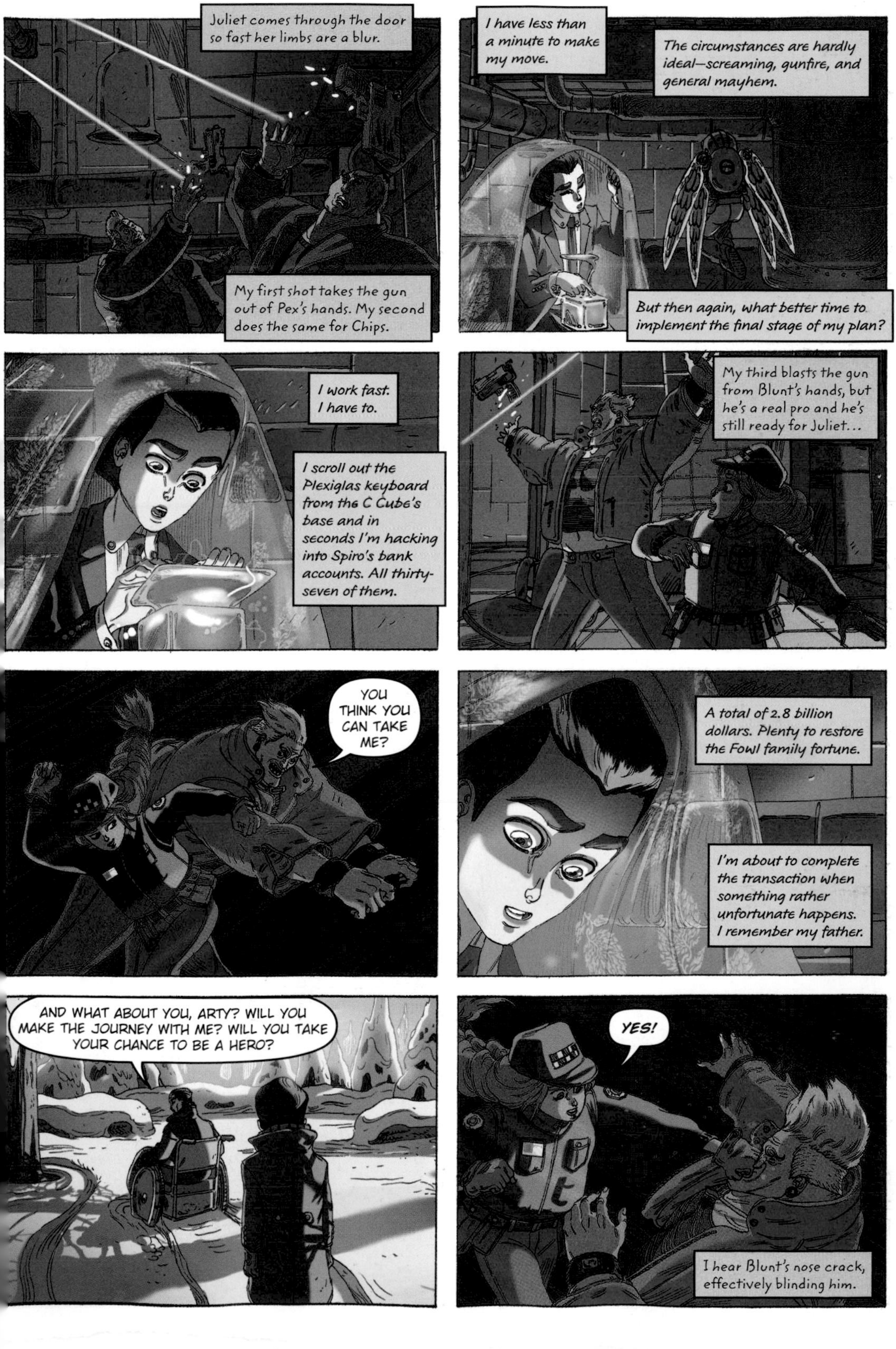
Juliet comes through the door so fast her limbs are a blur.
My first shot takes the gun out of Pex's hands. My second does the same for Chips.
I have less than a minute to make my move.
The circumstances are hardly ideal—screaming, gunfire, and general mayhem.
But then again, what better time to implement the final stage of my plan?
I work fast. I have to.
I scroll out the Plexiglas keyboard from the C Cube's base and in seconds I'm hacking into Spiro's bank accounts. All thirty-seven of them.
My third blasts the gun from Blunt's hands, but he's a real pro and he's still ready for Juliet...
YOU THINK YOU CAN TAKE ME?
A total of 2.8 billion dollars. Plenty to restore the Fowl family fortune.
I'm about to complete the transaction when something rather unfortunate happens. I remember my father.
AND WHAT ABOUT YOU, ARTY? WILL YOU MAKE THE JOURNEY WITH ME? WILL YOU TAKE YOUR CHANCE TO BE A HERO?
YES!
I hear Blunt's nose crack, effectively blinding him.

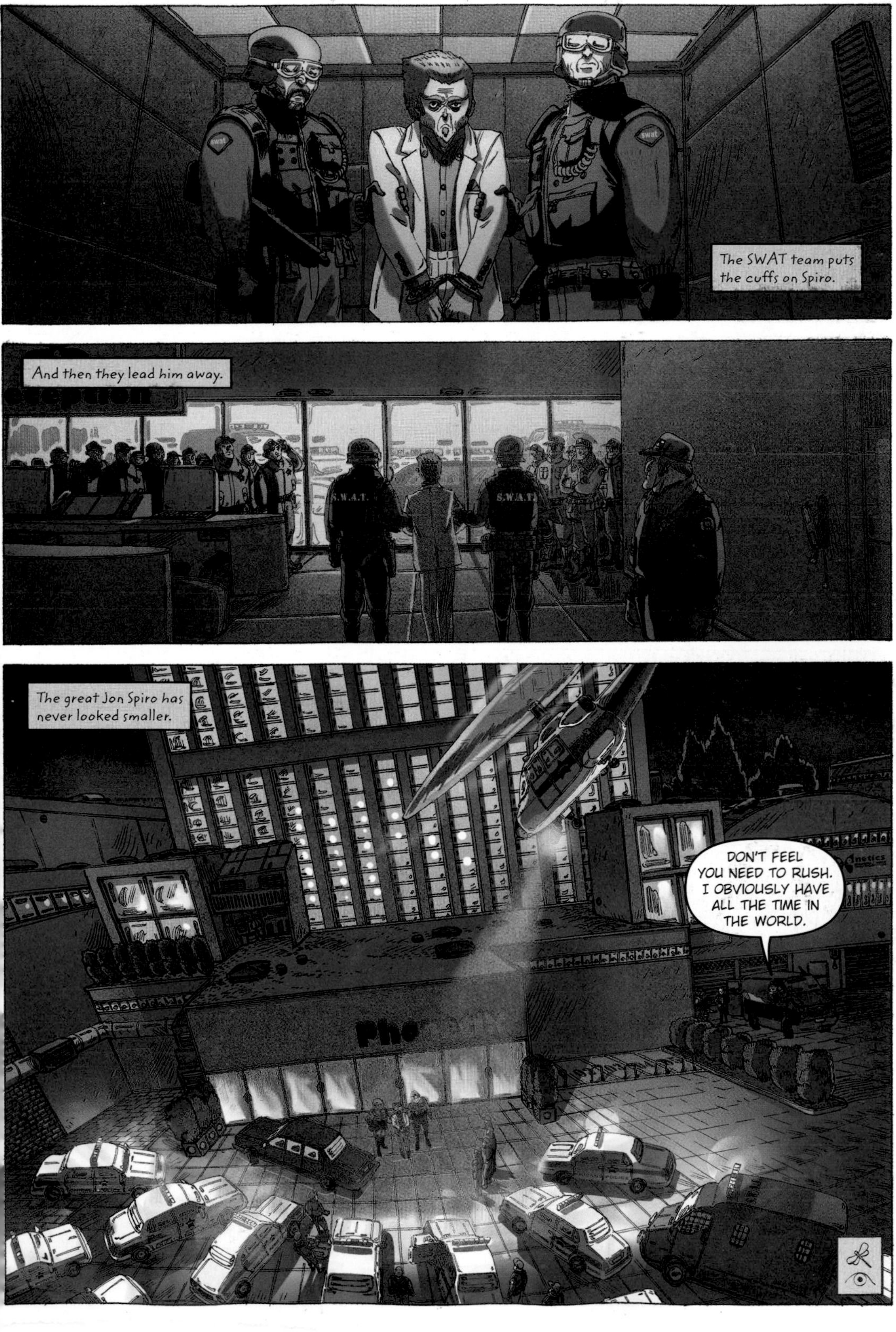
The SWAT team puts the cuffs on Spiro.
And then they lead him away.
The great Jon Spiro has never looked smaller.
DON'T FEEL YOU NEED TO RUSH. I OBVIOUSLY HAVE ALL THE TIME IN THE WORLD.

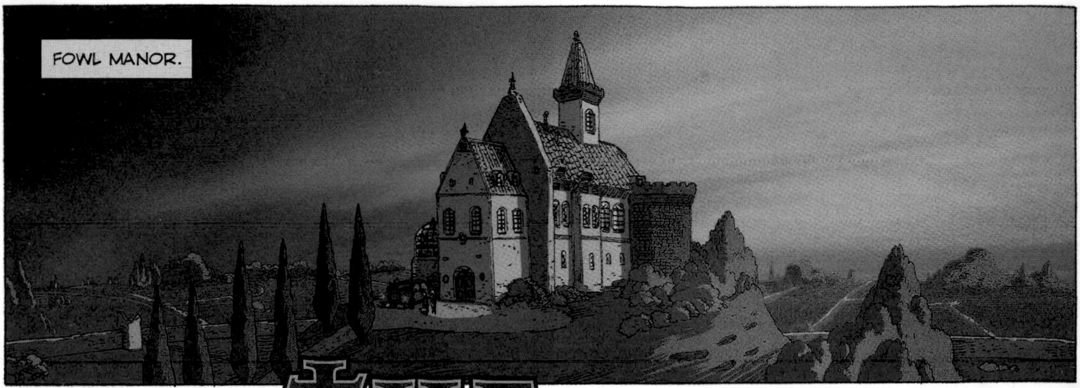
FOWL MANOR.

CHAPTER 11: THE INVISIBLE MAN

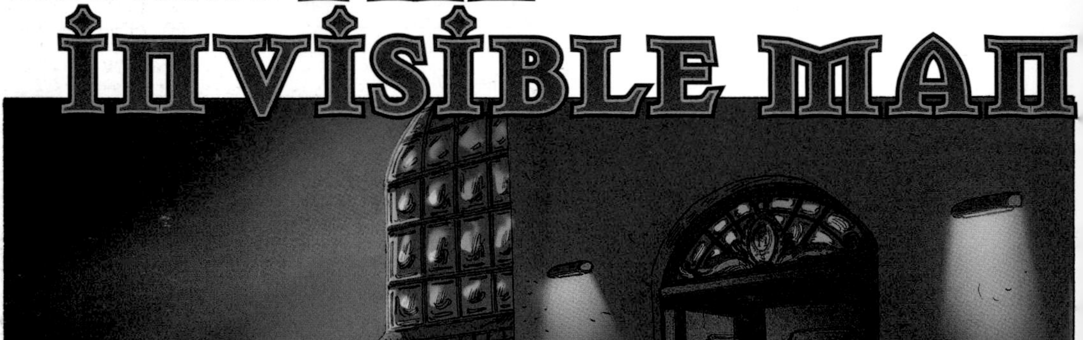

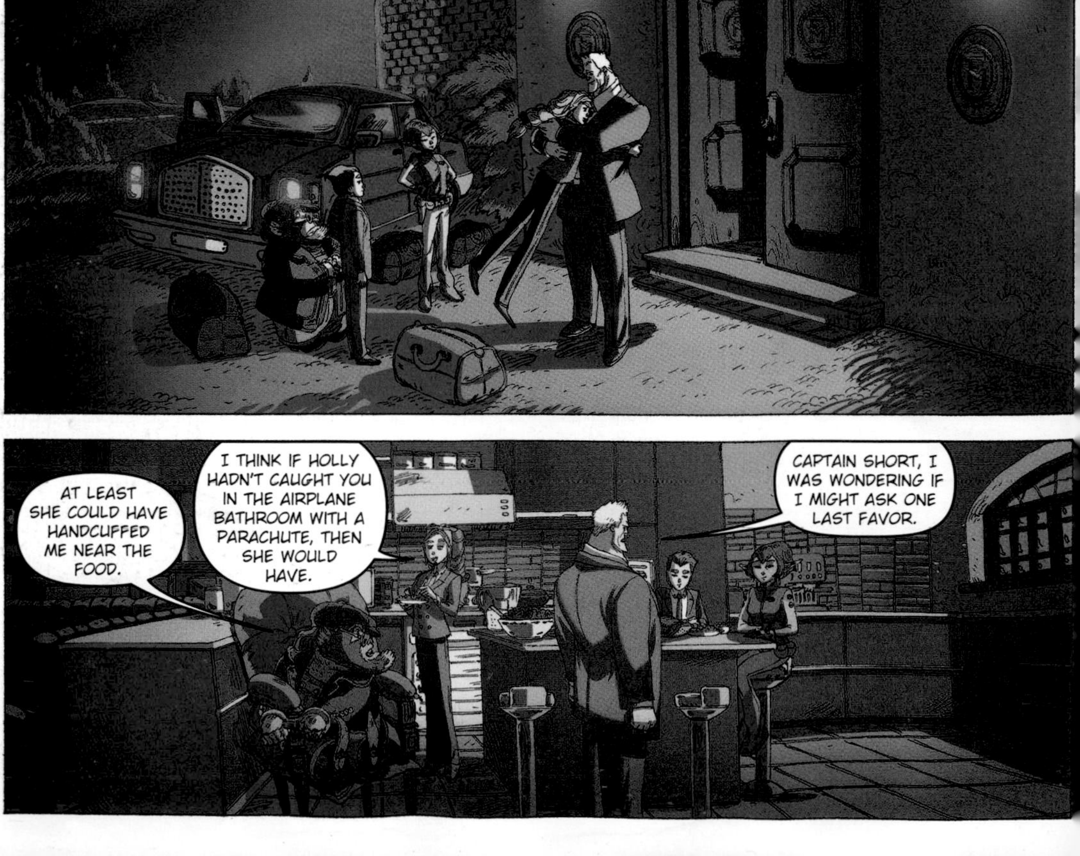
AT LEAST SHE COULD HAVE HANDCUFFED ME NEAR THE FOOD.
I THINK IF HOLLY HADN'T CAUGHT YOU IN THE AIRPLANE BATHROOM WITH A PARACHUTE, THEN SHE WOULD HAVE.
CAPTAIN SHORT, I WAS WONDERING IF I MIGHT ASK ONE LAST FAVOR.

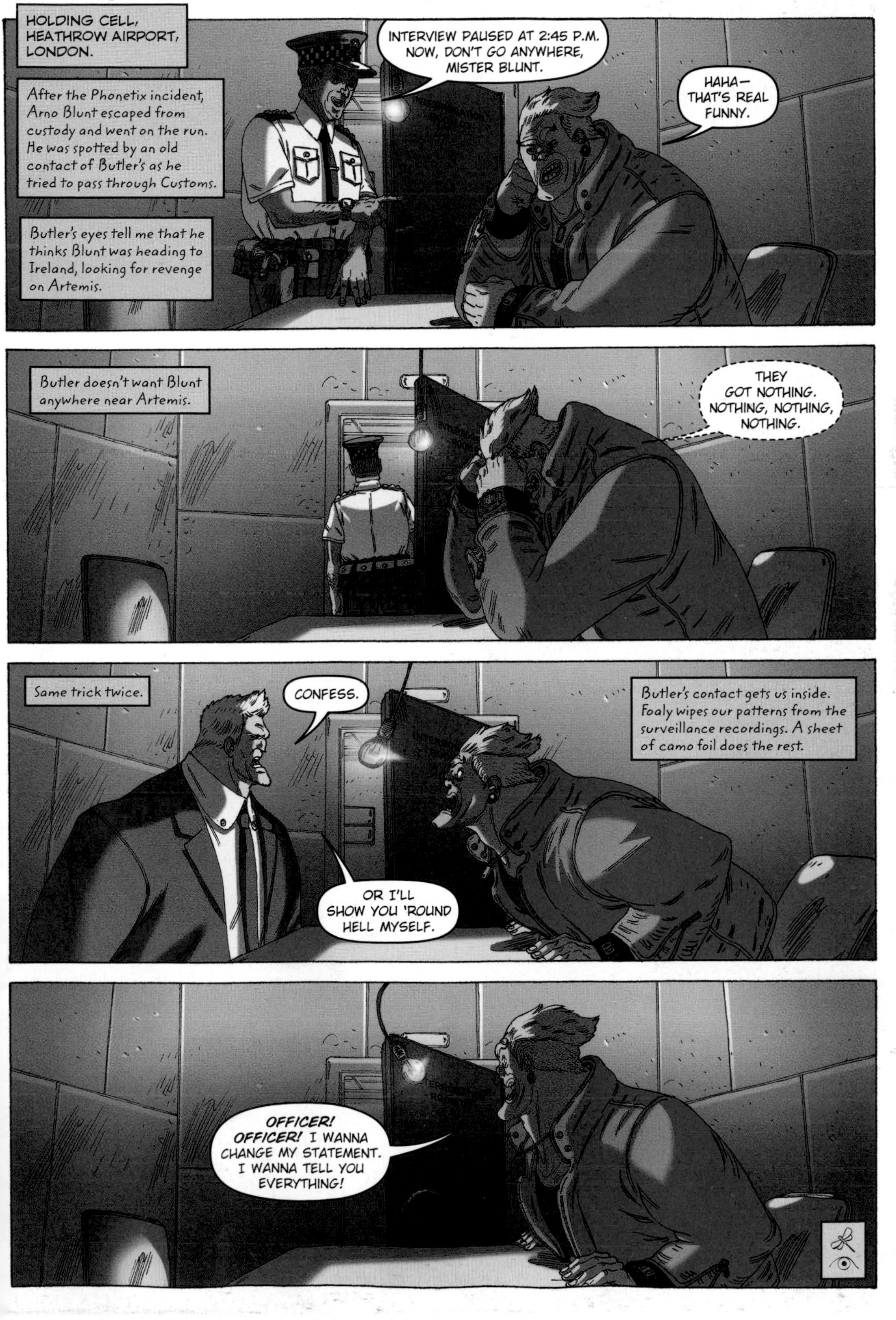
HOLDING CELL, HEATHROW AIRPORT, LONDON.
After the Phonetix incident, Arno Blunt escaped from custody and went on the run. He was spotted by an old contact of Butler's as he tried to pass through Customs.
Butler's eyes tell me that he thinks Blunt was heading to Ireland, looking for revenge on Artemis.
INTERVIEW PAUSED AT 2:45 P.M. NOW, DON'T GO ANYWHERE, MISTER BLUNT.
HAHA— THAT'S REAL FUNNY.
Butler doesn't want Blunt anywhere near Artemis.
THEY GOT NOTHING. NOTHING, NOTHING, NOTHING.
Same trick twice.
CONFESS.
Butler's contact gets us inside. Foaly wipes our patterns from the surveillance recordings. A sheet of camo foil does the rest.
OR I'LL SHOW YOU 'ROUND HELL MYSELF.
OFFICER! OFFICER! I WANNA CHANGE MY STATEMENT. I WANNA TELL YOU EVERYTHING!

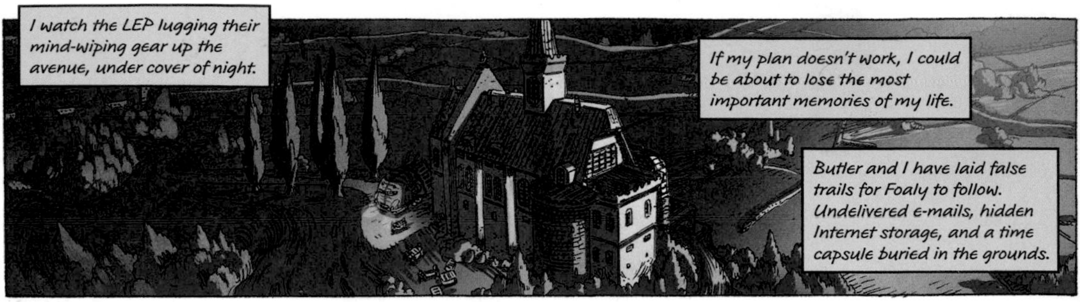
I watch the LEP lugging their mind-wiping gear up the avenue, under cover of night.
If my plan doesn't work, I could be about to lose the most important memories of my life.
Butler and I have laid false trails for Foaly to follow. Undelivered e-mails, hidden Internet storage, and a time capsule buried in the grounds.

CHAPTER 12: MIND WIPE

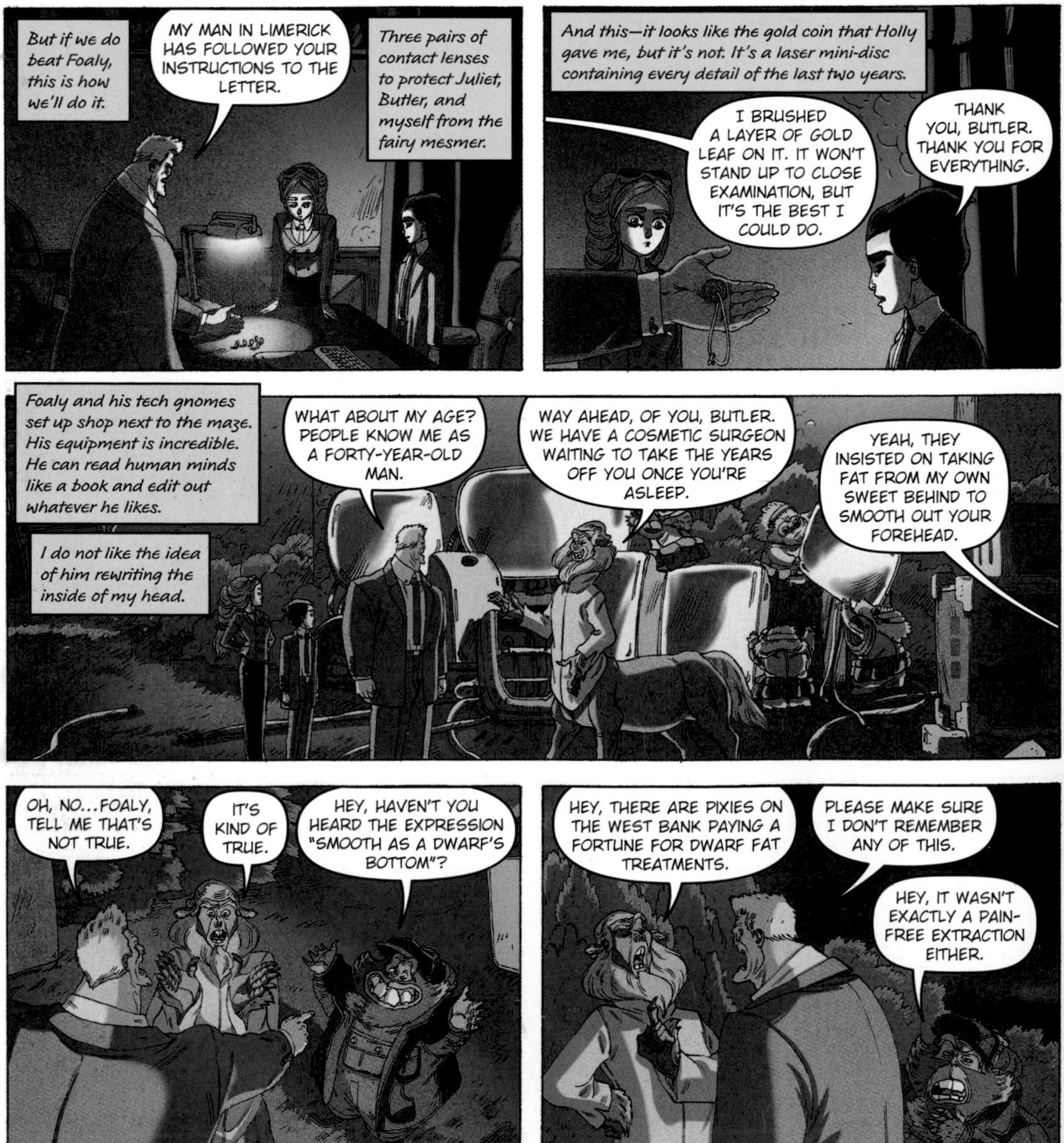
But if we do beat Foaly, this is how we'll do it.
MY MAN IN LIMERICK HAS FOLLOWED YOUR INSTRUCTIONS TO THE LETTER.
Three pairs of contact lenses to protect Juliet, Butler, and myself from the fairy mesmer.
And this—it looks like the gold coin that Holly gave me, but it's not. It's a laser mini-disc containing every detail of the last two years.
I BRUSHED A LAYER OF GOLD LEAF ON IT. IT WON'T STAND UP TO CLOSE EXAMINATION, BUT IT'S THE BEST I COULD DO.
THANK YOU, BUTLER. THANK YOU FOR EVERYTHING.
Foaly and his tech gnomes set up shop next to the maze. His equipment is incredible. He can read human minds like a book and edit out whatever he likes.
I do not like the idea of him rewriting the inside of my head.
WHAT ABOUT MY AGE? PEOPLE KNOW ME AS A FORTY-YEAR-OLD MAN.
WAY AHEAD, OF YOU, BUTLER. WE HAVE A COSMETIC SURGEON WAITING TO TAKE THE YEARS OFF YOU ONCE YOU'RE ASLEEP.
YEAH, THEY INSISTED ON TAKING FAT FROM MY OWN SWEET BEHIND TO SMOOTH OUT YOUR FOREHEAD.
OH, NO... FOALY, TELL ME THAT'S NOT TRUE.
IT'S KIND OF TRUE.
HEY, HAVEN'T YOU HEARD THE EXPRESSION "SMOOTH AS A DWARF'S BOTTOM"?
HEY, THERE ARE PIXIES ON THE WEST BANK PAYING A FORTUNE FOR DWARF FAT TREATMENTS.
PLEASE MAKE SURE I DON'T REMEMBER ANY OF THIS.
HEY, IT WASN'T EXACTLY A PAIN-FREE EXTRACTION EITHER.

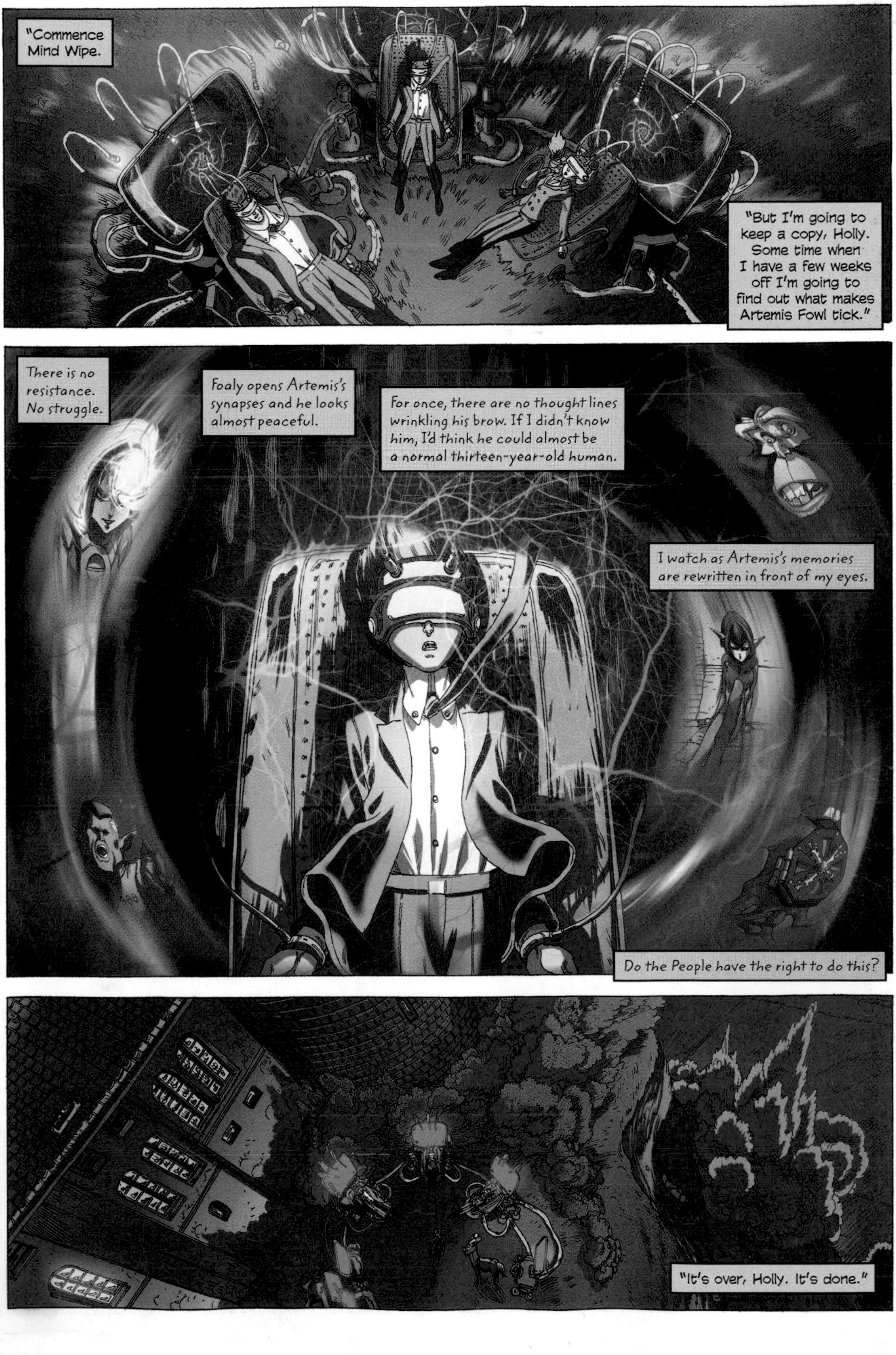
"Commence Mind Wipe.
"But I'm going to keep a copy, Holly. Some time when I have a few weeks off I'm going to find out what makes Artemis Fowl tick."
There is no resistance. No struggle.
Foaly opens Artemis's synapses and he looks almost peaceful.
For once, there are no thought lines wrinkling his brow. If I didn't know him, I'd think he could almost be a normal thirteen-year-old human.
I watch as Artemis's memories are rewritten in front of my eyes.
Do the People have the right to do this?
"It's over, Holly. It's done."

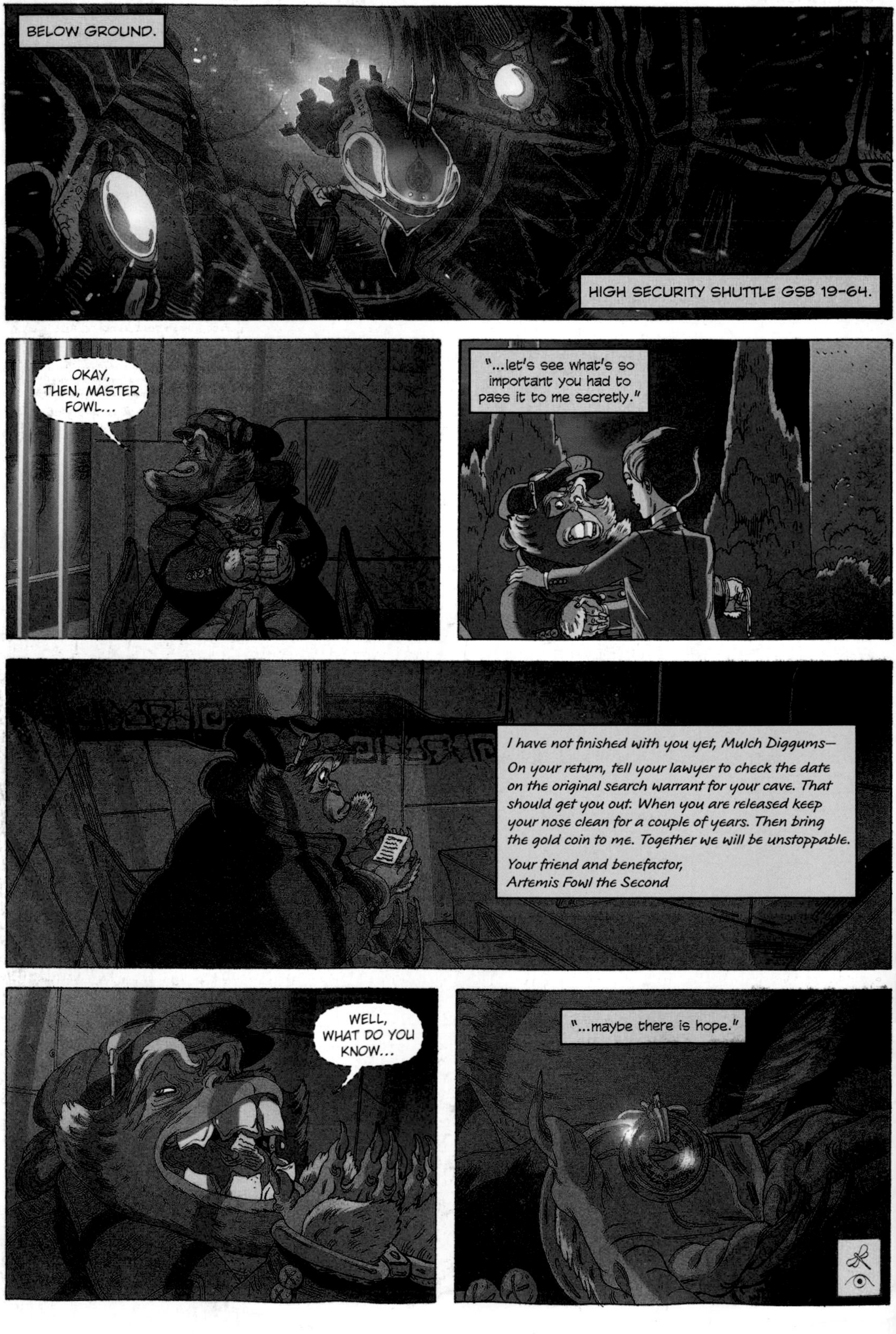
BELOW GROUND.
HIGH SECURITY SHUTTLE GSB 19-64.
OKAY, THEN, MASTER FOWL...
"...let's see what's so important you had to pass it to me secretly."
I have not finished with you yet, Mulch Diggums—
On your return, tell your lawyer to check the date on the original search warrant for your cave. That should get you out. When you are released keep your nose clean for a couple of years. Then bring the gold coin to me. Together we will be unstoppable.
Your friend and benefactor,
Artemis Fowl the Second
WELL, WHAT DO YOU KNOW...
"...maybe there is hope."

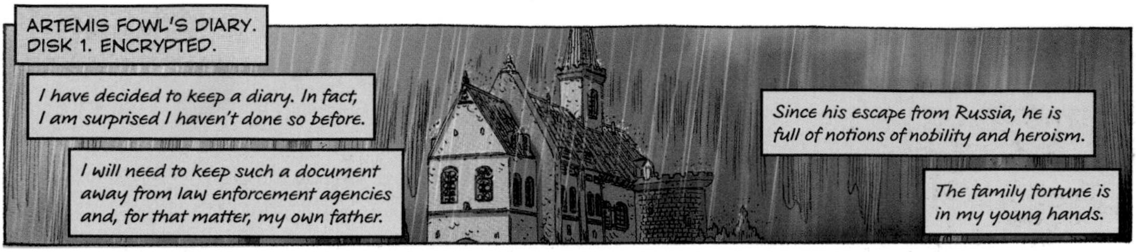
ARTEMIS FOWL'S DIARY. DISK 1. ENCRYPTED.
I have decided to keep a diary. In fact, I am surprised I haven't done so before.
I will need to keep such a document away from law enforcement agencies and, for that matter, my own father.
Since his escape from Russia, he is full of notions of nobility and heroism.
The family fortune is in my young hands.

EPILOGUE I

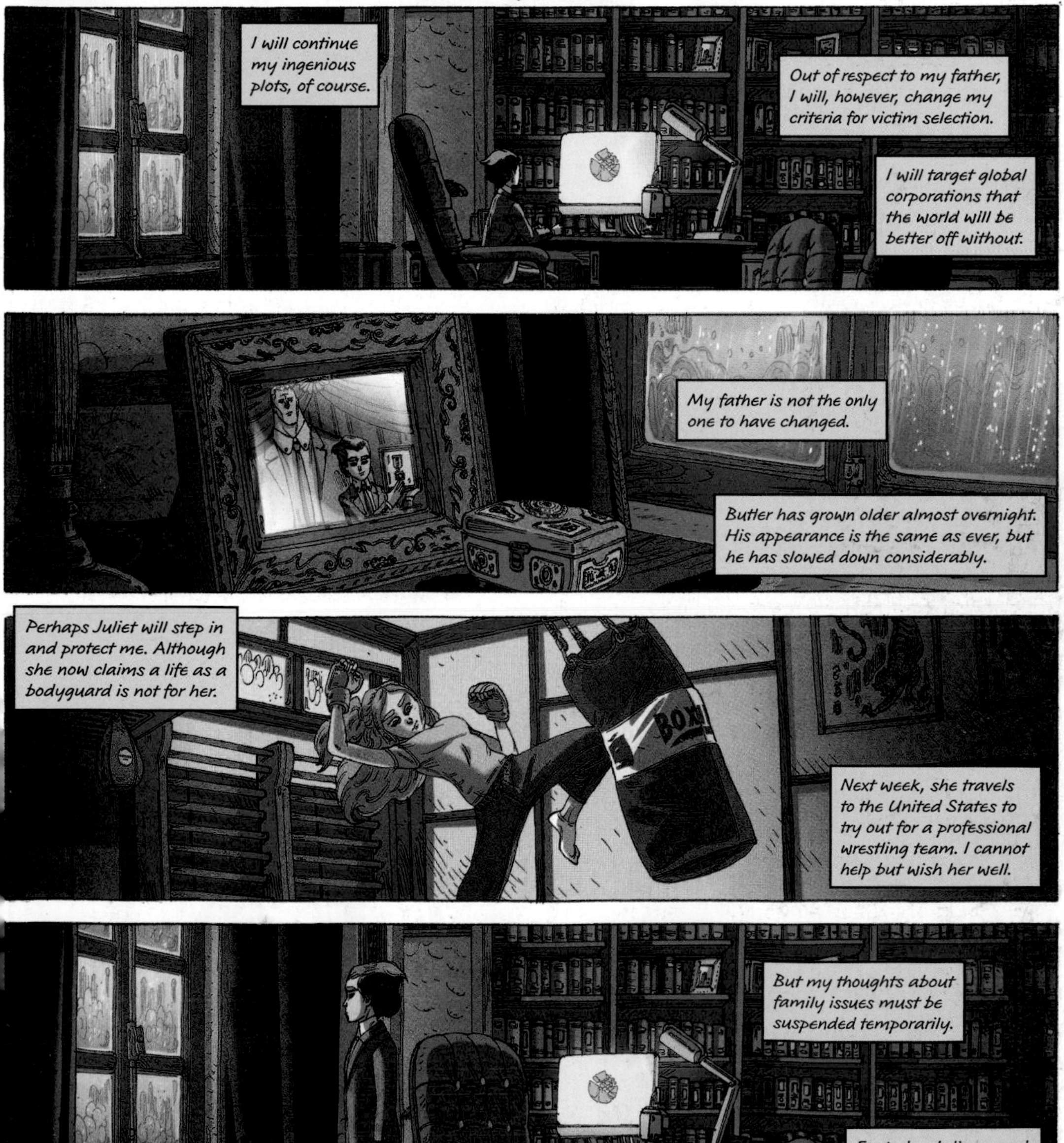
I will continue my ingenious plots, of course.
Out of respect to my father, I will, however, change my criteria for victim selection.
I will target global corporations that the world will be better off without.
My father is not the only one to have changed.
Butler has grown older almost overnight. His appearance is the same as ever, but he has slowed down considerably.
Perhaps Juliet will step in and protect me. Although she now claims a life as a bodyguard is not for her.
Next week, she travels to the United States to try out for a professional wrestling team. I cannot help but wish her well.
But my thoughts about family issues must be suspended temporarily.
For today I discovered that I am the victim of a conspiracy.

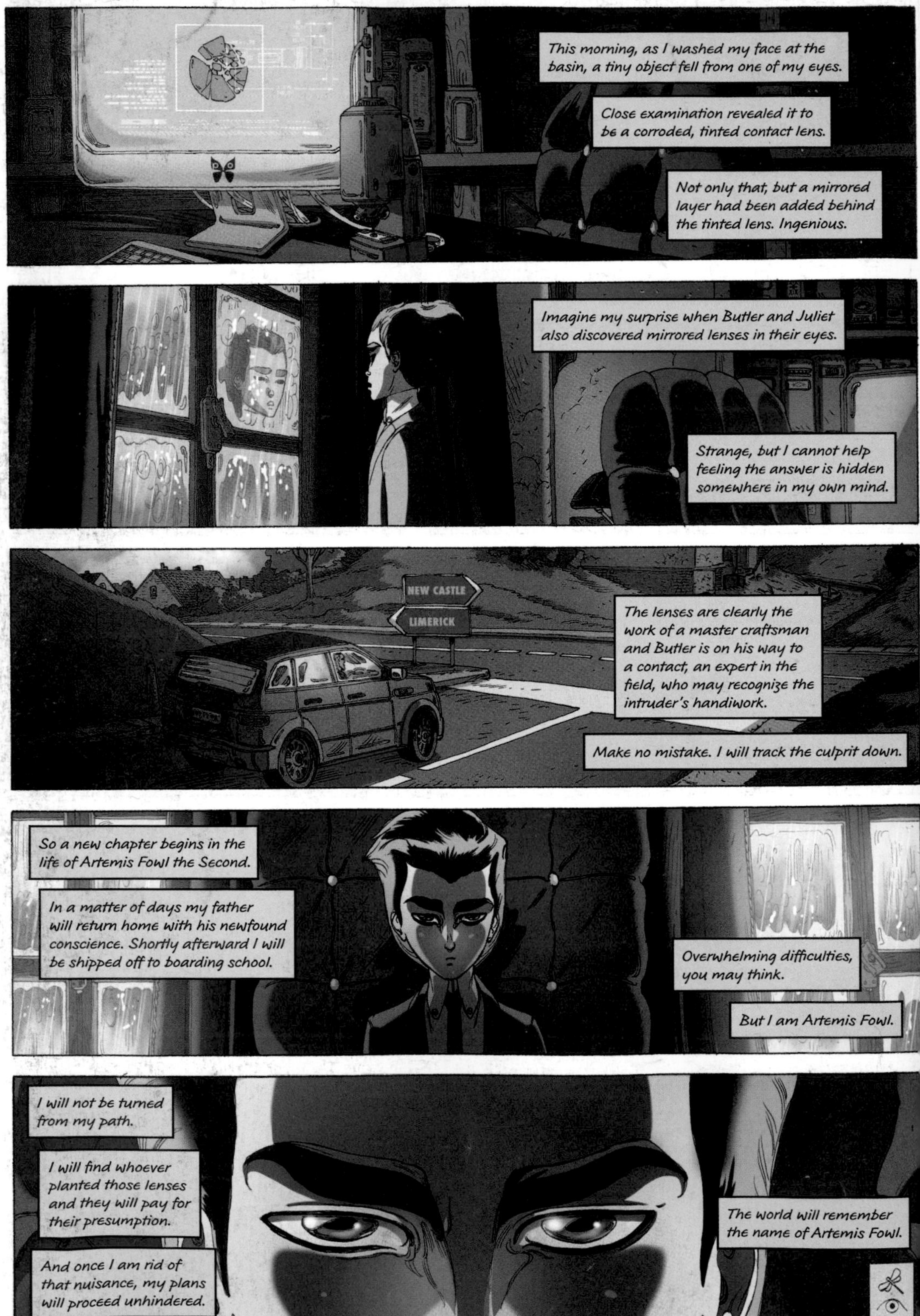
This morning, as I washed my face at the basin, a tiny object fell from one of my eyes.
Close examination revealed it to be a corroded, tinted contact lens.
Not only that, but a mirrored layer had been added behind the tinted lens. Ingenious.
Imagine my surprise when Butler and Juliet also discovered mirrored lenses in their eyes.
Strange, but I cannot help feeling the answer is hidden somewhere in my own mind.
NEW CASTLE
LIMERICK
The lenses are clearly the work of a master craftsman and Butler is on his way to a contact, an expert in the field, who may recognize the intruder's handiwork.
Make no mistake. I will track the culprit down.
So a new chapter begins in the life of Artemis Fowl the Second.
In a matter of days my father will return home with his newfound conscience. Shortly afterward I will be shipped off to boarding school.
Overwhelming difficulties, you may think.
But I am Artemis Fowl.
I will not be turned from my path.
I will find whoever planted those lenses and they will pay for their presumption.
And once I am rid of that nuisance, my plans will proceed unhindered.
The world will remember the name of Artemis Fowl.

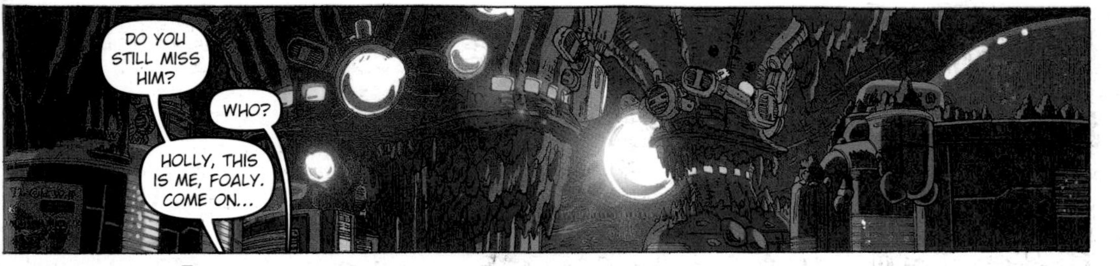
DO YOU STILL MISS HIM?
WHO?
HOLLY, THIS IS ME, FOALY. COME ON...

EPILOGUE II

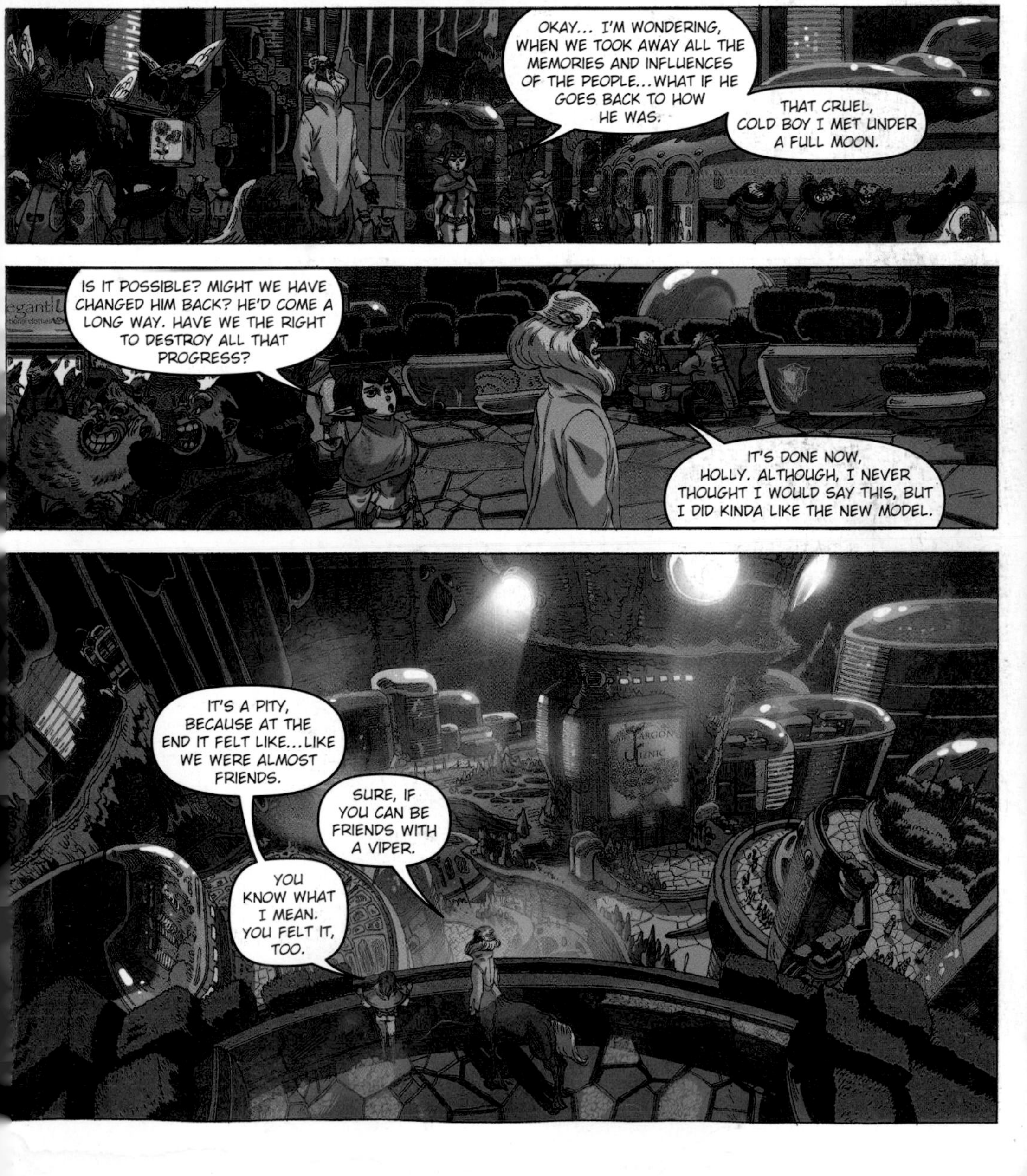
OKAY... I'M WONDERING, WHEN WE TOOK AWAY ALL THE MEMORIES AND INFLUENCES OF THE PEOPLE...WHAT IF HE GOES BACK TO HOW HE WAS.
THAT CRUEL, COLD BOY I MET UNDER A FULL MOON.
IS IT POSSIBLE? MIGHT WE HAVE CHANGED HIM BACK? HE'D COME A LONG WAY. HAVE WE THE RIGHT TO DESTROY ALL THAT PROGRESS?
IT'S DONE NOW, HOLLY. ALTHOUGH, I NEVER THOUGHT I WOULD SAY THIS, BUT I DID KINDA LIKE THE NEW MODEL.
IT'S A PITY, BECAUSE AT THE END IT FELT LIKE...LIKE WE WERE ALMOST FRIENDS.
SURE, IF YOU CAN BE FRIENDS WITH A VIPER.
YOU KNOW WHAT I MEAN. YOU FELT IT, TOO.

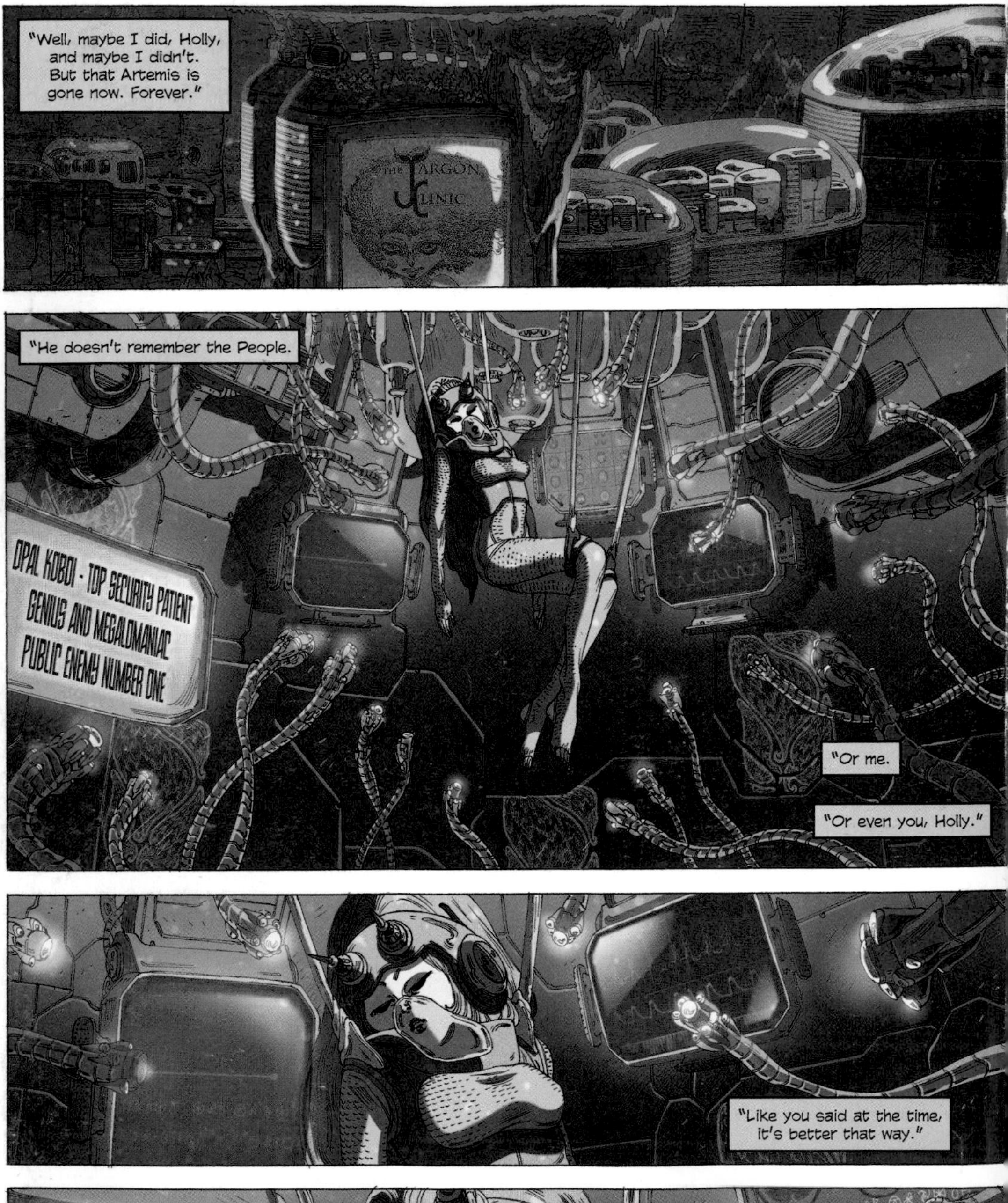
"Well, maybe I did, Holly, and maybe I didn't. But that Artemis is gone now. Forever."
THE ARGON CLINIC
"He doesn't remember the People.
OPAL KOBOI - TOP SECURITY PATIENT
GENIUS AND MEGALOMANIAC
PUBLIC ENEMY NUMBER ONE
"Or me.
"Or even you, Holly."
"Like you said at the time, it's better that way."
BEEEEEEEEEEP
"After all, why would the People ever want Artemis Fowl back?"

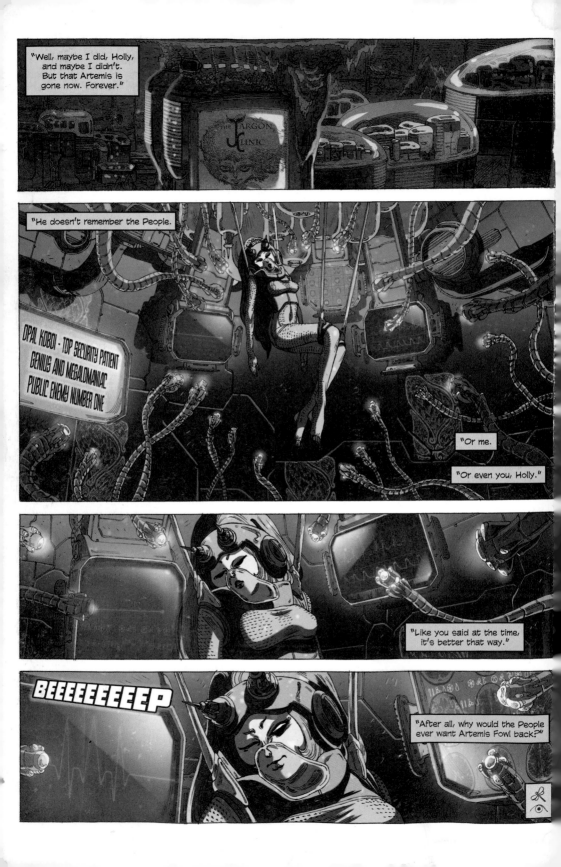